Forbidd

Marc

Dedications

This dedication is specially for you, Nicki. Although we originated from the same street, our bond has transcended beyond mere proximity throughout the years. Your unwavering support and commitment to my aspirations have been unparalleled over the past three decades. I am indebted to you more than you can fathom. Here's to another 30 years of cherished friendship.

Book Cover Dedication

Olivia (@oliviaprodesign on Fiverr)
https://www.fiverr.com/s/yL9x9e

Chapter 1: The Viking and His Dog

In the vast expanse of the Nordic lands, where the winds carried tales of bravery and conquest, lived a rugged Viking named Erik. He was a man of great strength and unwavering courage, known far and wide for his prowess in battle. But behind his fearsome exterior, Erik possessed a heart that yearned for companionship and connection.

At the edge of their village, Erik and his loyal canine companion, Thór, would often embark on grand adventures together. Thór, a magnificent wolfhound with a coat as dark as the night, possessed a keen intellect and unmatched loyalty, making him the perfect partner for the intrepid Viking.

On a chilly morning, as the sun began to peek over the horizon, Erik and Thór set out on their usual journey. The wind whispered through the towering pines, carrying the scent of pine needles and fresh dew. Erik reveled in the serenity of nature, finding solace in the company of his faithful companion.

As they ventured deeper into the lush forest, the sound of a distant stream reached their ears. Erik followed the babbling melody, eager to quench his thirst and let Thór frolic in the crystal-clear waters. A gentle mist hung over the stream, as if nature itself had conspired to create a mystical ambiance.

It was then that Erik spotted movement at the water's edge. His curiosity piqued, he approached cautiously, his hand resting on the hilt of his trusty sword. To his surprise, he found a girl, her golden locks cascading over her shoulders, delicately dipping her hand into the water. She seemed to be lost in her own thoughts, unaware of Erik's presence.

Thór, ever vigilant, stood by Erik's side, his keen senses detecting the stranger's arrival. But instead of barking or growling, the wise hound watched with a gentle curiosity, as if understanding the significance of this unexpected encounter.

Erik's heart skipped a beat as his eyes met the girl's for the first time. Her emerald eyes shimmered like the northern lights, reflecting a world of hidden depths and untold stories. He was captivated by her beauty, drawn to her like a moth to a flame. His pulse quickened, and he knew in that instant that his life would never be the same again.

But the realization hit Erik like a swift blow. A pang of sadness washed over him as he noticed the delicate ring adorning the girl's finger—a sign of her commitment to another. The realization that she was already married threatened to extinguish the flicker of hope within Erik's heart.

Erik and Thór lingered in the shadows, observing the girl from afar. They couldn't tear their gaze away from her, their thoughts consumed by her presence. They found themselves entangled in a bittersweet dance of forbidden desires and unspoken longing.

As the sun began its descent, casting a warm golden hue upon the land, Erik knew he had to retreat from the clandestine encounter. With a heavy heart, he silently bid farewell to the girl who had ignited a fire within his soul.

Little did he know that their paths would intertwine once more, and the flames of their forbidden love would continue to burn brighter, defying the boundaries of duty and society. The bond forged between a Viking, his loyal dog, and a girl torn between love and loyalty would shape their lives in ways they could never have imagined.

Chapter 2: The Village Feast

In the heart of the Viking village, nestled amidst rugged mountains and sprawling meadows, preparations were underway for a grand feast to celebrate the victorious return of the warriors. The air was alive with anticipation, and the aroma of roasting meat wafted through the village, enticing all who caught its scent.

Erik, still enraptured by the memory of the girl he had encountered by the stream, found himself lost in a sea of bustling villagers. Despite his inner turmoil, he knew he couldn't ignore the call of camaraderie and celebration. With Thór faithfully at his side, he made his way toward the lively gathering.

The village square bustled with activity, adorned with vibrant banners and flickering torches that illuminated the faces of joyous revelers. Tables laden with food and drink lined the perimeter, groaning under the weight of succulent boar, freshly baked bread, and flagons of mead.

Erik, clad in his weathered armor, blended seamlessly into the boisterous crowd. His broad smile revealed a glimmer of excitement as he sought familiar faces among his fellow warriors. They exchanged tales of valor and triumph, regaling one another with embellished accounts of their exploits.

As the feast reached its crescendo, a hush fell over the crowd, signaling the arrival of the village chieftain. Draped in regal furs, his grizzled beard cascading down his chest, the chieftain raised his goblet high, his voice booming across the square. He offered words of gratitude for the warriors' bravery and paid tribute to those who had fallen in battle, their sacrifices forever etched into the village's history.

With each toast, the atmosphere brimmed with a mixture of jubilation and solemn remembrance. Erik raised his own goblet, his mind wandering back to the girl who had bewitched his thoughts. He wondered if she too was present, caught in the merriment and yet burdened by the weight of her own unfulfilled desires.

As the night wore on, the festivities took on a life of their own. The village square transformed into a swirling dance floor, alive with spinning bodies and the sounds of joyous laughter. Musicians played lively tunes on their instruments, their melodies reaching every corner of the celebration.

Erik, caught up in the revelry, allowed himself a fleeting moment of respite from the thoughts of the girl. He danced with vigor and abandon, his movements mirroring the flickering flames of the bonfire. Thór joined in, his paws tapping to the rhythm, bringing a touch of canine grace to the festivities.

Amidst the swirling crowd, a familiar scent reached Erik's nostrils. He turned, his heart leaping within his chest, and there she stood —the girl who had captivated his every waking thought. Her eyes sparkled with the same enchantment that had enthralled him by the stream, and a smile played upon her lips as their gazes met.

Their connection was electric, a silent acknowledgment of the unspoken bond that tethered their hearts. Erik fought against the tide of emotions that threatened to overwhelm him. He yearned to take her hand, to sweep her away from the revelry and whisper the depths of his longing into her ear.

But the constraints of honor and her marital ties weighed heavily upon Erik's conscience. He couldn't bear the thought of causing her pain or tarnishing her reputation. And so, with a heavy sigh, he tore his gaze away, leaving the girl standing amidst the mirth and revelry.

The night wore on, the feast slowly winding down as the villagers retreated to their homes. Erik and Thór wandered through the emptying square, their steps heavy with the weight of unfulfilled desires. They knew that their encounter with the girl had marked the beginning of a tumultuous journey—one filled with heartache, longing, and the constant struggle between duty and love.

As they left the village square behind, their souls filled with equal parts hope and trepidation, Erik and Thór embarked on a silent vow to honor the girl's memory, even if their hearts could not forget her. Little did they know that the threads of fate were already conspiring to weave their destinies together once again, setting the stage for a tale of love that would endure against all odds.

Chapter 3: A Chance Encounter

The passage of time had done little to quell the ember of longing that burned within Erik's heart. Days turned into weeks, and weeks into months since the village feast, yet the image of the girl remained etched in his mind like an indelible mark. Each morning, as the sun bathed the land in its warm glow, Erik couldn't help but wonder if he would ever cross paths with her again.

One fateful day, as Erik and Thór traversed a dense forest, their footsteps stirring a carpet of fallen leaves, destiny granted them an unexpected meeting. The crisp autumn air whispered through the branches, carrying with it a symphony of rustling leaves and the distant call of wildlife.

Erik paused to catch his breath, leaning against the trunk of an ancient oak tree, when a gentle voice floated through the air. "Is someone there?" it asked, tinged with a mixture of curiosity and caution.

Erik's heart skipped a beat as he recognized the voice. It was her—the girl who had taken residence within his thoughts, her presence now resonating beyond his dreams. With a mixture of trepidation and hope, he stepped forward, emerging from the shadows into her line of sight.

Their eyes locked, a shared recognition passing between them like a secret unspoken. The girl's emerald eyes widened with a mixture of surprise and delight, mirroring the emotions that coursed through Erik's veins. Thór, ever the loyal companion, wagged his tail enthusiastically, sensing the significance of this moment.

"I... I didn't expect to see you again," the girl whispered, her voice laced with both joy and apprehension. "What brings you to this part of the forest?"

Erik took a deep breath, his words carefully chosen. "Fate, perhaps, or a desire to be near you once more," he replied, his voice tinged with vulnerability. "Since our encounter, my thoughts have been consumed by your memory. I couldn't resist the pull to seek you out."

A mixture of emotions flickered across the girl's face—longing, hesitation, and a flicker of regret. "Our meeting was a forbidden chance, Erik," she admitted, her voice laden with sorrow. "I am bound by vows of marriage, and my loyalty lies with another."

Erik nodded, understanding the weight of her words. "I, too, am torn by conflicting loyalties," he confessed. "But the connection we share cannot be denied. It is a flame that refuses to be extinguished."

Silence enveloped them, the forest seemingly holding its breath, as they grappled with the complexities of their hearts. The girl's eyes brimmed with unshed tears, reflecting the anguish of a love that dared not speak its name.

"I cannot promise you a future," she finally whispered, her voice barely audible. "But I cannot deny the hold you have over me, the way you make my heart beat with a fierceness I have never known."

Erik reached out, his hand trembling with both fear and determination, and gently touched her cheek. "Though the path ahead may be fraught with obstacles, I am willing to face them for a chance at something true and extraordinary," he declared.

Their gaze held, unspoken promises mingling in the air. Time seemed to stand still as they stood on the precipice of a choice that would forever alter their lives.

In that fleeting moment, the girl reached out, her hand meeting Erik's, their fingers intertwining in a silent declaration of the love that bound them. They knew that the road ahead would not be easy, that their hearts would be tested, but they were prepared to face whatever came their way, united in their shared longing.

Thór, sensing the gravity of the moment, nestled against their legs, offering his silent support. He would be there for them, a steadfast companion throughout their journey, his unwavering loyalty a beacon of hope.

And so, within the embrace of nature's sanctuary, Erik and the girl, their destinies intertwined, set forth on a path filled with both passion and peril, their love an ember burning bright amidst the darkness. Little did they know that their chance encounter would be the catalyst for a love story that would echo through the annals of time, leaving an indelible mark on the tapestry of their lives.

Chapter 4: The Mysterious Girl

In the wake of their chance encounter, the mysterious girl became an enigma that danced on the periphery of Erik's consciousness. Her presence lingered like a wisp of mist, both captivating and elusive. He yearned to know more about her, to unravel the secrets hidden beneath her ethereal facade.

Days turned into weeks, and with each passing moment, Erik's curiosity grew. He sought solace in the company of Thór, confiding in his loyal companion as they roamed the sprawling landscape. Together, they traversed dense forests, climbed towering cliffs, and braved treacherous waters, their shared adventures a welcome distraction from the constant pull of the girl's memory.

One misty morning, as Erik stood on a windswept cliff, gazing out at the vast expanse of the sea, a familiar voice interrupted his reverie. "Erik," it whispered, carried by the whispering wind.

Startled, Erik turned to find the girl standing beside him, her presence as enigmatic as ever. She wore a cloak of seafoam green, her eyes sparkling with an intensity that mirrored the turbulent waves crashing against the rocks below.

"Who are you?" Erik asked, his voice filled with equal parts curiosity and longing. "What secrets do you carry, hidden within the depths of your being?"

A gentle smile played upon the girl's lips, her gaze fixed on the horizon. "I am a tapestry of contradictions," she replied cryptically. "Bound by duty and circumstance, yet yearning to break free from the chains that bind me."

Erik's heart ached with understanding, the weight of their forbidden love bearing down upon them. "Tell me your name," he pleaded, his voice tinged with desperation.

The girl hesitated, her eyes flickering with a mixture of hesitation and surrender. "Call me Freya," she finally whispered, her voice carrying the weight of her own secrets.

Freya—the name reverberated within Erik's soul, resonating with a sense of destiny and ancient tales. It suited her, he thought, for she possessed a certain otherworldly quality that seemed to transcend time itself.

As the days turned into nights, Freya began to share fragments of her life with Erik, carefully weaving together the tapestry of her existence. She spoke of her marriage to a nobleman, a union forged for the sake of political alliances, but devoid of love. Her voice trembled as she revealed the longing that had seeped into her heart, a yearning for a connection that transcended the confines of duty.

Erik listened, his heart breaking for the sacrifices she had made, the compromises that had chiseled away at her spirit. He vowed to be her refuge, a sanctuary from the storm that raged within her. Though the path they walked was fraught with danger and uncertainty, they clung to the flicker of hope that burned bright within their souls.

Thór, always attuned to their emotions, remained a steadfast pillar of support. His unwavering loyalty was a balm to their wounded hearts, a reminder that love, in all its complexities, was worth fighting for.

And so, Erik and Freya continued to traverse the rugged lands together, their bond deepening with each shared moment. The weight of their unspoken desires grew heavier, like a tempest brewing on the horizon, threatening to engulf them in its relentless storm.

Little did they know that their journey had only just begun—a journey that would test their devotion, challenge their resolve, and force them to confront the very essence of their identities. The mysterious girl and the Viking, bound together by a love that defied conventions, stood poised on the precipice of destiny, ready to face whatever trials lay ahead.

Chapter 5: Introducing Thór, the Viking's Loyal Dog

Thór, with his regal stature and unwavering loyalty, had been a steadfast presence in Erik's life long before the fateful encounter with Freya. As they navigated the intricacies of their forbidden love, the faithful wolfhound remained a pillar of strength and a confidant to both Erik and Freya.

Born of a noble lineage of hunting dogs, Thór possessed an innate sense of duty and a deep bond with Erik. His sleek black coat shimmered in the sunlight, his piercing eyes reflecting a wisdom that surpassed his canine form. Erik often marveled at the depth of their connection, grateful for the companionship Thór offered in a world fraught with challenges.

Thór's role extended beyond that of a mere pet; he was Erik's guardian, his silent protector. Together, they traversed the rugged terrain of their homeland, their bond unyielding in the face of adversity. Whether scaling treacherous cliffs, braving stormy seas, or venturing into uncharted territories, Thór was a constant companion, lending both courage and solace.

Freya, too, recognized the significance of Thór's presence. She had witnessed the unwavering loyalty with which he stood by Erik's side, an embodiment of their unbreakable bond. She marveled at the innate understanding between the Viking and his noble companion, a connection that transcended words.

In the quiet moments they stole away from prying eyes, Erik and Freya often found solace in Thór's company. They would sit by the crackling fire, Thór nestled contentedly at their feet, his deep breaths punctuating the hushed conversations that flowed between them. In his observant eyes, they found an unspoken assurance that their love was worth fighting for, a reminder that their souls were intertwined in a tapestry woven with devotion and steadfastness.

Thór's loyalty extended beyond the confines of their hidden encounters. His keen senses detected danger lurking in the shadows, alerting Erik and Freya to potential threats. His fierce growls and bared teeth served as a warning, a testament to the depth of his commitment to their safety.

As the weight of their forbidden love grew heavier, Thór's presence became a beacon of hope, a reminder that even in the face of adversity, love could endure. His loyalty was a steadfast reminder that they were not alone in their journey, that there was strength in unity and unwavering trust.

Though the path ahead remained uncertain and fraught with danger, Erik, Freya, and Thór faced it together, bound by a love that defied societal norms. In the depths of their shared trials, they found solace in each other's arms, drawing strength from the unwavering loyalty of the canine companion who had witnessed their love blossom and would stand by them until the end.

As they embarked on the next chapter of their journey, Erik and Freya vowed to cherish the bond they shared, holding tight to the love that had ignited their souls. With Thór faithfully at their side, they faced the challenges that lay ahead, fortified by the enduring connection that bound their hearts together—the Viking, the mysterious girl, and the loyal dog whose presence would forever be a testament to the power of love and devotion.

Chapter 6: A Glimpse of Forbidden Love

In the veil of secrecy, Erik and Freya stole fleeting moments to indulge in the intoxicating embrace of their forbidden love. Hidden away from prying eyes, they found solace in the sanctuary of a secluded grove— a haven where the constraints of duty and societal expectations seemed to fade into insignificance.

Under the canopy of towering trees, dappled sunlight cast playful patterns on their entwined bodies. Erik's touch ignited a fire within Freya's soul, his lips tasting of desire and whispered promises. The world around them faded into a distant blur as they surrendered to the intoxicating pull that bound them.

Their encounters were brief, their stolen moments precious. Erik reveled in the feel of Freya's delicate hands against his weathered skin, while she savored the strength of his embrace, seeking refuge in the shelter of his arms. The world outside their clandestine sanctuary ceased to exist as they reveled in the tenderness of their connection.

Yet, even in their moments of bliss, a sense of trepidation lingered. They were acutely aware of the consequences that loomed over their heads—a tempest waiting to shatter their fragile haven. The weight of guilt and societal expectations pressed upon them, each stolen touch a bittersweet reminder of the complexity of their love.

Thór, ever the silent observer, stood guard at the edge of the grove, his vigilant eyes scanning the surroundings, ensuring their secret remained hidden. His presence, though unspoken, provided them with a sense of security—a steadfast guardian whose loyalty remained unswerving.

As the seasons changed and the grove transformed from vibrant greens to fiery hues, Erik and Freya's love deepened. Each encounter etched a mark upon their souls, a testament to their courage and resilience in the face of impossible odds. Their shared moments became lifelines, anchoring them amidst the storm that raged within their hearts.

Yet, the ache of their forbidden love remained. Freya's heart yearned for a life unconstrained, where she could freely choose the path her heart desired. Erik, too, grappled with the knowledge that their love, though passionate, was shrouded in shadows. He longed for a future where they could walk hand in hand, free from the chains that bound them.

Their stolen moments became a refuge from the harsh realities of the outside world—a fleeting escape from the constraints that threatened to suffocate their love. In those stolen glances and gentle caresses, they found solace, allowing their hearts to be swept away by the current of their shared desires.

But with each encounter, their hunger for more grew—a hunger that would soon demand a choice, a decision that would shape the course of their lives. The time for secret trysts and stolen kisses was drawing to an end, and the weight of their love bore down upon them, beckoning them to take a stand against the forces that sought to tear them apart.

As the sun set on another stolen moment, Erik and Freya clung to the fading remnants of their sanctuary. The grove, once a haven of forbidden love, transformed into a haunting memory, forever imprinted in their hearts. Their gaze lingered, their souls intertwined, as they silently vowed to face the world together —to confront the challenges that lay ahead and defy the odds that threatened to extinguish the flame that burned within them.

With Thór faithfully at their side, the Viking and the mysterious girl prepared to face the impending storm, their love emboldened by the glimpses of paradise they had shared. Though the path was fraught with uncertainty, they were determined to seize their own destiny—a destiny where their love would triumph, and the forbidden would be embraced with the strength of their devotion.

Chapter 7: The Married Woman

Within the confines of her lavish estate, surrounded by opulence and the echoes of whispered secrets, Freya, the married woman, grappled with the weight of her commitment. Bound by vows to a nobleman she did not love, she found herself torn between the confines of duty and the allure of a love that dared not speak its name.

As the days stretched into weeks, Erik's presence became a constant presence in Freya's thoughts. She found herself lost in the labyrinth of their stolen moments, yearning for the warmth of his embrace and the solace of his whispered promises. Each passing day deepened her awareness of the love she harbored, a love that defied the boundaries imposed upon her.

Freya's heart, like a captive bird, fluttered against the gilded cage of her marriage. The walls that enclosed her threatened to suffocate her spirit, to extinguish the flame that Erik had ignited within her. She longed for freedom—to cast aside the chains of her societal obligations and follow the path that her heart craved.

In the privacy of her chamber, Freya traced the contours of her wedding band, a symbol of the life she was expected to lead—a life devoid of passion, but one filled with privilege and comfort. The weight of her choices bore down upon her, a heavy burden she carried in silence.

The nobleman she was wed to, a man of stature and influence, remained oblivious to the battle waging within Freya's heart. He indulged in the pursuits of power and prestige, leaving her to navigate the intricacies of their life together, her desires and dreams relegated to the recesses of her soul.

But Erik, with his strength and unwavering devotion, had awakened a dormant part of Freya—a part she had long believed lost to the winds of time. In him, she saw a kindred spirit, a soul yearning for a love that transcended societal constraints. The longing within her grew stronger with each passing day, threatening to unravel the carefully constructed facade she presented to the world.

Yet, as Freya grappled with her desires, a sense of guilt gnawed at her conscience. She was acutely aware of the pain her choices could inflict on those caught in the crossfire of her emotions. The specter of betrayal loomed over her, casting a shadow on the love she and Erik shared.

In the solitude of her thoughts, Freya sought solace in the memory of their stolen moments —the stolen glances, the lingering touches, the stolen kisses that ignited a fire within her. Each encounter had etched a mark upon her heart, a testament to the strength of their connection. But with each stolen breath, the burden of secrecy grew heavier, threatening to drown her in a sea of deceit.

Thór, attuned to Freya's inner turmoil, provided a comforting presence—a loyal companion who offered solace without judgment. His steady gaze and gentle nuzzles were a reminder that love, in its many forms, demanded sacrifice and courage.

As Freya gazed out upon the lush gardens of her estate, a garden that bloomed with forbidden desires, she knew that a crossroads lay ahead. She yearned for a love unburdened by constraints, a love that could be declared freely, but the path to such freedom was shrouded in uncertainty.

With a determined resolve, Freya steeled herself for the choices that awaited her. The road ahead was treacherous, rife with heartache and difficult decisions. But she refused to let her love wither away in the shadows. In her heart, she knew that the fire that burned between her and Erik was worth fighting for—that their love, though forbidden, had the power to illuminate their lives with a brilliance that defied the darkness.

As the winds of change whispered through the corridors of her estate, Freya, the married woman, prepared to confront the forces that threatened to extinguish her love. With Erik by her side and the loyal Thór offering unwavering support, they stood poised on the precipice of a decision that would reshape their lives—a decision that would either bind them together in eternal love or plunge them into the depths of despair.

Chapter 8: Unsettling Thoughts

Unsettling thoughts swirled within Erik's mind like a tempestuous storm, threatening to engulf him in doubt and uncertainty. The weight of their forbidden love pressed upon him, as he grappled with the knowledge that Freya's heart was bound by the shackles of a loveless marriage. He wondered if he was merely a temporary respite—a flicker of light amidst the darkness that consumed her.

As he wandered the rugged lands, his loyal companion Thór by his side, Erik found himself tormented by questions that gnawed at his soul. Was he a fool to believe in a love that defied convention? Could their connection withstand the relentless scrutiny of society? The answers eluded him, casting a shadow of doubt over the path they had chosen.

In the depths of night, Erik's sleep was plagued by haunting dreams that merged reality and fiction. He would wake with a start, beads of sweat clinging to his brow, his heart pounding within his chest. The dreams taunted him, presenting alternate versions of their story, each more painful and tragic than the last.

Thór, sensing his master's inner turmoil, offered a comforting presence. The canine companion's steady gaze and unwavering loyalty served as a reminder that love, even in the face of uncertainty, was worth fighting for. In Thór's eyes, Erik found a reflection of his own unwavering devotion—a bond that went beyond the realm of words.

As the days turned into weeks, Erik found himself torn between the longing for Freya's presence and the torment of their impossible love. He yearned for her touch, her whispered confessions of affection, yet the knowledge of the complexities that lay before them lingered like a shadow in his heart.

He sought solace in the solitude of nature, where the wind whispered untold tales and the landscapes echoed with the wisdom of generations. Amidst towering cliffs and cascading waterfalls, Erik found a respite from the cacophony of conflicting thoughts. He would sit in quiet contemplation, allowing the majesty of the natural world to guide his unsettled mind.

One such day, as he stood at the edge of a precipice, the wind tugged at his cloak, carrying with it a sense of introspection. Erik closed his eyes, the world around him fading into a mere murmur. In the depths of that moment, clarity emerged from the chaos of his thoughts.

He realized that their love, though forbidden and uncertain, was a testament to their authenticity—a force that could not be contained by societal norms. Love, he understood, defied logic and reason. It was a primal force that surged through their veins, drawing them together like two celestial bodies locked in an eternal dance.

With renewed conviction, Erik embraced the unsettling thoughts that had plagued him. He knew the path ahead would be treacherous, rife with challenges and sacrifices. But the fire within his heart burned brighter than ever, urging him to push forward, to fight for a love that transcended boundaries.

Thór, attuned to his master's newfound resolve, wagged his tail in approval. In his loyal eyes, Erik found validation—a reminder that love was a force that demanded courage, resilience, and unwavering belief.

Armed with a newfound clarity, Erik prepared to face the trials that awaited them. With each step, his heart became a beacon of determination, lighting the way for a love that dared to defy the odds. They would face the storm together, weathering the uncertainties and braving the consequences, for the love they shared was a force that could not be silenced.

In the depths of his soul, Erik knew that their love would test their mettle, but he was ready to confront the challenges head-on. With Thór by his side, he would stand beside Freya, the woman whose heart beat in harmony with his own, and forge a path through the tumultuous sea of their desires. Their love, though shrouded in uncertainty, would stand as a testament to the indomitable spirit that resided within their souls.

Chapter 9: A Shared Moment

In the fading light of a crisp winter's day, Erik and Freya found themselves drawn to the solitude of a frozen lake. The world around them was hushed, as if nature itself held its breath, offering a sacred space for their shared moment.

Hand in hand, they ventured onto the ice, their footsteps leaving imprints upon the pristine surface. The chill in the air seemed to mirror the fragile balance they walked—a delicate dance between their hearts' desires and the constraints of their circumstances.

As they reached the center of the lake, a sense of calm settled upon them. The stillness of the frozen expanse reflected the quiet intensity of their emotions—a silence that held a thousand unspoken words.

Erik turned to Freya, his eyes searching hers, as if seeking affirmation in the depths of her gaze. The weight of their love pressed upon him, mingling with the trepidation that had plagued him in moments of doubt. But in that shared moment, he found solace—a respite from the tumultuous sea of uncertainty.

Freya, too, felt the weight of their love bearing down upon her. She had spent countless nights wrestling with the consequences of their desires, questioning the path they had chosen. Yet, in Erik's presence, a sense of clarity settled within her, like the calm after a storm.

Silent understanding passed between them, their souls entwined in a dance of unspoken longing. The air crackled with an electric charge, as if the universe itself recognized the significance of their connection.

With a tenderness that defied the bitter cold, Erik cupped Freya's face in his hands, his touch a balm against the uncertainties that plagued them. Time seemed to stand still as he leaned in, his lips brushing against hers—a gentle union that spoke volumes, transcending the limitations of language.

In that shared moment, their hearts sang in harmony. The world around them faded into insignificance as their souls became entangled, interwoven by a love that refused to be confined by the boundaries of their circumstances.

As they pulled away, a tear escaped Freya's eye, glistening like a precious gem upon her cheek. It held within it a mixture of joy and sorrow—a recognition of the beauty and pain that accompanied their forbidden love.

Erik wiped away the tear, his touch feather-light, filled with a tenderness that words could never convey. With a silent promise in his eyes, he vowed to cherish every stolen moment, to honor the love that bound them, regardless of the obstacles that lay ahead.

Hand in hand, they ventured back toward the shore, leaving behind their shared moment on the frozen lake. The world awaited them, fraught with challenges and uncertainty, but their hearts beat as one—a testament to the depth of their devotion.

Thór, ever the silent witness to their love, stood at the water's edge, his tail wagging in approval. In his canine wisdom, he understood the significance of the shared moment—the fragile connection that they had dared to forge amidst a world that sought to tear them apart.

As Erik, Freya, and Thór ventured onward, their steps echoing in harmony, they carried within them the memory of that shared moment—a precious reminder of the love that burned within their souls. Together, they faced the unknown, bound by a love that defied the limitations of their circumstances, their hearts beating with a fierce determination to seize their own destiny.

Chapter 10: A Troubled Heart

Within the depths of his being, Erik's heart swirled with conflicting emotions. Despite the strength of his love for Freya, doubts crept into his thoughts, casting shadows of uncertainty over their future.

As he traversed the rugged terrain, Thór by his side, Erik grappled with the weight of their forbidden love. The world seemed to conspire against them, threatening to unravel the delicate thread that bound their hearts together. The sacrifices they had made, the risks they had taken, all weighed heavily upon him.

In the solitude of nature's embrace, Erik sought solace, hoping that the winds would carry away the troubling thoughts that tormented his soul. But they clung to him, persistent and unyielding, whispering doubts that eroded the foundations of his resolve.

He questioned whether their love was a mere illusion—a flicker of hope in a reality that demanded they remain apart. The consequences of their choices loomed larger than ever, threatening to upend their lives and trample the fragile love they had nurtured.

Thór, attuned to Erik's troubled heart, offered a silent presence, his unwavering loyalty providing a semblance of stability. He nuzzled against his master, his warmth and understanding a comforting balm.

In the midst of his turmoil, Erik sought guidance from the wisest voices he could find. He sought counsel from the village elder, a figure revered for his wisdom and insight. The elder listened with empathy, his weathered face a testament to a life lived and lessons learned.

With a voice tinged with both compassion and caution, the elder spoke of the complexities of love. He warned Erik of the perils that lay ahead, the price they may have to pay for defying societal expectations. But he also spoke of the transformative power of love, of the profound joy that could blossom from embracing one's true desires.

The elder's words offered Erik a glimmer of clarity in the midst of his confusion. Love, he realized, was a tumultuous journey, fraught with uncertainty. It demanded bravery and sacrifice, but it also held the potential for profound happiness.

In the wake of their conversation, Erik stood at a crossroads—a precipice between the known and the unknown. The doubts that had clouded his mind began to dissipate, replaced by a renewed sense of purpose and determination. He would not let fear dictate their path. Love, he decided, was worth every risk they had taken.

With a resolute heart, Erik sought out Freya, their destinies forever intertwined. He would stand beside her, ready to face whatever challenges came their way. Their love, he realized, was a force that defied convention— a flame that burned bright amidst the darkness.

As he approached her, a mixture of trepidation and unwavering love filled his being. In that moment, he resolved to cast aside the doubts that had plagued him. They would weather the storms together, forging a path of their own making.

Thór, sensing Erik's newfound resolve, stood at his side, offering his silent support. In his loyal eyes, Erik found reassurance—a reminder that their love was a force to be reckoned with, a bond that transcended the boundaries imposed upon them.

With their hearts aligned and their determination ablaze, Erik and Freya stood poised to face the challenges that lay ahead. The troubled whispers in Erik's heart faded into the background as they embarked on a journey fueled by a love that refused to be silenced. Hand in hand, they would navigate the uncertainties of their path, fortified by the strength of their bond and the unwavering loyalty of their faithful companion, Thór.

Chapter 11: The Viking's Restless Nights

Restless nights descended upon Erik like a relentless tempest, their turbulent winds tossing and turning him in a sea of uncertainty. As he lay in the darkness, his mind haunted by a myriad of thoughts, he found sleep an elusive companion.

Visions of Freya, both fleeting and vivid, danced behind his closed eyelids. Her captivating presence infiltrated his dreams, intertwining with the reality he yearned for. But the line between dreams and reality blurred, leaving Erik disoriented and yearning for clarity.

With each passing night, his restless mind wrestled with conflicting emotions. Doubts gnawed at the edges of his consciousness, casting shadows upon the love that burned within him. The weight of their forbidden desires weighed heavily upon his heart, testing the strength of his resolve.

In the solitude of the midnight hour, Thór sensed his master's turmoil, his warm body pressed against Erik's side, offering comfort in the absence of words. The canine companion's presence brought solace, a constant reminder of the love that bound them together—a love that transcended the realms of human understanding.

Erik sought solace in the vastness of nature, wandering beneath the moon's gentle glow, his footsteps echoing through the stillness of the night. The whispers of the wind carried fragments of his thoughts, whispered secrets shared with the heavens above.

He sought guidance in the wisdom of the stars, their distant light a beacon amidst the darkness. Through silent contemplation, he searched for answers that eluded him, hoping to find a path that would lead him to a love unencumbered by societal constraints.

In the depths of his sleepless nights, Erik revisited the moments he and Freya had shared—the stolen kisses, the lingering touches, the unspoken promises. Each memory etched a mark upon his soul, fueling his determination to defy the forces that sought to extinguish their love.

But doubts, like persistent shadows, persisted. The reality of their situation loomed before him—a reality that could potentially shatter their dreams and leave them with hearts bruised and broken. The weight of responsibility pressed upon him, urging caution and consideration.

As the restless nights continued, Erik turned inward, searching for the strength to confront his fears head-on. The doubts that plagued his heart became stepping stones toward a deeper understanding of his own desires. He knew that love demanded sacrifice and courage, but he also knew that it held the power to transcend the limitations imposed by society.

With the first light of dawn, a glimmer of clarity pierced the veil of Erik's restless nights. The realization settled within him, a quiet certainty that resonated in every fiber of his being. He had made his choice—he would embrace the love that burned within him, ready to face whatever challenges lay ahead.

Thór, sensing Erik's newfound resolve, greeted the dawn with an air of quiet celebration. His loyal eyes held a knowing gleam, a recognition of the strength that lay within his master's heart.

Armed with a renewed sense of purpose, Erik prepared to confront the uncertainties that awaited him. He would face the world unafraid, his love for Freya a shield against the doubts that had plagued him. Restless nights would no longer hold sway over his spirit, for he knew that true love was worth every sleepless hour.

With a steadfast heart and Thór at his side, Erik ventured forth into the world, ready to embrace the challenges and joys that awaited him. The restless nights would forever remain a testament to the depth of his devotion—a reminder that love, in its rawest form, demanded courage and an unwavering belief in the power of the heart.

Chapter 12: A Friendly Gesture

In the midst of the turmoil that consumed Erik's heart, an unexpected act of kindness brought a glimmer of solace to his troubled soul. It came in the form of a friendly gesture from a familiar face—an old friend from his village named Gunnar.

Gunnar, a burly Viking with a jovial disposition, had been a steadfast companion during Erik's youth. Their paths had diverged over the years, but fate had now brought them together once again.

On a crisp autumn morning, as Erik wandered through the village with Thór by his side, he caught sight of Gunnar's unmistakable figure near the village square. It seemed as if time had stood still, for the genuine warmth in Gunnar's eyes mirrored the friendship they had shared in their youth.

With a broad smile, Gunnar called out to Erik, his voice booming through the air. The weight of Erik's troubles momentarily lifted as they embraced, their shared history permeating the air with a sense of camaraderie.

Over a hearty meal and frothy mugs of ale, Erik and Gunnar reminisced about the adventures of their youth. They laughed and shared stories, their laughter punctuating the air like music, momentarily drowning out the burdens that weighed upon Erik's heart.

Gunnar, ever perceptive, sensed the turmoil that Erik carried within him. With a gentle touch on Erik's arm, he leaned in, his voice filled with empathy. "I see the weight you bear, my friend. Know that I am here to listen, should you wish to unburden your soul."

Erik's heart swelled with gratitude for the offer of a sympathetic ear. He hesitated for a moment, unsure of how much to reveal, but the sincerity in Gunnar's eyes put him at ease.

And so, Erik shared the complexities of his love for Freya, the forbidden desires that consumed him, and the doubts that plagued his restless nights. Gunnar listened intently, his presence a calming balm amidst the storm of Erik's emotions.

After a moment of thoughtful silence, Gunnar spoke with unwavering support. "Love, my friend, is a force that often defies reason and societal norms. It is a flame that burns within us, demanding to be acknowledged. Though the path ahead may be treacherous, the joy and fulfillment it offers are worth every struggle."

His words resonated deeply with Erik, reaffirming the conviction he had nurtured within his own heart. To hear such unwavering support from an old friend reminded him that his love for Freya was not a fleeting infatuation, but a flame that burned with an undeniable intensity.

Encouraged by Gunnar's perspective, Erik felt a renewed sense of determination. The weight of his troubles seemed lighter, as if the burdens he carried were shared between them. In that moment, he realized the power of friendship—the ability to offer solace and guidance in times of need.

As their conversation drew to a close, Erik thanked Gunnar for his understanding and support. The simple act of reconnecting with an old friend had offered him a glimmer of hope amidst the tumult of his emotions.

With a firm embrace and promises to stay in touch, Erik and Gunnar bid each other farewell. Erik walked away with a newfound sense of strength, his heart uplifted by the kindness and wisdom bestowed upon him.

Thór, who had been quietly observing the exchange, trotted alongside Erik, his presence a constant reminder of the loyalty and unwavering support they shared.

As Erik continued his journey, he carried with him the memory of the friendly gesture—a reminder that even in the face of adversity, friendship and understanding could provide solace. The road ahead remained uncertain, but armed with the knowledge that he was not alone, Erik faced the challenges with renewed courage and an open heart.

Chapter 13: The Secret Meeting

Under the cover of night, when the moon cast its ethereal glow upon the land, Erik and Freya arranged a clandestine meeting, their hearts beating in sync with the anticipation of stolen moments. They yearned to be together, if only for a brief respite from the world that sought to keep them apart.

With Thór as their faithful guardian, they ventured to a secluded clearing nestled within the dense forest—a hidden sanctuary known only to them. The rustling of leaves and the hushed whispers of nature accompanied their steps, as if the world itself conspired to shield their forbidden love.

As Erik arrived at the meeting place, his pulse quickened. A mixture of nerves and excitement danced within him, his mind teeming with thoughts of Freya. He longed to see her, to hold her in his arms, and to lose himself in the depths of their shared desires.

And then, she appeared—a vision of beauty amidst the moonlit glade. Freya, her eyes reflecting a mixture of longing and trepidation, took a tentative step toward Erik. The air crackled with electricity, the unspoken connection between them pulsating with a fervor that defied reason.

Without a word, they closed the distance between them, their bodies drawn together by an invisible force. In that moment, the world ceased to exist, leaving only their love and the unspoken promises that hung in the air.

Erik reached out, his hand trembling with anticipation, and brushed his fingers against Freya's cheek. It was a gentle caress—a gesture that spoke volumes, conveying the depth of his affection without the need for words. In the dim light, their eyes locked, silently affirming the bond they shared.

Thór, ever the watchful companion, stood nearby, his presence offering a sense of security amidst the vulnerability of their clandestine meeting. He remained on guard, a symbol of their devotion and a silent witness to their love.

As they stood in that sacred space, their minds and hearts intertwined, Erik and Freya found solace in each other's arms. They reveled in stolen kisses and tender embraces, their connection transcending the boundaries of time and space.

In their shared moment, they were free—the weight of the world lifted, if only for a fleeting instance. The worries and uncertainties that plagued them were momentarily forgotten, replaced by the sheer bliss of their union.

Words whispered like soft melodies in the stillness of the night, their voices carrying promises of enduring love and unwavering dedication. They bared their souls, sharing dreams and fears, strengthening the bond that had been forged against all odds.

As the moon continued its ascent, marking the passage of time, Erik and Freya reluctantly parted, their hearts heavy with the knowledge that their secret meeting must come to an end. But the memory of their stolen moments remained etched upon their souls, a guiding light in the darkness that awaited them.

With a final, lingering touch, Erik and Freya bid each other farewell, their eyes filled with a mixture of longing and hope. The world beckoned them back, demanding they resume their separate lives, but the fire of their love burned brighter than ever, urging them to find a way to defy the constraints that sought to tear them apart.

Hand in hand, Erik and Thór made their way back through the forest, the echoes of their secret meeting still resonating within their hearts. They carried the memory of their stolen moments—a testament to the strength of their love and a reminder that their connection was worth fighting for.

The secret meeting had ignited a flame within them, a flame that would continue to burn, guiding their footsteps through the labyrinth of challenges that lay ahead. In the depths of their souls, they knew that their love was a force that could not be extinguished, and they vowed to navigate the treacherous path together, united in their shared desires and unwavering devotion.

Chapter 14: Conflicting Loyalties

Conflicting loyalties waged a relentless battle within Freya's heart, tearing at her with an intensity that threatened to consume her. The weight of her commitment to her marriage, her duty to her family, and the fervent love she held for Erik clashed like titans in her mind, leaving her adrift in a sea of indecision.

As she moved through the motions of her daily life, the echoes of their secret meeting lingered in her thoughts, whispering of stolen kisses and shared dreams. Her heart yearned for Erik, but the chains of obligation tugged at her, reminding her of the repercussions their love could bring.

Guilt settled deep within Freya's core, its grip tightening with each passing day. She felt the weight of betraying her husband, a man she had once pledged her life to. She questioned her own integrity, torn between her longing for a love that set her soul ablaze and the responsibilities she had willingly accepted.

In the quiet of her chamber, Freya sought refuge from the chaos that swirled around her. She gazed upon the reflection in her mirror, her eyes tracing the contours of her face—a face that had known both joy and anguish. She wondered if her desires made her selfish, if the love she harbored for Erik was worth the pain it inflicted upon those entangled in her web of secrets.

Thór, sensing Freya's turmoil, rested his head upon her lap, offering a silent comfort. His loyalty, unwavering and unconditional, served as a reminder of the bond she shared with her husband—a bond that, in her heart, she struggled to reconcile with the fervor of her love for Erik.

Conflicting loyalties vied for dominance within her soul—the loyalty to a marriage that had lost its spark, and the loyalty to a love that held the promise of passion and fulfillment. Each path seemed to lead to a different destination, each choice leaving a trail of heartache in its wake.

In the stillness of the night, as she lay upon her bed, sleep eluded her. Her mind became a battlefield, the ghosts of her choices haunting her every thought. Her heart ached for resolution, for a way to reconcile the fragments of her desires and responsibilities.

With the dawn of a new day, Freya rose with a newfound determination. She resolved to confront the conflicting loyalties that had tormented her, to seek clarity amidst the chaos that consumed her. It was a path fraught with uncertainty, but she knew that she could no longer remain trapped in the shadows, her heart pulled in two opposing directions.

Erik, Thór, and the life they represented called to her, promising a love that soared beyond the boundaries of convention. Yet, her husband, her family, and the commitments she had made whispered cautionary tales, reminding her of the pain their choices could unleash.

In the depths of her conflicted heart, Freya knew that a decision loomed—one that would shape the course of her life. She yearned for the courage to confront her emotions head-on, to find a resolution that honored both her obligations and her desires.

As Freya stepped into the world, her gaze fixed upon the horizon, she prepared to face the challenges that awaited her. Conflicting loyalties would no longer hold her captive. With Thór by her side and the echoes of her love for Erik resonating within her, she ventured forth, determined to forge a path that would honor her truth—a path where her loyalties would align, and her heart would find solace amidst the tumultuous sea of conflicting desires.

Chapter 15: Unspoken Desires

Unspoken desires simmered beneath the surface of Erik and Freya's interactions, a potent undercurrent that pulsed with a fervor that refused to be contained. Their stolen glances and fleeting touches held a depth of meaning that words could not convey, each gesture a testament to the fire that burned within their souls.

In the quiet moments they stole, their hearts beat in unison, the unspoken desires between them hanging heavy in the air. Their conversations, once filled with playful banter and shared dreams, now carried a weighty subtext—a dance of longing and restraint.

Erik, his eyes filled with adoration whenever he looked upon Freya, yearned to hold her close, to revel in the embrace of their love. But he understood the delicacy of their situation, the boundaries that threatened to confine them. His desires remained unspoken, locked within the depths of his being, patiently awaiting the day they could be unleashed.

Freya, too, held unspoken desires that danced beneath her skin, swirling with both anticipation and trepidation. She longed to feel Erik's touch, to lose herself in the depths of their shared passion. But the weight of her obligations and the consequences that loomed ahead kept her desires tightly contained, hidden from the world and even from Erik himself.

In the moments they stole away, a silent language passed between them—an intimate connection that transcended words. Their eyes spoke volumes, each lingering gaze a confession of the desires that coursed through their veins. They reveled in the electricity that sparked between their fingertips, the unspoken promise of a love that yearned to be fully realized.

Thór, ever the silent observer, sensed the unspoken desires that swirled around his human companions. His presence provided a comforting solace, a reminder that their love was worth the patience and sacrifices it demanded. In his canine wisdom, he understood that their desires were bound by a delicate balance, waiting for the opportune moment to be unleashed.

As the days turned into weeks, Erik and Freya found solace in the stolen moments they shared—a stolen touch in the market square, a stolen kiss beneath the moon's watchful gaze. Their unspoken desires intensified with each passing encounter, fueling the flame that burned within them.

But as the intensity of their love grew, so did the weight of their unspoken desires. Each unspoken word became a burden, threatening to consume them from within. They yearned for a day when the walls that confined their love would crumble, and the desires that had been locked away would be unleashed with the force of a hurricane.

In the depths of the night, as they lay separate and longing, Erik and Freya found solace in their dreams. In the realm of dreams, their desires were given voice, their bodies and souls entwined without the constraints of reality. It was a bittersweet respite—a taste of the passion they longed to share.

But dreams could only provide temporary solace. Erik and Freya knew that the day would come when their desires would no longer remain unspoken, when the truth of their love would be laid bare for the world to see. They could only hope that when that day arrived, it would bring with it the freedom they so desperately craved.

With unspoken desires burning within them, Erik and Freya stood poised on the precipice of their fate. The path ahead remained uncertain, but their hearts beat with a resolute determination. They would continue to steal moments, nurturing the flame of their love, until the day when their desires could be unleashed—a day when their unspoken desires would become a symphony of passion, and their love would no longer be confined to whispers and stolen glances.

Chapter 16: The Viking's Dilemma

The weight of the Viking's dilemma pressed upon Erik's shoulders, burdening his spirit with a gravity that threatened to consume him. The love he harbored for Freya was an inferno that raged within, burning brighter with each passing day. Yet, the constraints of their circumstances loomed large, demanding a resolution that tore at the fabric of his being.

As he ventured across the rugged landscape, his faithful companion Thór by his side, Erik's mind spun with conflicting thoughts. The path he had chosen, the love he held dear, seemed entangled in a web of obligations and consequences. His heart ached for Freya, but the weight of his choices threatened to crush the joy he found in their connection.

In the solitude of nature's embrace, Erik sought solace, hoping that the winds of the wild would carry away the burden that weighed upon him. He climbed the highest peaks, seeking perspective amidst the sweeping vistas that stretched before him. But the answers he sought remained elusive, leaving him adrift in a sea of uncertainty.

Thór, ever attuned to his master's turmoil, offered a steadfast presence. His soulful eyes held unwavering loyalty, reminding Erik that love was a force worth fighting for—a force that transcended the boundaries of society and demanded the courage to pursue one's desires.

As the days wore on, Erik found himself torn between the promise of their love and the consequences that loomed like a specter. The whispers of the village, the disapproval of society, clawed at the edges of his consciousness, threatening to poison the love he held so dear.

He yearned to declare his love for Freya, to embrace her openly and cast aside the chains that bound them. But the weight of responsibility, the knowledge of the hearts they would break and the lives they would disrupt, held him back. The Viking's dilemma tore at his heart, leaving him to grapple with the consequences of his desires.

In the quiet of his chamber, Erik retreated into introspection. He stared into the flickering flames of the hearth, their dance mirroring the turmoil within him. His mind became a battleground, where love clashed with duty, and desire waged war against reason.

The words of the village elder echoed in his thoughts, his voice a guiding presence in Erik's darkest moments. The elder's wisdom had illuminated the path before, reminding Erik that love demanded bravery and sacrifice. But the Viking's dilemma persisted, its weight heavy upon his shoulders.

With a heavy heart, Erik acknowledged the complexity of their situation. The road ahead would be treacherous, paved with heartache and uncertainty. Their love would be tested, their souls bared to the scrutiny of the world. He knew that the choices he made would ripple outward, impacting the lives of those around them.

But as he gazed into the flames, the ember of hope ignited within him. He could not deny the strength of his love for Freya, nor the intensity of the connection they shared. The Viking's dilemma would not smother the fire that burned within his soul, for he understood that their love was a force that defied logic and reason—a force that demanded to be acknowledged.

Erik vowed to navigate the treacherous path with integrity and compassion, seeking a resolution that honored both his love for Freya and the responsibilities he carried. Their journey would not be without sacrifices, but he would face the challenges with an open heart and an unwavering devotion to the truth that resided within him.

As he emerged from the depths of his contemplation, a sense of clarity settled upon Erik's shoulders. The Viking's dilemma still weighed heavily, but he carried it with renewed purpose. With Thór by his side, his faithful companion and symbol of unwavering loyalty, Erik resolved to confront the choices that lay ahead. Love, he understood, demanded courage—the courage to forge a path that embraced their desires while acknowledging the complexities of their reality.

The Viking's dilemma would continue to cast its shadow, testing Erik's resolve and challenging the very foundations of their love. But he would face it head-on, with the strength of his heart and the guidance of his steadfast companion. For in the face of uncertainty, he knew that love would be the guiding light, illuminating their path and leading them towards a future where the Viking's dilemma would be but a memory of the trials they overcame.

Chapter 17: The Tangled Web

A tangled web of secrets and emotions spun tighter around Erik and Freya, ensnaring their hearts in a web of complexity and uncertainty. Their love, once a flame that burned bright and pure, now flickered amidst the shadows of their clandestine encounters.

Each stolen moment, every lingering touch, fed the intricate threads of their tangled web, weaving a tapestry of desire and restraint. They yearned for a love unburdened by secrecy, yet the constraints of their circumstances held them captive, leaving them to navigate the labyrinthine paths of their emotions.

As they ventured forth, hand in hand, Thór a silent sentinel by their side, the weight of their secrets bore down upon them. The village buzzed with whispered rumors, the sharp glances of onlookers dissecting their every move. They walked a delicate tightrope, teetering between the truths they held in their hearts and the façades they maintained for the sake of appearances.

Erik's longing for Freya grew with each passing day, an ache that could no longer be contained within the confines of their secret encounters. His heart yearned to declare their love to the world, to cast aside the tangled web that ensnared them. Yet, he understood the consequences of such an act—a tempest that would unleash chaos and disrupt the lives of those around them.

Freya, too, grappled with the intricacies of their predicament. Her desire to be with Erik burned brightly, but the fear of losing everything she held dear held her back. The tendrils of duty and obligation tightened their grip, entwining her in the tangled web they had woven. The truth threatened to unravel their carefully constructed lives, leaving devastation in its wake.

In the midst of their internal turmoil, Erik and Freya sought solace in the sanctuary of their shared moments. They stole fleeting encounters amidst the cover of night, their gazes filled with unspoken promises. Their lips brushed against each other's in stolen kisses, igniting sparks that danced along the tangled threads that bound them.

Thór, ever the loyal companion, stood by their side, a constant reminder of the love they shared. His presence offered a glimmer of hope amidst the tangled web—a reminder that love, even when ensnared in complexities, could weather the storm and emerge stronger on the other side.

As the days turned into weeks, the burden of the tangled web grew heavier. Erik and Freya found themselves at a crossroads, their choices carrying the potential to unravel the delicate tapestry they had woven. They yearned for a resolution, for a way to untangle the threads that kept their love concealed.

In the depths of their souls, they knew that the time for decisions drew near. They could no longer bear the weight of the secrets and the constraints that held them back. The tangled web demanded unraveling, even if it meant facing the unknown consequences that awaited them.

With a shared determination, Erik and Freya vowed to confront the tangled web together, hand in hand. They would untangle the threads one by one, no matter the challenges that lay ahead. Their love, forged amidst the intricacies of their lives, would be their guiding light—a beacon that would illuminate the path towards a future unburdened by secrecy and restraint.

As they ventured forth, their hearts alight with hope, they knew that the road would be arduous. But armed with their unwavering devotion and the strength of their love, Erik and Freya embarked on a journey that would test their resolve and reshape their destinies.

The tangled web that had ensnared them would no longer dictate their choices. Instead, they would weave a new tapestry— one of love, authenticity, and freedom. With each thread untangled, their love would emerge more vibrant and resilient, ready to withstand the storms that lay ahead. Together, they would rewrite their story, unraveling the tangled web that had bound them, and embracing a future where their love would shine unencumbered by the constraints of the past.

Chapter 18: The Girl's Inner Turmoil

Deep within the recesses of Freya's heart, an inner turmoil waged a relentless battle, tearing at the seams of her existence. The conflict between her love for Erik and her commitment to her marriage consumed her, leaving her entangled in a web of emotions that threatened to suffocate her spirit.

As she moved through her daily routines, a hollow ache gnawed at the core of her being. The weight of her desires pressed heavily upon her, filling her thoughts with an intoxicating mix of longing and guilt. Her heart yearned for Erik, his presence an ember that burned brightly amidst the ashes of her fading marital flame.

In the quiet solitude of her chamber, Freya found refuge from the cacophony of external pressures. Her gaze fixed upon the reflection in her mirror, where she saw not only her physical self but also the reflection of her conflicted soul. Her heart teetered on the precipice of a choice that could alter the course of her life forever.

Unspoken words reverberated within her, their echoes like whispers of temptation. She questioned her own desires, wrestling with the morality of her yearning for Erik's touch, his love. The vows she had taken, the commitment she had made, weighed heavily upon her conscience, a constant reminder of the life she had built—a life that now felt like a gilded cage.

Thór, ever watchful, sensed Freya's inner turmoil, his soulful eyes brimming with understanding. He nestled close to her, offering solace in his silent presence. His unwavering loyalty and unconditional love provided a lifeline amidst the storm, reminding her that she was not alone in her struggle.

The girl's inner turmoil continued to wage its relentless battle, the scales of her heart tipping precariously between the desires that consumed her and the responsibilities she had sworn to uphold. She wondered if it was selfish to want more, to yearn for a love that set her soul ablaze. Guilt clawed at her, threatening to strangle the flickering flame of hope that burned within.

In the depths of the night, as sleep evaded her, Freya sought solace in the embrace of her dreams. In those fleeting moments, the walls that confined her desires crumbled, and she found herself lost in the arms of Erik. Their love blossomed in the realm of the subconscious, unburdened by the weight of societal expectations.

But with the first light of dawn, reality seeped back into her consciousness, and the girl's inner turmoil resurfaced with renewed force. She yearned for a resolution, for a way to reconcile the conflicting desires that threatened to tear her apart.

With each passing day, Freya realized that her heart held the answers she sought. The girl's inner turmoil was not a sign of weakness but a testament to the depth of her emotions and the complexity of the human experience. Love, she understood, had the power to transcend boundaries, but it also demanded the courage to face the consequences of its pursuit.

In the stillness of her chamber, Freya made a solemn vow to herself—a promise to honor her truth and navigate the turbulent waters of her emotions with integrity. She knew that the path ahead would be treacherous, fraught with difficult choices and potential heartache. But she was no longer willing to let her inner turmoil hold her captive.

With Thór as her steadfast companion and her love for Erik burning brightly within, Freya prepared to face the challenges that lay ahead. She would find the strength to untangle the web of conflicting desires, to forge a path that honored her heart's yearnings while respecting the lives she had built.

The girl's inner turmoil remained, an ever-present reminder of the complexities of her choices. But within the depths of her being, a newfound resolve stirred—a quiet certainty that her love for Erik was worth the battles she would face. With courage as her guide, she would navigate the tumultuous currents of her emotions, seeking a resolution that would set her free from the chains of inner conflict.

In the crucible of her inner turmoil, Freya would discover her own truth—a truth that would empower her to embrace the love that set her soul ablaze, and to chart a course towards a future where the depths of her desires and the authenticity of her heart would find harmonious balance.

Chapter 19: The Weight of Obligation

The weight of obligation pressed heavily upon Erik's shoulders, a burden that threatened to bend him under its immense gravity. His commitment to his village, his duties as a Viking, and the responsibilities he held to his family tugged at his conscience, intertwining with the desires that burned within his heart.

As he stood upon the village's outskirts, his gaze sweeping across the fields and homes he had sworn to protect, Erik felt the weight of expectation settle upon him. The honor of his ancestors, the legacy of his bloodline, demanded his unwavering dedication. But beneath the armor of duty, his heart longed for a love that defied the confines of his obligations.

Each step he took, each decision he made, carried the weight of a thousand lives. The village relied on him, its protector and defender. His kin looked to him for guidance and strength. The weight of obligation pressed upon him, a constant reminder that his desires must be held in check, confined within the boundaries set by society.

Thór, his loyal companion, stood steadfast by his side, his presence offering a silent solace. The dog's unwavering loyalty was a reminder of the sacrifices Erik had made and the responsibilities he held. Thór's watchful eyes seemed to understand the internal struggle that consumed his master, offering a comforting presence amidst the storm of conflicting emotions.

In the solitude of the forest, Erik sought solace, the towering trees bearing witness to his inner turmoil. He stood amidst nature's grandeur, the whisper of the wind carrying his thoughts to the heavens above. He wondered if his desires were selfish, if his yearning for a love that defied convention was a betrayal of the obligations he bore.

But as he contemplated the weight of obligation, a flicker of rebellion stirred within Erik's soul. He recognized that a life dictated solely by duty and responsibility would be devoid of the passion and fulfillment his heart craved. Love, he understood, held the power to transcend the limitations imposed by societal expectations, to ignite a fire that burned brighter than any duty could ever impose.

With each passing day, the weight of obligation became entangled with the desires that fueled his love for Freya. He yearned to break free from the chains that held him back, to embrace a love unburdened by the weight of societal conventions. But the consequences loomed large—a ripple effect that would impact not only his own life but the lives of those he held dear.

In the quiet moments of reflection, Erik grappled with the choices that lay before him. He understood that his actions would have far-reaching consequences, that the path he chose would forever alter the course of his life and the lives of those entwined in his journey. The weight of obligation tugged at his heartstrings, threatening to suppress the flame of love that burned within him.

But in the depths of his being, Erik recognized that true fulfillment could only be achieved when one honored the desires that resonated within the core of their being. Love, he realized, demanded the courage to navigate the treacherous waters of conflicting obligations, to find a way to honor both his responsibilities and the yearnings of his heart.

With Thór as his steadfast companion, Erik resolved to carry the weight of his obligations with grace and integrity. He would honor his commitments, protecting his village and providing for his family. But within the folds of his heart, he would nurture the flame of his love for Freya, seeking a path that would allow them to forge a future unburdened by the weight of societal expectations.

In the face of the weight of obligation, Erik found strength—the strength to defy the constraints imposed upon him and to chart a course that honored his truth. He understood that the journey ahead would be fraught with challenges, but armed with love and a steadfast heart, he vowed to navigate the intricacies of duty and desire, forging a path where obligations and love could coexist in harmonious balance.

Chapter 20: The Unforgettable Kiss

In the depths of twilight, where the sky blazed with hues of orange and purple, Erik and Freya found themselves drawn together once more. The weight of their unspoken desires had grown unbearable, their hearts aching for release. It was in this moment, amidst the fading light, that destiny conspired to grant them an unforgettable kiss.

As they stood in a secluded grove, shadows dancing around them, the air tingled with anticipation. The tension between them was palpable, like a taut string waiting to be plucked. Their gazes locked, conveying a depth of understanding that words could never express.

Erik reached out, his hand trembling with equal parts desire and trepidation, and gently cupped Freya's cheek. His touch sent a jolt of electricity through both of them, an undeniable connection that transcended the boundaries of the physical world. In that fleeting moment, time stood still.

Their lips met in a kiss that was at once tender and fervent, a collision of pent-up longing and unbridled passion. It was a kiss that spoke of a love that had been kept at bay for far too long, a love that refused to be silenced any longer.

In that single act, the world around them faded into insignificance. The whispers of the village, the weight of obligations, the constraints of their circumstances—all were forgotten, swallowed by the intensity of their embrace. It was a moment that etched itself into their souls, forever imprinted upon their memories as the kiss that unleashed their love upon the world.

Thór, their steadfast witness, stood guard a short distance away, his eyes conveying a mixture of understanding and approval. In that moment, he seemed to acknowledge the depth of their connection, recognizing that their love was no longer a flame confined to whispers and stolen moments but a force that demanded to be acknowledged.

As the kiss lingered, time resumed its course, and Erik and Freya reluctantly parted. Their eyes, filled with a mixture of ecstasy and sorrow, locked for a moment longer, silently communicating the depth of their emotions. The unspoken promises that passed between them were etched into their souls, a vow to continue defying the constraints that sought to keep them apart.

The unforgettable kiss became a touchstone —a beacon of hope amidst the uncertainty that lay before them. It served as a reminder that their love was not a fleeting fantasy but a flame that burned with an intensity that could not be extinguished.

With hearts ablaze, Erik and Freya walked away from that sacred grove, forever changed by the weight and power of their unforgettable kiss. It would become the fuel that propelled them forward, igniting their determination to navigate the challenges that lay ahead.

In the depths of their souls, they carried the imprint of that kiss—a symbol of their love's undeniable strength. It would serve as a guiding light, guiding them through the labyrinth of conflicting desires and obligations, towards a future where their love could flourish, unshackled by the chains of societal expectations.

With Thór by their side, a loyal companion and a symbol of unwavering devotion, Erik and Freya embraced the knowledge that their unforgettable kiss marked a turning point. They vowed to seize the moments that awaited them, to defy the odds and honor the flame of their love, until the day when their lips would meet once more, sealing their fate in an embrace that would leave no doubt of the depths of their love.

Chapter 21: A Risky Proposition

In the wake of their unforgettable kiss, Erik and Freya found themselves standing at a precipice—a threshold between the safety of their current lives and the unknown realm of possibilities that lay before them. The flame of their love burned brighter than ever, compelling them to consider a risky proposition that could forever alter the course of their destinies.

As they sought refuge in the solitude of the forest, Erik's gaze fixed upon Freya, his eyes filled with a mixture of longing and determination. He could no longer deny the depth of his feelings, nor the undeniable connection they shared. With a resolve that quivered beneath his skin, he spoke the words that had been simmering within him:

"Freya, my love, let us dare to defy the chains that hold us back. Let us face the risks together and embrace a future where our love can bloom without restraint."

Freya's heart raced within her chest as Erik's proposition hung in the air. The weight of the decision loomed large, the consequences of their actions a specter that whispered cautionary tales in her mind. But her love for Erik, the yearning that resonated within her, demanded a leap of faith.

She met his gaze, her eyes shimmering with a mixture of fear and hope. "Erik, to embark upon such a path would require immense courage and sacrifice. The web of obligations that binds us cannot be easily undone. Are we prepared to face the storm that may follow?"

Erik's voice held an unwavering resolve. "Freya, I understand the risks that lie ahead. But the love we share is worth every challenge we may encounter. Together, we can weather the tempest and forge a future where our hearts are free to love without restraint."

Thór, ever the loyal guardian, sensed the weight of the moment. His eyes shifted from Erik to Freya, as if silently acknowledging the gravity of their proposition. His presence offered a sense of steadfast support, a reminder that they were not alone in their journey.

In the face of uncertainty, Erik and Freya made a pact—a commitment to dare greatly and pursue a life guided by their love. They recognized that the path ahead would be fraught with obstacles and sacrifices, but the fire that burned within them demanded to be honored.

With a shared determination, they forged a plan. They would gather their strength and confront the web of obligations head-on, seeking a way to untangle the threads that held them back. Their love would be their compass, guiding them towards the life they dreamed of—a life where they could be together, unburdened by the weight of secrecy and the constraints of their current existence.

Word by word, action by action, they would dismantle the tangled web that had ensnared them. They would engage in heartfelt conversations, seeking understanding and support from those who held influence in their lives. Their honesty would serve as a testament to the authenticity of their love, and their unwavering commitment would demonstrate their willingness to face the consequences.

With their hearts aflame and Thór by their side, Erik and Freya prepared to embark on a journey that would test the limits of their courage. They were aware that the path they chose might lead to uncharted territories, where their love would be both celebrated and challenged. But they embraced the risks, for they knew that a life lived in pursuit of love was a life truly worth living.

As they took their first steps, their souls alight with hope, they understood that the risky proposition they embraced was not without its uncertainties. However, armed with their unwavering love and the strength of their connection, they ventured forth, ready to defy the odds and carve their own destiny.

The path ahead would be arduous, and the weight of their decision would continue to bear down upon them. But Erik and Freya were resolved to face whatever awaited them, hand in hand. With hearts intertwined and the fire of their love burning brightly, they would seize the opportunity to embrace a future that defied the limitations imposed upon them—a future where their love could flourish and their souls could find true fulfillment.

Chapter 22: The Viking's Decision

The weight of the risky proposition hung heavy upon Erik's shoulders, demanding a decision that would forever shape the course of his life. In the depths of his being, he understood that the time for hesitation had passed—a choice had to be made, regardless of the potential consequences.

As he stood upon the cliffs overlooking the roaring sea, Erik's gaze fixated on the horizon, his mind a whirlwind of conflicting thoughts and emotions. The call of his heart, the relentless yearning for a life with Freya, battled against the echoes of his responsibilities, the ties that bound him to his village and his kin.

Thór, his loyal companion, sat quietly by his side, the embodiment of unwavering loyalty. His presence offered a silent reassurance, a reminder that Erik's decisions were not made in isolation. The weight of the Viking's legacy, the expectations of his ancestors, tugged at his spirit, interwoven with the desires that burned within his soul.

In the solitude of nature's embrace, Erik sought clarity. The crashing waves and the salty breeze seemed to carry whispers of wisdom, nudging him towards a resolution that aligned with his truth. He closed his eyes, allowing the tranquility of the moment to envelop him, hoping for guidance from the forces that shaped his destiny.

Images of Freya's radiant smile, their stolen moments of bliss, flickered through his mind. Her love had ignited a fire within him, a fire that refused to be extinguished. The Viking's decision became clear—a life without Freya, a life confined to the limitations of duty and obligation, would be a life devoid of true fulfillment.

With a resolute determination, Erik turned his gaze from the horizon to face the path that lay before him. The risky proposition, once a daunting prospect, now held a glimmer of hope—a beacon that illuminated the possibilities that awaited him. He knew that pursuing a future with Freya would require immense sacrifices, that their journey would be strewn with challenges and uncertainties. But he could no longer deny the calling of his heart.

Thór, sensing the Viking's resolve, rose to his feet and nudged Erik gently, as if to affirm his decision. In his canine wisdom, he understood that the bonds of loyalty extended beyond the confines of tradition and duty. Love, he silently conveyed, was a force that transcended societal expectations —a force that demanded the Viking's unwavering courage.

With a steady heart, Erik walked back to the village, his steps resolute and purposeful. He sought out those whose counsel he trusted, whose support he knew would be instrumental in navigating the uncharted waters that lay ahead. He confided in his closest allies, explaining his decision with honesty and vulnerability, laying bare the depths of his love for Freya.

Some listened with understanding, their eyes reflecting a mixture of empathy and concern. Others resisted, their voices echoing cautionary tales of the risks involved. Yet, Erik remained steadfast, honoring the truth that resided within him. He acknowledged the weight of his obligations but emphasized that a life without love would be a life half-lived.

In the face of resistance, Erik remained resolute. He knew that not everyone would understand or support his decision, but he could no longer deny the fire that burned within him. With Thór by his side, a symbol of loyalty and devotion, he prepared to embark on a journey that would redefine his existence —a journey that would bring him closer to the love he held dear.

As the village buzzed with whispers and speculation, Erik steeled himself for the challenges that lay ahead. He knew that his decision would ripple outward, impacting the lives of those around him. But he took solace in the knowledge that true fulfillment could only be found by embracing the desires of his heart, even if it meant defying societal expectations.

The Viking's decision had been made—a decision fueled by love and the longing for a life with Freya. He would forge a new path, one that honored both his responsibilities and the calling of his soul. With determination as his compass and love as his guiding light, Erik prepared to chart a course towards a future that defied the limitations imposed upon him—a future where his heart could find solace and his spirit could soar.

Chapter 23: The Forbidden Tryst

Erik and Freya, having made their daring decisions, found themselves drawn to a hidden grove deep within the forest—a sanctuary where they could embrace their love in secret. It was here, amidst the lush foliage and the symphony of nature's whispers, that they arranged a forbidden tryst, a stolen moment of bliss that would forever be etched in their memories.

As the sun dipped below the horizon, casting a golden glow upon the land, Erik arrived at the grove, his heart pounding with anticipation. The air was charged with electricity, crackling with the tension of their forbidden love. He scanned the surroundings, his eyes searching for any sign of Freya's presence.

And there she stood, a vision of ethereal beauty, bathed in the fading light. Freya's eyes sparkled with a mix of excitement and trepidation, mirroring the emotions that churned within Erik's own soul. With a graceful step forward, she closed the distance between them, their gazes locking in a silent understanding.

In the embrace of the grove, they surrendered to the intensity of their desires, the allure of their love. Their hearts beat in syncopation, their bodies drawn together like magnets, as they melted into each other's arms. Time ceased to exist as they reveled in the stolen moments they had fought so bravely to claim.

Their lips met in a dance of passion and longing—a forbidden union that ignited a fire within their souls. Every touch, every caress, spoke of a love that defied the boundaries imposed upon them. The world around them faded into insignificance as they sought solace in the arms of one another.

Thór, the ever-watchful companion, stood guard at the edge of the grove, a silent witness to their forbidden tryst. His presence offered a sense of both comfort and caution, a reminder of the risks they were taking and the consequences that awaited their actions. Yet, in his loyal gaze, Erik and Freya found a source of reassurance—a silent permission to embrace the love that burned within them.

In the midst of their stolen encounter, Erik and Freya reveled in the knowledge that this moment was theirs and theirs alone. It was a declaration of their defiance, a testament to the strength of their love. They immersed themselves in the ecstasy of their connection, their bodies entwined, as if trying to fuse their very souls together.

With each passing second, their forbidden tryst intensified, a crescendo of emotions that swirled around them like a tempest. In that moment, the weight of their choices, the risks they had taken, seemed irrelevant. They were consumed by the passion that blazed within them, a flame that refused to be extinguished.

But as the moon began its ascent, casting a silver glow upon their entangled bodies, reality began to seep back into their consciousness. The forbidden tryst had to end, their time together limited. Reluctantly, Erik and Freya untangled themselves, their breaths ragged with a mix of desire and sorrow.

With a final lingering touch, they exchanged a look filled with unspoken promises—a vow to endure the challenges that lay ahead, no matter the sacrifices they may face. With a heavy heart, they bid each other farewell, retreating back into the world that sought to keep them apart.

As Erik and Freya parted ways, the grove remained as a sanctuary of their love—a place where the forbidden tryst had etched its mark upon their souls. They carried the memory of their stolen moments within them, fueling their resolve to navigate the storm that awaited them, to forge a future where their love could exist unburdened by secrecy and restraint.

With Thór as their silent confidant, they embarked on separate paths, their hearts forever intertwined. The forbidden tryst had ignited a flame that would guide them through the darkness, fueling their determination to defy the odds and embrace a love that defied the constraints of their world.

As they retreated into the night, the forbidden tryst remained a bittersweet memory—a reminder of the depths of their passion and the risks they were willing to take. Their souls carried the weight of their stolen encounter, a testament to the indomitable power of love, and a reminder that their hearts would forever yearn for the day when their love would no longer be confined to stolen moments, but would shine freely for all to see.

Chapter 24: The Rush of Passion

In the wake of their forbidden tryst, Erik and Freya found themselves caught in a whirlwind of emotions—a torrent of desire and longing that refused to be contained. The taste of their stolen moments lingered upon their lips, igniting a rush of passion that consumed their thoughts and propelled them forward.

Every glance exchanged, every brush of their fingertips, ignited a fire that burned brighter than ever. The magnetic pull between them grew stronger, their souls intertwining in a dance that defied the constraints of their circumstances. They were captivated by a love that knew no boundaries, no limits.

As the days turned into weeks, Erik and Freya yearned for more than stolen moments. The flame of their passion demanded to be kindled, to blaze brightly in the open, unshackled by the shadows. They longed for a life where their love could flourish without fear or reservation.

In the depths of the night, under the cloak of darkness, they found solace in secret rendezvous. Their encounters were marked by a sense of urgency, as if time itself conspired against them. With each stolen moment, their bodies became a canvas upon which their passion painted its vivid strokes.

The rush of passion coursed through their veins, their hearts beating in sync with the rhythm of their desires. They surrendered to the intoxicating spell of their love, their bodies becoming conduits of an electric energy that sparked with every touch, every kiss.

Thór, their ever-loyal companion, bore witness to their union, his presence offering a silent understanding. He stood guard, a symbol of their devotion and a reminder of the risks they faced. His watchful eyes seemed to convey a message—an unspoken plea to tread carefully, to protect the fragile flame of their love.

Erik and Freya understood the risks that came with succumbing to the rush of passion. Their actions, veiled in secrecy, threatened to upend the lives they had known. But the fire that burned within them refused to be contained. Their love demanded to be fully embraced, to be set free from the confines of the shadows.

In the moments of stolen bliss, they found respite from the weight of their obligations, from the expectations that had bound them for so long. It was in the embrace of their passion that they discovered a profound sense of freedom—a liberation that only their love could offer.

With each encounter, the rush of passion surged, leaving them both breathless and hungry for more. They became addicts, intoxicated by the heady elixir of their desires. The world outside their clandestine haven seemed to fade away, the walls closing in on the space they shared, as if conspiring to keep them locked in their passionate embrace.

Yet, amidst the euphoria, a bittersweet undercurrent flowed. They were acutely aware that the rush of passion they experienced came at a cost—a cost measured in stolen moments, hidden glances, and the constant threat of discovery. The boundaries of their secret love became both their sanctuary and their prison.

In the depths of their hearts, Erik and Freya grappled with the weight of their choices. They knew that the rush of passion, though exhilarating, could not sustain them indefinitely. They yearned for a love that could exist openly, a love that transcended the clandestine encounters that had become their norm.

With each stolen moment, they became more resolute in their determination to forge a future where their love could flourish in the light of day. The rush of passion, once a seductive force that consumed their every thought, now fueled their courage to break free from the chains that bound them.

Together, they would navigate the storm of uncertainty, driven by the rush of passion that had awakened within them. With Thór as their steadfast companion and their love as their guiding light, Erik and Freya would find the strength to defy the odds, to embrace the unknown, and to rewrite the narrative of their love—a narrative where their passion would no longer be confined to stolen moments, but would radiate with an unyielding brilliance that could not be dimmed.

Chapter 25: The Guilt and Remorse

The rush of passion had awakened a love that Erik and Freya could no longer deny, but as they continued their clandestine encounters, an undercurrent of guilt and remorse began to seep into their hearts. They found themselves grappling with the consequences of their actions, the weight of their choices bearing down upon them.

In the quiet moments of solitude, when the rush of passion subsided and reality crept in, Erik's conscience stirred. The weight of the obligations he had cast aside in pursuit of his love gnawed at him, whispering reminders of the lives he had disrupted. Guilt twisted his gut, each stolen moment with Freya becoming a painful reminder of the promises he had broken.

Freya, too, felt the weight of remorse settle upon her like a heavy cloak. She loved Erik with a passion that burned bright, but her commitment to her marriage and the vows she had taken cast a shadow over their union. The guilt gnawed at her soul, reminding her of the promises she had made and the potential pain she was causing to others.

Their love, once a beacon of hope, now bore the burden of their guilt. They questioned the righteousness of their actions, the morality of their choices. The consequences of their forbidden affair loomed large, threatening to shatter the fragile paradise they had built.

Thór, their ever-loyal companion, sensed their inner turmoil, his watchful eyes filled with a mix of understanding and concern. He stood by their side, offering solace in his presence, a silent reminder that their guilt was not without cause. The dog's unconditional love served as a gentle nudge, urging them to confront the remorse that threatened to consume them.

Erik and Freya knew that their love was not without consequences, that the path they had chosen had ripple effects that extended beyond their own desires. Their guilt was a testament to their awareness of the pain they may be causing, both to their spouses and to the community they were a part of.

In the depths of their hearts, they yearned for a way to reconcile their love with the remorse that tugged at their souls. They sought redemption, a path that would allow them to honor their desires while acknowledging the pain they had caused. The weight of their guilt became a catalyst for change, a call to action that could no longer be ignored.

With heavy hearts, Erik and Freya made a pact to confront their guilt head-on. They resolved to face the consequences of their actions, to take responsibility for the pain they had caused, and to seek a path of healing and forgiveness.

In the days and weeks that followed, they began the process of reconciliation. They engaged in honest conversations, addressing the hurt they had inflicted upon their spouses, their families, and themselves. They acknowledged their remorse and sought forgiveness, understanding that true redemption required sincere efforts to make amends.

Thór, ever the loyal companion, stood by their side throughout their journey of redemption. His presence served as a reminder of the capacity for unconditional love and forgiveness. His watchful eyes conveyed a message of hope, assuring Erik and Freya that the path to redemption was within their grasp.

As they faced the consequences of their actions, Erik and Freya gradually began to rebuild the lives they had disrupted. They offered support and empathy to their spouses, seeking to heal the wounds they had inadvertently caused. They leaned on their community, humbly accepting the repercussions of their choices and working towards rebuilding trust.

The weight of guilt and remorse slowly began to lift, replaced by a sense of accountability and a commitment to make things right. Though the scars of their actions would forever remain, Erik and Freya embraced the opportunity for growth and transformation. They understood that true redemption required not only remorse but also action—a dedication to learn from their mistakes and strive to be better individuals.

With each step forward, Erik and Freya found solace in the knowledge that their guilt had not defined them but rather propelled them towards a path of self-discovery and redemption. Their love, once marred by remorse, now became a catalyst for personal growth, a force that inspired them to become more compassionate, understanding, and resilient.

United in their pursuit of redemption, Erik and Freya moved forward, determined to forge a future where their love could exist with integrity and authenticity. Thór, ever faithful, remained by their side, a symbol of unwavering loyalty and a constant reminder of the capacity for forgiveness and the transformative power of love.

.

Chapter 26: A Love Unfulfilled

As Erik and Freya confronted the consequences of their actions and sought redemption, they realized that the path they had chosen had come at a steep price. Their love, once vibrant and all-encompassing, had become a bittersweet reminder of what could never be fully realized—a love unfulfilled.

The weight of their remorse and the repercussions of their affair cast a shadow over their hearts, dimming the flame of their passion. The guilt they carried with them became an unwelcome companion, a constant reminder of the pain they had caused to their spouses, their families, and themselves.

Erik and Freya understood that their love could never be fully actualized within the boundaries of their current lives. Their commitments and responsibilities to others stood as insurmountable obstacles, forever separating them from the life they had envisioned together.

In the moments of solitude, they grappled with the heart-wrenching truth—a love that burned so fiercely, yet could never be fully realized. The pain of their unfulfilled desires became a haunting presence, a reminder of the sacrifices they had made and the dreams they had relinquished.

Thór, their steadfast companion, offered solace as he sensed their inner turmoil. His unwavering loyalty served as a reminder that their love, though unfulfilled, had not been in vain. His presence provided a comforting anchor in the storm of their emotions, a reminder that their connection had touched their souls in profound ways.

As Erik and Freya navigated the tumultuous waters of their emotions, they sought solace in the memories they had created—the stolen moments, the rush of passion, and the unwavering love that had once consumed them. They cherished those memories, for they were the remnants of a love that had transcended the boundaries of their circumstances.

Though their love remained unfulfilled, Erik and Freya recognized the importance of cherishing what they had shared. They understood that even in the midst of their pain, their connection had brought them moments of true bliss and awakened depths of emotion that would forever shape their lives.

In the face of their unfulfilled love, Erik and Freya found solace in the knowledge that they had grown as individuals. They had experienced the exhilaration of a love that defied conventions, and in doing so, they had learned valuable lessons about themselves, their desires, and the complexities of the human heart.

With time, the intensity of their passion began to fade, replaced by a profound sense of gratitude for the transformative power of their love. Though they yearned for a different outcome, they understood that the lessons learned and the growth achieved were not in vain.

Erik and Freya remained in each other's lives, albeit in a different capacity. Their connection had evolved into a deep friendship—a bond that held both understanding and respect for the choices they had made. They provided support and solace to one another, a reminder that the love they shared, though unfulfilled, had forever imprinted itself upon their souls.

Thór, the constant witness to their journey, continued to be their loyal companion. His presence served as a reminder that love, even when unfulfilled, could bring about moments of profound connection and personal growth. He reminded them that the pain of an unfulfilled love did not diminish its significance but rather enriched their understanding of the complexities of the human experience.

In the depths of their hearts, Erik and Freya carried the weight of their unfulfilled love, forever marked by the flame that had burned so brightly. Though their paths had diverged, the imprint of their connection remained—a testament to the power of love, the depths of human desire, and the resilience of the human spirit.

As they navigated the complexities of their lives, Erik and Freya held onto the memories of their love, cherishing them as treasures that would forever define a chapter of their existence. Their unfulfilled love became a testament to their capacity to feel deeply, to experience the joys and pains of life in all their intricate shades.

In the face of their unfulfilled desires, they learned to embrace the beauty and the sadness that love could bring—a poignant reminder that even when love is unfulfilled, its presence can shape and transform us in ways that nothing else can.

Chapter 27: The Girl's Conflicted Heart

Freya's heart was a battlefield, torn between the love she held for Erik and the commitments she had made to her marriage. Each beat echoed with a cacophony of conflicting emotions, her desires clashing with her sense of duty.

In the stillness of the night, she sought solace under the moon's gentle glow. The cool breeze whispered through the trees, carrying with it the weight of her choices. Her mind became a labyrinth of contemplation, a maze of uncertainty.

On one path, she glimpsed the vivid memories of her moments with Erik—the stolen kisses, the rush of passion, and the bond they had forged. Their connection had ignited a flame within her, one that refused to be extinguished. The thought of a life with Erik sparked a warmth that resonated deep within her soul.

But on another path, she confronted the reality of her marriage—the vows she had taken, the promises she had made. Guilt coursed through her veins like a poison, clouding her thoughts and weighing heavily on her conscience. The pain she would inflict upon her spouse and the potential destruction of her family became an unbearable burden to bear.

Thór, ever the loyal companion, offered comfort in his silent presence. He stood beside her, a symbol of loyalty and devotion, a reminder of the unwavering love that existed in her life beyond Erik. His watchful eyes conveyed a mixture of understanding and support, urging her to listen to the whispers of her heart and find a path towards resolution.

Freya longed for a way to reconcile her desires with her obligations. She yearned for a life where love and duty could coexist harmoniously—a life where she could honor her own heart while respecting the commitments she had made.

In the depths of her conflicted heart, Freya began to seek clarity. She engaged in introspection, soul-searching that demanded courage and honesty. She questioned her motivations, the roots of her discontent, and the consequences of her actions.

As she delved deeper into her inner turmoil, she realized that her conflicting desires were not simply a matter of choosing between Erik and her marriage. It was a matter of finding her own voice, her own path to happiness and fulfillment. She acknowledged that her happiness did not solely lie in the hands of another but within her own power to shape her destiny.

Freya confronted the guilt that had plagued her, addressing the pain she would cause to those she cared for deeply. She understood that decisions made in pursuit of love were not without consequences, that her actions could wound and scar those she held dear. The weight of that understanding tempered her resolve, reminding her of the importance of compassion and empathy in her choices.

In the silence of her contemplation, Freya found strength. She discovered that true resolution lay in seeking a path of integrity and authenticity—a path that honored her desires while remaining mindful of the impact on others. She resolved to communicate openly, to engage in difficult conversations with both Erik and her spouse, to seek understanding and forgiveness.

With Thór by her side, a beacon of steadfast support, Freya embarked on a journey of self-discovery and healing. She would navigate the complex landscape of her conflicted heart, embracing the courage to confront her choices head-on. She understood that her decisions would shape not only her own happiness but also the lives of those intertwined with hers.

The path ahead remained uncertain, fraught with challenges and difficult decisions. But as Freya took her first steps towards resolution, she carried within her a newfound clarity—an understanding that love, when intertwined with duty and responsibility, demanded courage, empathy, and unwavering self-reflection.

In the depths of her conflicted heart, Freya vowed to find a way to honor her own desires while acknowledging the consequences of her actions. She sought a path where love and duty could coexist, where her heart and her commitments could find a delicate balance.

With Thór as her loyal companion and the echoes of her conflicting emotions still reverberating within her, Freya embarked on a journey of self-discovery—a journey that would test her resilience, challenge her perceptions, and lead her towards a resolution that would bring peace to her conflicted heart.

Chapter 28: The Viking's Torment

Erik's tormented soul battled against the consequences of his actions, his heart aching with the weight of guilt and remorse. The love he held for Freya burned like a relentless flame within him, yet the pain of betraying his vows and the havoc he had wreaked upon his family gnawed at his conscience.

Every waking moment was a torment, his mind haunted by the choices he had made. The image of his spouse, the one he had promised to cherish and protect, haunted his thoughts, their hurt etched deep within his soul. The shattered trust and the potential devastation he had caused weighed heavily upon him.

In the depths of his despair, Erik sought solace in the solitude of nature. The vast expanse of the wilderness offered a temporary respite from the turmoil of his emotions. Amidst the towering trees and the rustling leaves, he cried out to the gods, pleading for guidance and forgiveness, seeking redemption for the pain he had inflicted.

Thór, his loyal companion, stood by his side, a steadfast presence that offered silent support. The dog's unwavering gaze conveyed a mixture of understanding and encouragement, reminding Erik of the need to confront his tormented soul and find a path towards healing.

Haunted by his torment, Erik began a journey of self-reflection. He delved into the depths of his own character, exploring the motivations and vulnerabilities that had led him astray. He confronted his weaknesses, acknowledging the flaws that had clouded his judgment and fueled his actions.

With each introspective step, Erik recognized the need for accountability. He confronted the pain he had caused, both to his spouse and to himself. He embraced the responsibility of facing the consequences of his choices, acknowledging that true growth required acknowledging and learning from his mistakes.

The Viking's torment was not merely a result of his own guilt, but also the profound love he held for Freya. His heart longed for a life with her, to explore the depths of their connection without the chains of secrecy and betrayal. Yet, the awareness of the pain and destruction their love had caused gnawed at his very core.

In the depths of his anguish, Erik yearned for a path towards redemption. He understood that his actions had shattered the trust of those he held dear, and he was determined to repair the fragments he had broken. He sought forgiveness, both from those he had hurt and from himself, recognizing that forgiveness was a crucial step on the path to healing.

With Thór as his unwavering companion, Erik embarked on a journey of atonement. He reached out to his spouse, baring his soul with honesty and vulnerability. He apologized for his betrayal, seeking understanding and offering reassurance of his commitment to repairing the damage he had caused.

The road to redemption was fraught with obstacles, resistance, and pain. Erik faced the consequences of his actions head-on, acknowledging that healing would be a process that required time and effort. Yet, within the depths of his tormented soul, a flicker of hope remained—a hope that through repentance and genuine efforts towards change, he could mend what had been broken.

As Erik navigated his torment, he committed himself to personal growth and self-improvement. He engaged in deep introspection, striving to understand the root causes of his actions and the lessons they held. He sought guidance from wise elders and sought solace in the teachings of his ancestors, drawing strength from their wisdom and the rich tapestry of Viking traditions.

In the depths of his remorse, Erik held onto the belief that his tormented soul could find redemption. He understood that healing would require patience, forgiveness, and a commitment to making amends. With each step on the path towards atonement, he hoped to rebuild not only his own character but also the trust of those who had been affected by his choices.

The Viking's torment became a catalyst for transformation. Through his journey of self-reflection and atonement, Erik endeavored to rise above the pain he had caused and embrace a life of integrity and honor. With Thór as his steadfast companion and the flicker of hope burning within, he set forth on a path that would lead him towards redemption, forgiveness, and ultimately, a newfound sense of peace.

Chapter 29: The Marriage Vows

In the wake of turmoil and heartache, the sacred vows that bound Erik's marriage stood as a beacon of hope amidst the darkness. The weight of his betrayal lay heavy upon his shoulders, but he knew that in order to find redemption, he must honor and rebuild the foundations of his commitment.

With a heavy heart and a newfound sense of purpose, Erik turned his attention to his spouse. He sought to reaffirm the vows that they had once spoken, the promises that had formed the bedrock of their union. He knew that healing would require not only repentance but also a genuine effort to rebuild the trust that had been shattered.

In a quiet moment, Erik approached his spouse with humility and a profound desire to make amends. He bared his soul, expressing the depth of his remorse and acknowledging the pain he had caused. He spoke from a place of genuine contrition, vowing to do whatever it took to rebuild their relationship.

Tears welled in the eyes of his spouse, a mixture of hurt, confusion, and cautious hope. The wounds inflicted by Erik's actions were still fresh, but his genuine remorse offered a glimmer of possibility—a flicker of belief that healing was indeed possible.

Together, they revisited their marriage vows, reciting the words that had once bound them together. They spoke of love, of commitment, and of the promises they had made to one another. In that sacred moment, Erik made a silent vow to honor those words with unwavering dedication and sincerity.

Thór, the loyal companion, bore witness to this heartfelt exchange. His presence served as a reminder of the unconditional love that existed within their union—a love that had been tested but not extinguished. He offered silent support, his steady gaze a symbol of hope and encouragement.

Erik understood that rebuilding trust would not happen overnight. It would require consistent effort, open communication, and a willingness to confront the scars left by his betrayal. He was committed to earning back the trust that had been lost, to proving his sincerity through his actions, day after day.

As the days turned into weeks and then months, Erik embraced the opportunity to demonstrate his growth and transformation. He became more attuned to his spouse's needs, actively listening and seeking to understand their perspective. He engaged in heartfelt conversations, fostering a safe space for honest communication and vulnerability.

Small gestures of love and consideration began to bridge the divide that had grown between them. Erik sought to show his spouse that he was committed to being the partner they deserved—a partner who recognized the value of their bond and was determined to make amends.

In his quest for redemption, Erik also engaged in self-reflection and self-improvement. He delved into the depths of his own character, addressing the flaws that had led him astray. He sought guidance from wise elders, seeking their wisdom and incorporating their teachings into his own journey of growth.

Through his dedication and genuine efforts towards rebuilding their relationship, Erik began to witness the slow but steady rekindling of the flame that had once burned brightly. Trust, like a delicate blossom, began to unfurl its petals, with tentative hope and cautious optimism.

Thór, ever present, stood as a symbol of the love and loyalty that Erik aspired to embody. The dog's unwavering support and companionship served as a reminder of the depths of commitment and the resilience of their bond.

As Erik and his spouse navigated the complex path of healing, their marriage vows became a guiding light, an anchor that held them steady amidst the storms they faced. They worked together to rebuild their foundation, to reshape their future, and to forge a love that was fortified by the trials they had endured.

In the process of healing their relationship, Erik and his spouse discovered that the scars left by his betrayal could become a testament to the strength of their love. They learned that forgiveness, though a difficult journey, had the power to mend the broken pieces and create something even more beautiful—a love that had been tested and emerged stronger.

Together, they embraced the path of reconciliation, knowing that the road ahead would not be without challenges. Yet, armed with renewed commitment, open hearts, and a shared understanding of the value of their vows, they embarked on a journey towards the restoration of their marriage—a journey guided by love, trust, and the unwavering desire to honor the sacred promises they had once made.

Chapter 30: The Girl's Desperate Plea

Freya's heart, burdened by the weight of her conflicted desires, reached a breaking point. The turmoil within her grew unbearable, and she found herself at a crossroads, torn between the love she held for Erik and the commitment she had made to her marriage.

In the depths of her despair, Freya realized that remaining in limbo was no longer an option. The torment of her conflicted heart had become too much to bear. With a trembling resolve, she sought out Erik, her voice quivering as she poured out her emotions.

In a secluded place where they had once found solace, Freya stood before Erik, her eyes filled with a mixture of desperation and longing. She spoke with raw vulnerability, her voice laced with the pain of unfulfilled love.

"Erik," she began, her voice quivering. "I am consumed by this torment, torn between the love I hold for you and the vows I have made. My heart aches, and I can no longer bear this anguish. Please, help me find a way forward."

Tears welled in Freya's eyes, mirroring the pain that Erik had carried within himself. In that moment, she pleaded for understanding, for guidance, and for a resolution that would bring peace to their tormented souls.

Erik, his own heart heavy with the weight of his choices, listened to Freya's desperate plea. He understood the depths of her anguish, for he too had wrestled with his own conflicted desires. Her words resonated with him, touching a chord that echoed with the longing and pain he held within his own soul.

With a mixture of tenderness and determination, Erik reached out to hold Freya's trembling hands. His voice, filled with sincerity, responded, "Freya, I too carry the weight of this torment within me. I understand the depth of your longing, and I share in your pain. Let us seek a way forward together, for the love that binds us demands that we face this storm united."

In that moment, a flicker of hope ignited within Freya's heart. She realized that they were not alone in their struggle, that they could navigate the tumultuous waters together. The desperate plea had opened a door to a path of understanding and resolution—a path that would require courage, compromise, and unwavering commitment.

Thór, the ever-watchful companion, stood by their side, his presence a symbol of loyalty and support. His calm gaze seemed to convey a silent reassurance, reminding them that their love, though tested, was worth fighting for.

Together, Erik and Freya vowed to confront their conflicting desires and seek a resolution that honored their commitments and their love. They recognized that finding a way forward would require difficult conversations, deep introspection, and a willingness to make difficult choices.

In the days that followed, Erik and Freya embarked on a journey of self-discovery and open communication. They explored the depths of their own hearts, seeking to understand the roots of their desires and the impact of their choices. They engaged in honest conversations, sharing their fears, hopes, and dreams, with the intention of finding a middle ground that would bring them solace.

Their desperate plea had opened the door to a renewed sense of purpose. They were no longer resigned to the torment of unfulfilled love but committed to finding a resolution that would honor their values, their commitments, and their own well-being.

In the face of uncertainty, Erik and Freya held onto the belief that their love was powerful enough to guide them through the storm. With each step forward, they would navigate the complexities of their desires and obligations, trusting in their shared commitment to find a way that would bring them both peace and fulfillment.

The desperate plea had sparked a journey of self-discovery and hope. With Thór by their side, a constant reminder of loyalty and unwavering love, Erik and Freya set forth on a path that would test their resilience, challenge their beliefs, and ultimately lead them towards a resolution that would honor both their hearts and their commitments.

Chapter 31: The Secrets Unveiled

As Erik and Freya delved deeper into their quest for resolution, the journey of self-discovery led them to unveil hidden truths that had remained buried beneath layers of secrecy. In their pursuit of understanding and healing, the secrets they had held close began to unravel, exposing vulnerabilities and shaping the path before them.

With trust and vulnerability as their guides, Erik and Freya found the courage to share the hidden parts of their lives. In a space of honesty and compassion, they revealed the struggles, fears, and traumas that had shaped them as individuals. The unveiling of these secrets opened a window into their souls, fostering a deeper understanding of each other's journeys.

Erik confessed the pain he had carried from his past, the wounds that had fueled his choices and led him astray. He bared his soul, sharing the vulnerabilities that had driven him to seek solace outside his marriage. The weight of his confession lifted, replaced by a newfound sense of accountability and a commitment to growth.

Freya, in turn, unveiled the complex emotions that had driven her into Erik's arms. She revealed the discontent that had simmered beneath the surface of her marriage, the longing for a connection that felt authentic and true. The secrets she had held no longer bound her, as she bravely faced the consequences of her desires.

In the space between them, the revelations formed bridges of understanding and empathy. Erik and Freya recognized that their journeys had been intertwined, that their choices were not made in isolation but were shaped by the complexities of their individual stories. Their secrets, once heavy burdens, became catalysts for deeper connection and a shared commitment to healing.

Thór, the ever-loyal companion, observed the unfolding revelations with a keen sense of understanding. He recognized that the unveiling of their secrets was a necessary step on their journey towards resolution. His presence provided a sense of grounding and assurance, a reminder that true growth required confronting the hidden truths that lay dormant within.

Together, Erik and Freya navigated the aftermath of the secrets unveiled. They held space for each other's pain and fears, offering support and understanding as they grappled with the implications of their revelations. They understood that healing required not only personal growth but also compassion for the scars left by their shared journey.

In the wake of the secrets unveiled, Erik and Freya began to reshape their perspectives. They recognized that their desires, though valid, needed to be grounded in a deeper understanding of themselves and their commitments. They questioned societal expectations and traditional notions of love and marriage, seeking a path that honored their individual truths.

Through their shared vulnerability, they learned to embrace the complexities of love and relationships. They understood that no union was without its imperfections, and that true strength lay in the ability to confront the shadows that lay hidden beneath the surface. They were committed to weaving a new narrative—one that honored their desires while remaining anchored in integrity and compassion.

As Erik and Freya ventured forward, the secrets unveiled became catalysts for personal growth and transformation. They embarked on a journey of self-reflection and self-improvement, recognizing that the unveiling of their secrets had opened a door to profound change.

With each step, they forged a path that embraced authenticity and open communication. Their shared commitment to growth and understanding became the foundation upon which they could build a love that was grounded in truth and compassion.

The secrets unveiled had illuminated the intricacies of their desires and the depths of their souls. Erik and Freya understood that the journey ahead would still be challenging, but armed with their newfound knowledge, they moved forward, ready to face the complexities of their intertwined lives with courage and an unwavering commitment to personal and shared growth.

Chapter 32: The Revelation

In the midst of their journey towards healing and understanding, Erik and Freya stumbled upon a revelation that would shake the very foundation of their world. A long-kept secret, buried deep within the annals of their shared history, came to light, sending shockwaves through their hearts and minds.

As they continued their conversations of honesty and vulnerability, a piece of the puzzle fell into place—a puzzle they had unknowingly been solving all along. An unexpected encounter with an elder in their community unveiled a truth that had remained hidden for years, a truth that would forever change their perception of themselves and their connection.

With bated breath and a mixture of trepidation and curiosity, Erik and Freya listened to the elder's words. The revelation unfolded like a forgotten tale, weaving together the threads of their past, their families, and their shared destiny.

It was revealed that Erik and Freya, whose paths had crossed seemingly by chance, were not strangers after all. Their connection ran deeper than they had ever imagined—it was rooted in a shared lineage, bound by ancestral ties that dated back generations.

As the elder's words hung in the air, Erik and Freya's minds raced with the implications of this revelation. They realized that the magnetic pull they had felt towards each other was not merely a product of chance or forbidden desire, but a reflection of a bond forged long before their time.

The weight of this newfound knowledge settled upon them, stirring a mix of awe, confusion, and a profound sense of destiny. They grappled with the realization that their love was not simply a transgression against their current lives, but an intricate tapestry woven by the threads of their shared heritage.

Thór, the ever-watchful companion, seemed to sense the gravity of the revelation. His gaze held a knowingness, as if he too understood the depth of the connection that had unfolded before them. In his presence, Erik and Freya found solace—a reminder that even amidst the chaos of their unraveling world, there was a steadfast presence that would guide them forward.

The revelation became a turning point in Erik and Freya's journey. It offered a new perspective, one that transcended the boundaries of their individual desires and obligations. It forced them to question the meaning of their connection, the intricacies of fate, and the significance of the love that had blossomed between them.

With this revelation, Erik and Freya embarked on a profound exploration of their shared history. They dove into the depths of their ancestral roots, seeking to understand the stories that had shaped their families and the invisible threads that had brought them together.

In their quest for understanding, they discovered tales of forbidden love, sacrifice, and the enduring power of connection. They realized that their own story was part of a larger narrative, one that had been played out across generations—a tapestry of love, heartache, and the pursuit of authenticity.

The revelation infused their journey with a renewed sense of purpose. Erik and Freya saw themselves as custodians of a legacy—a legacy that demanded they honor the sacrifices of their ancestors while forging a path that honored their own desires and convictions.

Armed with the weight of their shared heritage, Erik and Freya's commitment to healing and growth took on a deeper significance. They understood that their love carried a profound responsibility—one that required them to navigate the complexities of their desires and obligations with grace and integrity.

As they ventured forward, they carried the revelation as both a burden and a blessing. It challenged them to embrace the fullness of their story, the richness of their shared history, and the transformative power of their love. The revelation became the catalyst for a deeper understanding of themselves, their connection, and the legacy they would leave behind.

Erik and Freya were no longer just two individuals entangled in a forbidden love— they were the embodiment of a tale written by the hands of their ancestors, a story that demanded to be told with authenticity and reverence.

Together, they set forth on a path that honored the revelation, embracing the weight of their shared heritage, and remaining steadfast in their commitment to chart a course that would weave their own story into the tapestry of their ancestors. Guided by the love that had brought them together, they faced the challenges ahead with a newfound clarity and determination.

Chapter 33: The Consequences of Betrayal

The revelation of Erik and Freya's shared heritage had brought them closer, yet it also amplified the consequences of their betrayal. As they confronted the weight of their actions, the ripples of their choices began to reverberate through their lives, affecting not only themselves but also those around them.

Erik and Freya grappled with the fallout of their betrayal, understanding the pain they had inflicted upon their spouses, families, and communities. The trust they had shattered could not be easily rebuilt, and they were faced with the reality that some wounds may never fully heal.

Their spouses, upon learning the truth, were devastated. The pain etched in their eyes mirrored the depth of the betrayal they had endured. The foundations of their marriages had been shaken, and they were left to navigate a tumultuous sea of anger, heartache, and shattered dreams.

Friends and community members, once pillars of support, struggled to comprehend the extent of the deception. Whispers and judgment hung in the air, casting a shadow over Erik and Freya's lives. They had become symbols of broken trust, their actions tarnishing their reputations and straining the relationships they had once cherished.

Thór, ever the loyal companion, offered solace to Erik and Freya as they grappled with the consequences of their betrayal. His unwavering presence served as a reminder of the unconditional love that existed within their lives, even in the face of their transgressions. He stood by their side, offering comfort without judgment.

In the midst of the storm, Erik and Freya recognized the need for accountability and remorse. They acknowledged the pain they had caused and took responsibility for their actions. Their love, once a source of joy and passion, had become a reminder of the damage they had wrought.

Seeking redemption, they engaged in acts of restitution and healing. They offered sincere apologies, seeking forgiveness from those they had hurt. They committed themselves to rebuilding trust through actions aligned with their words, knowing that true redemption would require patience, consistency, and unwavering dedication.

The consequences of their betrayal forced Erik and Freya to confront their own demons and grow as individuals. They embarked on a journey of self-reflection and transformation, delving into the depths of their own souls to address the flaws and vulnerabilities that had led them astray.

They sought guidance from wise elders, engaging in deep introspection and embracing the wisdom of those who had weathered similar storms. They learned to confront their own shadows, to navigate the complexities of desire and obligation with integrity and compassion.

Together, they faced the judgments and whispers of their community with resilience and grace. They recognized that they could not control others' perceptions or the duration of the consequences they faced. Instead, they focused on their own growth, seeking to emerge from the shadows of their mistakes as stronger, wiser individuals.

The consequences of betrayal were not easily overcome, but Erik and Freya refused to let their past define their future. They remained committed to personal growth and building a foundation of trust, understanding that healing would take time and effort from all parties involved.

Through their commitment to accountability and growth, they began to rebuild fragments of what had been broken. Slowly, trust was rekindled, wounds began to heal, and a semblance of stability returned to their lives. Their journey towards redemption was marked by small victories and moments of healing, serving as reminders of the resilience of the human spirit.

As they faced the consequences of their betrayal, Erik and Freya found solace in the shared belief that true growth and transformation were possible even in the face of their gravest mistakes. With Thór by their side, a symbol of unwavering loyalty, they resolved to learn from their past and forge a future defined by integrity, forgiveness, and a commitment to authenticity.

The consequences of betrayal would forever leave an indelible mark on their lives. However, Erik and Freya embraced the opportunity for growth and redemption, recognizing that the journey towards healing required confronting the consequences head-on, holding themselves accountable, and striving to become better versions of themselves.

Chapter 34: A Broken Promise

In the wake of their betrayal and the consequences they faced, Erik and Freya were confronted with the painful realization of a broken promise—a promise they had made to themselves and to each other in the depths of their love and longing.

The weight of their actions weighed heavily upon them, tarnishing the once-bright flame of their forbidden love. The trust they had shattered had left scars that ran deep, eroding the foundation of their connection. The broken promise served as a painful reminder of the pain they had inflicted upon themselves and those they held dear.

As they stood at this crossroads, Erik and Freya confronted the truth that their actions had betrayed not only their spouses and their community but also their own integrity. The promises they had made to honor their commitments and respect the sanctity of their marriages had been cast aside in the pursuit of their desires.

Thór, their loyal companion, stood beside them, his presence a reminder of the unwavering loyalty that they had forsaken in their pursuit of a love that defied the boundaries of their obligations. His watchful eyes conveyed a mix of empathy and sorrow, mirroring the weight of their broken promise.

With heavy hearts, Erik and Freya recognized the need for profound self-reflection and soul-searching. They questioned the choices they had made and the impact those choices had on their own moral compasses. They confronted the pain they had caused to themselves and to others, acknowledging the depth of their betrayal.

In the depths of their remorse, they vowed to learn from their mistakes and to honor the promises they had broken. They recognized that true growth and redemption could only be achieved through a commitment to integrity and authenticity. Their broken promise became a catalyst for self-transformation—a call to reevaluate their values and realign their actions with their moral compasses.

Erik and Freya knew that rebuilding trust, both within themselves and with others, would require consistent effort and unwavering dedication. They recognized that words alone could not heal the wounds they had inflicted, but rather, their actions would be the measure of their sincerity and growth.

Together, they recommitted themselves to the promises they had made—to honor their commitments, to respect the boundaries of their marriages, and to seek a path of integrity and honesty. They embraced the challenging road ahead, knowing that the journey of redemption would demand courage, perseverance, and the willingness to face the consequences of their choices head-on.

In the eyes of their spouses, they sought forgiveness, knowing that it would be a long and arduous road to rebuild the shattered trust. They engaged in heartfelt conversations, offering heartfelt apologies and demonstrating through their actions a renewed commitment to change.

Their broken promise served as a constant reminder of the importance of accountability and the fragility of trust. It became the cornerstone upon which they would rebuild their lives, shaping their actions, and guiding their decisions with unwavering integrity.

As Erik and Freya embarked on this path of redemption, they knew that the road would not be easy. The scars of their betrayal would forever be etched upon their hearts, a reminder of the pain they had caused. Yet, armed with remorse and a renewed sense of purpose, they committed themselves to healing, growth, and the mending of the broken promise they had once made.

In the shadow of their broken promise, they found solace in the belief that true transformation was possible. Through their commitment to self-improvement and their relentless pursuit of integrity, they aimed to forge a future defined by honor, compassion, and a renewed sense of the promises they would make and keep.

The broken promise became a catalyst for a new chapter in their lives—one of humility, redemption, and a steadfast commitment to rebuilding trust, not only with others but also within themselves. With Thór by their side, a constant reminder of loyalty and the resilience of love, they took their first steps towards a future where their actions would reflect the promises they had once made, and where the wounds of betrayal could slowly begin to heal.

Chapter 35: The Girl's Struggle

Freya found herself engulfed in a profound struggle, torn between the love she held for Erik and the consequences of their actions. The weight of her choices bore heavily upon her, as she grappled with the aftermath of the broken promise and the impact it had on her life and the lives of those around her.

In the depths of her soul, Freya confronted a whirlwind of emotions—guilt, remorse, and a deep sense of longing. The echoes of her betrayal reverberated through her heart, challenging her sense of self and forcing her to question the boundaries of love, commitment, and personal integrity.

Every decision became a battlefield within her mind. She questioned the path she had chosen and the pain it had caused. The conflicting desires within her waged an internal war, leaving her feeling lost and uncertain of the way forward.

The consequences of her actions seeped into every aspect of her life. The once vibrant connections she had with her spouse and her community now felt strained and distant. She felt the weight of their judgment and the piercing gaze of disappointment, which only intensified her struggle.

Thór, sensing her anguish, offered unwavering support and companionship. His presence served as a constant reminder that she was not alone in her journey, that amidst the turmoil, she still had the capacity to heal and grow. His gentle nature offered solace, a respite from the storm that raged within her.

Amidst the chaos of her emotions, Freya sought clarity and guidance. She turned to introspection, diving into the depths of her own heart and confronting the vulnerabilities and flaws that had led her astray. She grappled with questions of identity and self-worth, yearning to reconcile her desires with her commitment to personal integrity.

Through the struggle, Freya began to recognize the importance of forgiveness—not only from those she had hurt but also from herself. She understood that growth and healing required acknowledging her mistakes, learning from them, and embracing a path of self-compassion.

She engaged in honest conversations with her spouse, laying bare her remorse and demonstrating her commitment to rebuilding trust. She sought to rebuild the foundations of their connection, knowing that it would take time and consistent effort to mend the wounds they had endured.

Freya's struggle was not only internal but also external. She faced the judgment and whispers of the community, grappling with the fear of being defined solely by her past actions. She was confronted with the challenge of proving her growth and sincerity in the face of skepticism.

As she navigated this tumultuous journey, Freya learned to embrace vulnerability as a source of strength. She began to let go of the shame that had consumed her, recognizing that she was more than her mistakes. She held onto the belief that redemption was possible, that through her struggle, she could emerge as a stronger, more compassionate individual.

Though the struggle remained, Freya refused to succumb to despair. She held onto the flicker of hope that burned within her, knowing that within the depths of her struggle, there was the potential for growth, healing, and the redemption she sought.

In the midst of her inner turmoil, Freya understood that the journey towards self-forgiveness and reconciliation would be a lifelong process. It required consistent effort, self-reflection, and a commitment to personal growth. She accepted that her struggle would shape her, molding her into a woman who had learned from her mistakes and strived to become the best version of herself.

With Thór by her side, Freya drew strength from his unwavering loyalty and the reminder that love, even in its most complicated forms, had the power to heal and transform. In the face of her struggle, she vowed to persevere, to confront the complexities of her desires and obligations with courage and authenticity.

Freya's struggle became a catalyst for personal growth and a deepened understanding of the complexities of love and commitment. With each step forward, she moved closer to finding peace within herself and reclaiming her sense of purpose. The struggle became a testament to her resilience, reminding her that even amidst the darkest moments, the human spirit has the capacity to endure, learn, and heal.

Chapter 36: The Viking's Agony

Erik, consumed by the weight of his actions and the consequences they had unleashed, found himself engulfed in a deep agony. The pain of his betrayal, coupled with the shattered trust and broken promises, tore at his soul, leaving him feeling lost and tormented.

The once vibrant spirit that had animated Erik now withered under the weight of remorse and self-condemnation. He grappled with the knowledge that his choices had caused immeasurable pain to those he held dear. The agony he felt reverberated through every fiber of his being, leaving him in a state of profound despair.

Guilt gnawed at Erik's conscience, a constant reminder of the pain he had inflicted. The once confident and determined Viking now wrestled with doubt and self-reproach. He questioned his own integrity, his ability to make sound decisions, and the irreparable damage he had wrought.

Thór, the ever-faithful companion, sensed Erik's agony. The loyal dog stood by his side, offering silent support and unconditional love.

His presence provided a sense of solace amidst the turmoil, reminding Erik that he was not alone in his suffering.

In the depths of his agony, Erik sought solace through self-reflection. He delved into the recesses of his soul, confronting the flaws and vulnerabilities that had led him astray. He faced his own shadows, seeking to understand the root of his desires and the choices that had brought him to this point.

With each passing day, Erik grappled with the consequences of his actions. He witnessed the pain in the eyes of his spouse, a reflection of the deep betrayal he had inflicted upon them. The once unbreakable bond between them had been fractured, and Erik felt the weight of their shattered trust.

The agony within Erik's heart deepened as he considered the impact of his betrayal on his community. Whispers and judgment followed him wherever he went, casting a shadow over his interactions and relationships. He saw the disappointment in the eyes of friends and family, the shattered image they once held of him.

Haunted by his actions, Erik engaged in acts of restitution and self-improvement. He committed himself to rebuilding trust through consistent effort and unwavering dedication.

He sought forgiveness, not only from those he had hurt but also from himself, knowing that true growth required acknowledging his mistakes and taking steps to rectify them.

His agony became a catalyst for introspection and transformation. Erik questioned the values he had held and the choices he had made, seeking to align his actions with his own moral compass. He confronted the depths of his remorse and, through his agony, discovered a newfound resolve to become a better man.

With every fiber of his being, Erik vowed to learn from his mistakes and make amends. He engaged in open conversations with his spouse, offering sincere apologies and demonstrating his commitment to change. He understood that rebuilding the foundations of their relationship would be a long and arduous journey, one that required patience, understanding, and unwavering dedication.

Amidst his agony, Erik began to grasp the transformative power of redemption. He recognized that the path to healing required confronting his own demons, seeking forgiveness, and taking tangible steps towards personal growth. His agony became a driving force for change, igniting a flicker of hope within him that redemption was indeed possible.

With Thór by his side, a constant reminder of loyalty and the resilience of love, Erik drew strength. The dog's unwavering presence offered comfort and encouragement, reminding him that he had the capacity to heal and rebuild, even in the face of his greatest mistakes.

Erik's agony served as a testament to the depth of his remorse and the desire to make things right. With each passing day, he moved forward with a renewed determination to become a man of integrity, a man who would confront the consequences of his betrayal head-on and work tirelessly to rebuild the trust he had shattered.

As he navigated the depths of his agony, Erik clung to the belief that even amidst the darkest moments, there was the potential for redemption. Through his remorse and the transformative power of his actions, he aimed to emerge from the depths of his agony as a changed man—one who had learned from his mistakes and embraced the opportunity for growth and healing.

Chapter 37: The Trials and Tribulations

Erik and Freya faced a series of trials and tribulations as they sought to rebuild their lives and navigate the aftermath of their betrayal. The path to redemption proved to be a challenging one, fraught with obstacles and moments of doubt.

Their commitment to personal growth and healing was tested at every turn. They encountered skepticism and judgment from their community, faced the consequences of their actions head-on, and wrestled with their own inner demons. Each trial they encountered served as a crucible, forging their resilience and determination.

Together, Erik and Freya confronted the skepticism and doubt that surrounded their journey of redemption. They understood that actions would speak louder than words, and they dedicated themselves to demonstrating consistent effort, transparency, and integrity. With each step forward, they aimed to rebuild trust and prove that their remorse was genuine.

The tribulations they faced also tested their resolve to honor the promises they had made

—to themselves, to their spouses, and to the bonds they had once held sacred. They confronted moments of temptation and uncertainty, where the remnants of their forbidden love threatened to resurface. But through their commitment to growth, they remained steadfast, resolute in their determination to choose the path of integrity.

In their journey towards redemption, Erik and Freya sought guidance from wise elders and sought solace in the support of those who understood the complexities of their struggle. They engaged in therapy and counseling, delving into the depths of their own psyches to uncover the root causes of their choices and to develop strategies for lasting change.

The trials and tribulations they encountered also required them to confront their own flaws and vulnerabilities. They acknowledged the wounds that had led them astray and made a conscious effort to address them. With humility, they accepted responsibility for their actions and committed themselves to personal growth and self-improvement.

Amidst the trials, Thór remained a steadfast presence, offering unwavering support and unconditional love. His companionship served as a reminder that even in the face of adversity, they were not alone. His watchful eyes mirrored the resilience and loyalty they aspired to embody.

Throughout their journey, Erik and Freya experienced moments of doubt and moments of profound growth. They recognized that the road to redemption was not linear, but rather, it was marked by peaks and valleys. They stumbled and faltered, but with each setback, they gained the strength to rise again.

Their commitment to healing extended beyond their personal journeys. They sought to repair the relationships they had damaged, engaging in open and honest conversations with their spouses, family members, and friends. They listened with empathy and offered heartfelt apologies, acknowledging the pain they had caused and demonstrating their genuine desire to make amends.

The trials and tribulations served as reminders of the fragility of trust and the complexities of human relationships. Erik and Freya learned to approach each challenge with humility, compassion, and a willingness to confront their own limitations. They recognized that redemption required more than just the absence of further transgressions—it demanded consistent effort, empathy, and a commitment to growth.

As they navigated the trials and tribulations, Erik and Freya embraced the belief that their journey of redemption was a lifelong process. They understood that healing and growth were not achieved overnight, but through perseverance, self-reflection, and a relentless pursuit of integrity.

With every trial they overcame, Erik and Freya emerged stronger and more resilient. They held onto the lessons learned, the wisdom gained, and the transformative power of their journey. Together, they faced the trials and tribulations with unwavering determination, knowing that true redemption lay in their unwavering commitment to personal growth, healing, and the rebuilding of trust.

Chapter 38: A Glimmer of Hope

Amidst the trials and tribulations that Erik and Freya faced on their journey of redemption, a glimmer of hope emerged, illuminating their path with newfound possibilities. In the midst of their struggle, they began to see the seeds of transformation taking root, offering a ray of light amidst the darkness.

As Erik and Freya committed themselves to personal growth and rebuilding trust, they started to witness the first signs of progress. The wounds they had inflicted upon their loved ones, though deep and lasting, began to show signs of healing. Tentative gestures of forgiveness were extended, bridging the chasms that had separated them.

Their spouses, once consumed by anger and heartache, saw the genuine remorse in Erik and Freya's actions. They recognized the sincerity of their efforts to change, to rebuild what had been shattered. With cautious optimism, they embraced the possibility of mending their broken relationships, albeit with the understanding that healing would take time and consistent effort.

Erik and Freya, fueled by this glimmer of hope, redoubled their commitment to personal growth and transformation. They engaged in self-reflection and sought therapy to address the underlying issues that had led them astray. With every step forward, they became more attuned to the intricacies of their desires, boundaries, and the importance of open and honest communication.

Thór, the ever-faithful companion, sensed the shift in energy. His presence served as a constant reminder of loyalty, resilience, and the possibility of renewal. With a wag of his tail and a gentle nudge, he encouraged Erik and Freya to continue their journey, reminding them that the glimmer of hope they had discovered was worth pursuing.

In the wake of this newfound hope, Erik and Freya also began to see the potential for growth within themselves. They recognized that their actions had not only hurt others but had also hindered their own personal development. As they confronted their own shadows and vulnerabilities, they discovered strength and resilience they hadn't known existed.

The glimmer of hope extended beyond their personal lives and affected their community as well. The whispers and judgment that once surrounded them began to soften, replaced by curiosity and a cautious willingness to witness their transformation. The community, recognizing the sincere efforts of Erik and Freya, started to embrace the possibility of forgiveness and healing.

With every small victory, the glimmer of hope grew brighter. Erik and Freya found solace in the progress they made, no matter how incremental. They understood that true redemption was a journey, not a destination, and that every step forward, no matter how small, was a testament to their resilience and determination.

Amidst the glimmer of hope, Erik and Freya also rediscovered the depth of their love for one another. Though their connection had been forged in tumultuous circumstances, they recognized that the love they shared was not without its complications. They navigated the complexities of their desires, embracing a newfound understanding of the boundaries that must be honored to rebuild trust and nurture their individual growth.

Together, they embraced the belief that true redemption was possible, even in the face of their gravest mistakes. They held onto the glimmer of hope, knowing that the journey ahead would still be filled with challenges, but that with dedication, self-reflection, and unwavering commitment, they could continue to move towards a future defined by integrity, growth, and the possibility of a love that was built on a foundation of trust.

As the glimmer of hope grew brighter, Erik and Freya were reminded that their journey of redemption was not just about repairing what had been broken but also about becoming better versions of themselves. They embraced the challenges and setbacks that lay ahead, knowing that the glimmer of hope would guide them through the darkest moments and propel them towards a future where healing, forgiveness, and personal growth were not only possible but also inevitable.

Chapter 39: The Girl's Confession

As the glimmer of hope continued to illuminate their path, Freya found herself compelled to make a confession—one that held the potential to further heal the wounds inflicted by her betrayal and pave the way for a more authentic future.

With a heavy heart, Freya gathered her courage and sought a private moment with her spouse. She knew that honesty was the only way forward, even if it meant risking the fragile progress they had made in rebuilding trust. The weight of her confession bore down on her, but she understood that it was a necessary step towards true healing and redemption.

In a quiet, intimate setting, Freya looked into her spouse's eyes, her voice trembling with a mix of fear and vulnerability. With every word she spoke, she bared her soul, revealing the depths of her remorse and the complexities of her emotions. She expressed her deepest regrets for her past actions and acknowledged the pain she had caused.

Freya's confession was not just an admission of guilt; it was an act of self-discovery and a testament to her commitment to personal growth. She shared her journey of introspection, the lessons she had learned, and the steps she had taken towards self-improvement. She assured her spouse that she was determined to become a better person and to honor the trust they had once shared.

In her confession, Freya expressed her love, not as an excuse for her actions but as a testament to the complexity of the human heart. She recognized that love, though powerful, did not justify her betrayal. Instead, she saw it as a catalyst for her own growth and a source of strength to navigate the challenges that lay ahead.

Freya's spouse listened with a mix of disbelief, anger, and a flicker of hope. They saw the sincerity in her eyes, the rawness of her emotions, and the genuine desire for redemption. Though the wounds of betrayal still ran deep, they understood that forgiveness was a process—one that required time, patience, and a willingness to continue rebuilding the trust that had been shattered.

Thór, always attuned to the emotional currents within the room, stood by Freya's side, his presence a symbol of unwavering loyalty and a silent reminder of the journey they had embarked upon. His gentle demeanor offered a sense of comfort amidst the storm of emotions, reinforcing the genuine remorse and commitment Freya conveyed through her confession.

Freya's confession marked a turning point in their journey of redemption. It opened the door for a deeper level of understanding, transparency, and communication. It set the stage for further healing and allowed her spouse to express their own feelings, fears, and hopes for the future.

As they navigated the aftermath of Freya's confession, both Freya and her spouse recognized the complexities of rebuilding their relationship. They acknowledged the deep wounds that had been inflicted and the ongoing challenges they would face on their journey towards healing.

Freya's confession also had a profound impact on her own sense of self. In opening up about her past actions, she confronted her own vulnerabilities and embraced a newfound authenticity. She vowed to continue working on herself, not only for the sake of her relationship but also for her own personal growth and well-being.

In the wake of the confession, Freya's spouse grappled with a mix of emotions—pain, anger, and a glimmer of hope. The road ahead remained uncertain, but they saw the sincerity in Freya's words and actions. They recognized that healing would take time and effort from both parties, and they were willing to explore the possibility of a renewed connection.

Together, they committed themselves to open and honest communication, setting boundaries, and rebuilding trust step by step. They sought guidance from therapists and counselors, using the resources available to them to navigate the complexities of their journey.

Freya's confession also had ripple effects throughout their community. The honesty and vulnerability she displayed inspired conversations about the complexities of love, commitment, and personal growth. Others who had experienced similar struggles found solace and hope in Freya's willingness to confront her mistakes and work towards redemption.

As the days turned into weeks and the weeks into months, Freya and her spouse continued to face challenges and setbacks. But they also experienced moments of profound connection, forgiveness, and growth. They embraced the understanding that healing was not a linear process, but a journey marked by ups and downs.

Thór, ever the steadfast companion, remained a source of comfort and support for Freya and her spouse. His presence served as a reminder that loyalty and love could endure, even in the face of the most difficult circumstances. His unwavering presence was a silent testament to the power of second chances and the resilience of the human spirit.

Freya's confession had set in motion a process of healing, growth, and transformation. It marked a pivotal moment in their journey towards redemption, a moment of truth and vulnerability that allowed them to confront their past and pave the way for a future defined by honesty, trust, and the possibility of a renewed love.

Together, Freya and her spouse embraced the challenges that lay ahead, knowing that the road to redemption would not be easy. But they held onto the glimmer of hope ignited by Freya's confession—the belief that, with unwavering commitment and a willingness to confront their past, they could forge a future that honored their promises, their growth, and their shared journey of redemption.

Chapter 40: A Love Conflicted

As Erik and Freya continued their journey towards redemption, they found themselves caught in the tangled web of a conflicted love. The glimmer of hope they had nurtured was now met with the complexities of their emotions and the realities of their commitments.

Their hearts remained entwined, their connection undeniable. But with every step forward, they were reminded of the consequences of their actions and the vows they had taken with their spouses. The love they shared was not easily compartmentalized, and they grappled with the conflicting desires that pulled them in different directions.

Erik, torn between his love for Freya and the commitment he had made to his spouse, felt the weight of his conflicting emotions. The passion and longing that had once burned brightly now flickered amidst the turmoil of guilt and loyalty. He questioned his own integrity, struggling to reconcile his desires with the promise he had made to honor his marriage.

Freya, too, found herself caught in the grip of a conflicted love. The depth of her feelings for Erik clashed with her commitment to her spouse and the responsibility she felt towards repairing the wounds of her betrayal. Her heart yearned for a love that defied boundaries, yet she understood the importance of honoring her promises and seeking forgiveness.

Thór, ever perceptive, observed the turmoil within his companions. He offered silent solace, his presence a reminder of the loyalty and unwavering support that transcended the complexities of human love. His steady companionship provided comfort and encouragement, reminding Erik and Freya that they were not alone in their struggle.

As Erik and Freya confronted their conflicted love, they engaged in open and honest conversations. They acknowledged the intensity of their connection, yet recognized the boundaries they needed to uphold. They spoke of their desires and dreams, but also of the commitments and responsibilities that anchored them to their respective spouses.

Their conflicted love brought forth a deep sense of self-reflection. They questioned the nature of love and its capacity to coexist with commitment. They delved into the complexities of desire, loyalty, and personal growth, seeking to understand the nuances that defined their own emotional landscape.

Together, Erik and Freya explored the potential for growth within the confines of their committed relationships. They dedicated themselves to strengthening the bonds with their spouses, engaging in acts of genuine love, compassion, and support. They recognized that healing and transformation were not solely dependent on their connection with each other, but also on their ability to nurture and repair the relationships they had damaged.

In their conflicted love, Erik and Freya found an opportunity for personal growth and self-discovery. They recognized that true love encompassed not just the passionate moments of connection, but also the willingness to confront difficult choices and prioritize the well-being of those they had once pledged their hearts to.

The journey towards redemption was further complicated by the conflicting emotions they experienced. They navigated moments of longing, sadness, and doubt, all the while grappling with the guilt that came with their conflicted love. It was a delicate balance, requiring constant self-reflection and a commitment to personal integrity.

Amidst the complexities, Erik and Freya clung to the belief that their conflicted love had the potential to teach them valuable lessons. They saw it as an opportunity to redefine their understanding of love, commitment, and the boundaries that must be honored. They sought to forge a future where their conflicted emotions could coexist with the growth and transformation they aspired to achieve.

With Thór by their side, Erik and Freya drew strength from the unwavering loyalty he embodied. They knew that their journey would not be without challenges, but they remained committed to navigating the complexities of their conflicted love with grace and integrity.

As they continued on their path towards redemption, Erik and Freya embraced the reality of their conflicted love, recognizing that it was a reflection of their own humanity and the complexities of the human heart. They held onto the hope that, in time, they would find a way to honor their commitments while nurturing the love that had brought them together—a love that now served as a catalyst for personal growth, understanding, and the pursuit of a more authentic and balanced future.

Chapter 41: The Viking's Resolve

Erik, faced with the complexities of his emotions and the conflicting desires that tugged at his heart, found himself at a crossroads. The time had come for him to make a choice—a choice that would define the trajectory of his journey towards redemption and the path he would walk.

In the depths of his soul, Erik grappled with the weight of his conflicted love and the responsibilities he held as a Viking, a husband, and a man committed to personal growth. The glimmer of hope that had guided him thus far now served as a beacon, illuminating the way forward with unwavering clarity.

With a resolve that burned brightly within him, Erik reaffirmed his commitment to honor his marriage vows and the promises he had made. He recognized that true growth and redemption required acknowledging the complexities of love, but also embracing the importance of integrity, loyalty, and personal responsibility.

Thór, sensing Erik's resolve, stood steadfastly by his side, his presence a symbol of loyalty and the unwavering support that would guide Erik through the challenges that lay ahead. The loyal dog mirrored Erik's determination, his watchful eyes conveying a shared commitment to forging a path defined by authenticity and personal growth.

Erik engaged in soul-searching and introspection, seeking to understand the depths of his desires and the implications of his choices. He confronted the turmoil within his heart and acknowledged the pain he had caused to both his spouse and Freya. With each moment of reflection, his resolve strengthened, grounding him in the realization that true redemption lay in honoring the promises he had made.

He embarked on a journey of self-improvement, dedicating himself to strengthening the bonds with his spouse and working tirelessly to rebuild the trust he had shattered. Through acts of compassion, understanding, and unwavering support, he aimed to show his spouse the depth of his remorse and the sincerity of his commitment to change.

Erik also recognized that nurturing his own personal growth was essential to his journey of redemption. He sought wisdom from wise elders, sought guidance from mentors, and engaged in acts of self-reflection that allowed him to confront his own flaws and vulnerabilities. He knew that by cultivating his own integrity and authenticity, he would become a better man—a man worthy of the trust and love of those around him.

In the face of the conflicting desires that had once consumed him, Erik found solace in the strength of his resolve. He understood that true growth required making difficult choices and prioritizing the well-being of others over his own desires. His resolve became a compass, guiding him through the challenges and temptations that would undoubtedly arise on his path.

Though the journey ahead would not be easy, Erik clung to the belief that his resolve would carry him through. He knew that there would be moments of doubt, moments when the allure of his conflicted love would beckon. But with unwavering determination, he vowed to stay true to his commitment, to honor his marriage, and to walk a path defined by integrity and personal growth.

With Thór by his side, Erik embraced the companionship and unwavering loyalty the faithful dog offered. Together, they embarked on the next chapter of their journey—a chapter shaped by Erik's unwavering resolve, his commitment to personal growth, and his dedication to rebuilding the bonds he had once broken.

As Erik moved forward, his resolve burning brightly within him, he held onto the hope that his choices would lead not only to his own redemption, but also to the healing and growth of those he had hurt. He recognized that by staying true to his resolve, he could pave the way for a future defined by integrity, compassion, and a love that was rooted in the strength of his commitments and the growth he had achieved.

Chapter 42: The Difficult Choice

Freya, faced with the complexities of her emotions and the conflicting desires that tugged at her heart, found herself standing at a crossroad. The time had come for her to make a choice—a choice that would shape the course of her journey towards redemption and the path she would follow.

In the depths of her soul, Freya grappled with the weight of her conflicted love and the commitments she held as a wife, a woman, and an individual seeking personal growth. The glimmer of hope that had guided her thus far now served as a guiding light, illuminating the way forward with unwavering clarity.

With a resolve that burned fiercely within her, Freya reaffirmed her commitment to honor her marriage vows and the promises she had made. She recognized that true growth and redemption required acknowledging the complexities of love while embracing the importance of integrity, loyalty, and personal responsibility.

Thór, sensing Freya's resolve, stood faithfully by her side, his presence serving as a symbol of unwavering loyalty and the strength that would carry her through the challenges to come. The loyal dog mirrored Freya's determination, his watchful eyes conveying a shared commitment to forging a path defined by authenticity and personal growth.

Freya embarked on a journey of self-discovery and self-improvement, dedicating herself to nurturing the bonds with her spouse and working tirelessly to rebuild the trust she had shattered. She engaged in open and honest communication, offering sincere apologies and demonstrating her commitment to change. Through acts of empathy, compassion, and understanding, she aimed to show her spouse the depth of her remorse and the sincerity of her resolve.

Freya also recognized the importance of nurturing her own personal growth on her journey towards redemption. She delved into the depths of her own vulnerabilities, seeking to understand the root causes of her choices and addressing them head-on. With each moment of introspection, her resolve strengthened, grounding her in the realization that true redemption lay in honoring the promises she had made.

In the face of the conflicting desires that had once entangled her heart, Freya found solace in the strength of her resolve. She understood that true growth required making difficult choices and prioritizing the well-being of others over her own desires. Her resolve became an anchor, guiding her through the challenges and temptations that would inevitably arise on her path.

Though the journey ahead would be arduous, Freya clung to the belief that her difficult choice would lead to her own redemption and the healing of those she had hurt. She acknowledged that there would be moments of doubt, moments when the allure of her conflicted love would call to her. But with unwavering determination, she vowed to stay true to her commitment, to honor her marriage, and to walk a path defined by integrity and personal growth.

With Thór faithfully by her side, Freya embraced the unwavering support and companionship the loyal dog offered. Together, they ventured into the next chapter of their journey—a chapter shaped by Freya's unwavering resolve, her commitment to personal growth, and her dedication to rebuilding the bonds she had once broken.

As Freya moved forward, her difficult choice guiding her, she held onto the hope that her actions would lead not only to her own redemption, but also to the healing and growth of those she had hurt. She recognized that by staying true to her resolve, she could pave the way for a future defined by integrity, compassion, and a love that was rooted in the strength of her commitments and the growth she had achieved.

Chapter 43: The Girl's Sacrifice

As Freya continued her journey towards redemption, she found herself faced with an agonizing decision—a sacrifice that would test the depth of her commitment and the strength of her resolve.

With her conflicted love still burning within her, Freya recognized that true growth and healing required more than just personal introspection and rebuilding trust. She understood that her actions had consequences that extended beyond her own desires and emotions.

In a moment of profound clarity, Freya realized that the greatest sacrifice she could make was to let go of her conflicted love and prioritize the well-being of all those involved. She understood that clinging to her own desires would only perpetuate the pain and turmoil that had already been caused.

With a heavy heart, Freya made the difficult choice to distance herself from Erik and focus on rebuilding the foundations of her marriage. She acknowledged the depth of her feelings for him but recognized that true redemption required letting go of the forbidden love that had ensnared her heart.

Thór, ever loyal and perceptive, stood by Freya's side as she grappled with her sacrifice. His gentle presence offered solace and support, reinforcing her resolve and reminding her of the strength she possessed. His unwavering loyalty mirrored the sacrifice she was making, as he, too, put aside his own desires to support her on her journey.

Freya's sacrifice was not born out of resignation or defeat, but rather out of a deep understanding of the consequences of her actions and the commitment she had made to her spouse. She recognized that true growth required acknowledging her mistakes, making amends, and prioritizing the well-being of all involved, even if it meant letting go of a love that had once consumed her.

In the wake of her sacrifice, Freya redoubled her efforts to rebuild trust and nurture her marriage. She engaged in acts of genuine love, compassion, and understanding, working tirelessly to demonstrate her commitment to change and her desire to heal the wounds that had been inflicted.

Freya's spouse, though still grappling with the pain of betrayal, witnessed the sincerity of her sacrifice. They recognized the depth of her remorse and the genuine efforts she was making to rebuild their relationship. Slowly, a flicker of hope ignited within them, bolstered by Freya's sacrifice and her unwavering commitment to their shared future.

The journey towards redemption continued, now marked by the bittersweet ache of Freya's sacrifice. She knew that her decision would not erase the past or instantly heal the wounds that had been inflicted. But in letting go of her conflicted love, she found a renewed sense of purpose and a commitment to honoring the promises she had made.

As Freya moved forward, she carried the weight of her sacrifice with grace and resilience. She knew that it was not a sacrifice in vain but rather a testament to her growth, her integrity, and her unwavering dedication to the path of redemption.

With Thór at her side, a reminder of the loyalty and strength that guided her, Freya embraced the difficult journey that lay ahead. She remained steadfast in her commitment to personal growth, rebuilding trust, and nurturing the love that had endured despite the tumultuous journey they had embarked upon.

Freya's sacrifice became a beacon of hope, inspiring others who faced similar challenges and reminding them that true redemption required making difficult choices and prioritizing the well-being of all involved. In her sacrifice, she found the strength to forge a future defined by integrity, growth, and a love that had been tested and transformed.

Chapter 44: The Viking's Desperation

Erik, confronted with the aftermath of Freya's sacrifice, found himself overwhelmed by a sense of desperation—a deep longing for the love he had lost and a yearning to reconcile the conflicting emotions that threatened to consume him.

The weight of Freya's sacrifice bore heavily on his heart. Though he had admired her strength and commitment to personal growth, he couldn't shake the profound sense of loss that had settled within him. The void left by the absence of their connection seemed insurmountable, and he felt adrift in a sea of conflicting desires and unfulfilled longing.

In his desperation, Erik sought solace in moments of solitude, seeking to understand the depths of his emotions and the implications of his choices. He grappled with the consequences of his actions and the impact they had on those he cared about most—the pain he had caused to both his spouse and Freya.

Thór, attuned to Erik's distress, offered his unwavering companionship, his presence a constant reminder of loyalty and the strength that resided within them both. With each comforting nudge and soulful gaze, Thór reminded Erik to stay grounded and encouraged him to navigate the depths of his desperation with resilience and determination.

As Erik faced the depths of his despair, he recognized the importance of confronting his emotions head-on. He engaged in introspection, seeking to understand the root causes of his desperation and the role it played in his journey of redemption. He confronted the complexities of his desires, acknowledging the pain he had caused and the responsibility he held to honor his commitments.

In his darkest moments, Erik was tempted to abandon his path of redemption, to succumb to the overwhelming pull of his conflicted love. But deep within his soul, he knew that such a choice would only perpetuate the pain and turmoil he had already caused. He understood that true growth required perseverance, even in the face of desperation.

With every ounce of determination, Erik resolved to channel his desperation into fuel for personal growth. He sought guidance from wise elders, seeking their wisdom and counsel as he navigated the complexities of his emotions. He engaged in acts of self-reflection, confronting his own flaws and vulnerabilities, and striving to become a better man—a man worthy of the trust and love of those around him.

Erik's desperation became a catalyst for change, igniting a fire within him to mend the broken pieces of his life and seek forgiveness from those he had hurt. He embarked on a renewed journey of introspection and personal growth, recognizing that the path to redemption required not only acknowledging his mistakes but also actively working to repair the damage that had been done.

With Thór faithfully by his side, Erik leaned on the unwavering support and companionship of his loyal dog. Thór's presence served as a constant reminder that even in the depths of despair, there was strength to be found and a path to be forged. The bond they shared offered solace amidst the turmoil, fueling Erik's determination to rise above his desperation and strive for a future defined by growth, integrity, and the possibility of redemption.

As Erik moved forward, his desperation transformed into a fierce resolve—a resolve to confront his emotions, repair the broken pieces of his life, and rebuild the trust he had shattered. He held onto the hope that through perseverance and unwavering commitment, he could find a way to navigate the depths of his despair and emerge on the other side, stronger and more deserving of the love and forgiveness he sought.

In the face of his desperation, Erik recognized that his journey of redemption was far from over. It was a path marked by challenges, but also by the potential for growth, healing, and the transformative power of love. With Thór by his side, he embraced the uncertainties that lay ahead, ready to confront his desperation with unwavering determination and a renewed commitment to personal growth.

Chapter 45: The Heartbreaking Farewell

As Erik and Freya continued on their separate paths of redemption, their hearts weighed heavy with the burden of their choices and the sacrifices they had made. Despite their resolve and commitment to personal growth, the ache of their parted ways remained a constant presence—a reminder of the love they had shared and the dreams they had dared to envision.

The time had come for Erik and Freya to bid each other a heartbreaking farewell—a farewell born out of a deep understanding that their conflicted love could not coexist with the commitments they had made to their spouses and the path towards redemption they had chosen.

With heavy hearts and tear-filled eyes, Erik and Freya met in a secluded spot, away from prying eyes and the judgment of others. Thór stood faithfully by Erik's side, sensing the emotional weight of the moment, while Freya took a deep breath, steeling herself for the inevitable pain that lay ahead.

Their eyes locked, conveying a multitude of unspoken emotions. The love they shared still burned brightly within them, but they knew that true growth required letting go of what they could not have. Their hearts ached as they confronted the depth of their feelings and the reality of the choices they had made.

In hushed tones and trembling voices, Erik and Freya spoke words of farewell—a bittersweet symphony of love, regret, and longing. They expressed their gratitude for the profound connection they had shared, acknowledging the impact they had on each other's lives. With tears streaming down their faces, they shared their hopes for a future filled with healing, growth, and the possibility of finding happiness within the boundaries of their commitments.

Thór, sensing the heartbreak that enveloped them, offered his silent support, his presence a reminder of the loyalty and unwavering love that transcended the constraints of human emotions. He nudged Erik gently, as if to convey that their shared journey would continue, albeit in separate paths.

With each passing moment, the weight of their farewell grew heavier, their hearts torn between the love they cherished and the commitment to honor their promises. They understood that saying goodbye was the ultimate act of love—the sacrifice of their own desires for the sake of the greater good.

As they embraced one final time, Erik and Freya clung to the shared memories that would forever be etched in their hearts. They vowed to carry the lessons they had learned from their time together and the growth they had achieved as individuals. Though their paths had diverged, they hoped that the love they had shared would find its way into the lives they had chosen to rebuild.

With a lingering touch, Erik and Freya bid their farewell, their hearts breaking in unison yet filled with a glimmer of hope. They understood that true growth required letting go of what they could not have, and in doing so, they embraced the possibility of a future defined by integrity, forgiveness, and the redemption they had sought.

As Erik and Freya walked away from each other, their footsteps marking the beginning of separate journeys, they carried the weight of their farewell with them. In their hearts, the love they had shared would forever be a poignant reminder of the depth of human emotions and the sacrifices made in the pursuit of redemption.

Thór, loyal to the end, stood by Erik's side, a source of comfort and strength as they continued their path towards growth and healing. Together, they embarked on the next chapter of their journey, honoring the farewell that had marked the end of one chapter and the beginning of another.

In the wake of the heartbreaking farewell, Erik and Freya found solace in the knowledge that they had chosen a path of integrity and personal growth. They held onto the hope that their farewell would not be in vain—that the love they had shared would inspire them to become better versions of themselves, to rebuild what had been broken, and to forge a future defined by authenticity, forgiveness, and the possibility of finding happiness within the boundaries of their commitments.

Chapter 46: The Longing

After the heartbreaking farewell, Erik and Freya found themselves engulfed by a profound sense of longing—a yearning that echoed in the depths of their souls, a reminder of the love they had shared and the connection they had forged.

As they continued on their separate paths, Erik and Freya discovered that the longing remained a constant presence in their lives. It followed them like a ghostly companion, whispering reminders of the moments they had once shared—the stolen glances, the gentle touches, and the profound understanding that had bound their hearts together.

In their solitude, Erik and Freya found solace in the memories they held dear. They replayed moments in their minds, savoring the depth of their connection and the beauty of their shared experiences. The longing grew in intensity, fueling their desire to find a way to reconcile the depth of their emotions with the commitments they had made.

Though they were apart, Erik and Freya discovered that their longing mirrored one another's—a shared ache that defied the boundaries of time and distance. In the quiet moments of the night, when the world slumbered, their thoughts intertwined, and their hearts reached out across the vast expanse that separated them.

Thór, ever perceptive, sensed the longing that gripped his companion's heart. With his steadfast presence, he offered a comforting presence, a reminder that the depth of their connection was not forgotten. His loyal gaze conveyed a silent understanding, acknowledging the complexities of human emotions and the unyielding power of love.

In their longing, Erik and Freya confronted the complexities of their desires and the implications of their choices. They grappled with the yearning that enveloped them, questioning whether it was a testament to their unresolved feelings or simply the remnants of a love that could never be fully realized.

They found themselves caught in a delicate dance—a dance between the love they still harbored and the commitment they had made to honor their marriages. The longing was both a source of comfort and a source of pain —a reminder of the connection they had cherished, yet a constant challenge to navigate the boundaries they had set.

Amidst the depths of their longing, Erik and Freya recognized the importance of self-reflection and personal growth. They engaged in acts of introspection, seeking to understand the root causes of their desires and the lessons that their longing held for them. Through self-discovery, they hoped to find clarity and the strength to navigate the complexities of their emotions.

Their longing also fueled their commitment to rebuilding the lives they had once shattered. Erik and Freya poured their energy into nurturing their relationships, working tirelessly to rebuild the trust that had been broken. They sought forgiveness, engaging in acts of compassion, and demonstrating their unwavering commitment to growth and transformation.

With each passing day, the longing persisted —a reminder of the depth of their emotions and the enduring impact of their connection. Erik and Freya understood that while they may never fully quell the longing, they could learn to embrace it as a reminder of the transformative power of love.

Thór, the steadfast companion, journeyed alongside them, offering his unwavering support and a reminder that love, even in its longing, could be a catalyst for personal growth and understanding. His presence was a testament to the resilience of the human spirit and the enduring power of the connections we forge.

In the depths of their longing, Erik and Freya held onto the hope that their separate paths of redemption would eventually lead them to a place of peace and acceptance. They understood that the longing they felt was a testament to the depth of their capacity to love and be loved.

As they continued their respective journeys, Erik and Freya vowed to embrace the longing as a guiding force, a reminder of the transformative power of love that had once touched their lives. With Thór by their side, they walked forward, each step a testament to their unwavering commitment to growth, understanding, and the pursuit of a future defined by the lessons learned from their shared longing.

Chapter 47: The Viking's Journey

Erik embarked on a profound journey of self-discovery and personal growth, determined to honor his commitments, find redemption, and navigate the complexities of his emotions. His path was paved with challenges and the echoes of the longing that still tugged at his heart, but he pressed forward with unwavering determination.

Guided by the lessons he had learned and the insights gained from his experiences, Erik sought wisdom from elders and mentors. He immersed himself in the wisdom of Viking sagas, drawing inspiration from the tales of courage, resilience, and honor. Through these stories, he discovered parallels to his own journey and found solace in the collective wisdom of those who had come before him.

Erik embraced the art of self-reflection, delving into the depths of his own vulnerabilities and flaws. He confronted his past actions with unflinching honesty, acknowledging the pain he had caused and the consequences of his choices. Through introspection, he unearthed the motivations behind his desires and worked towards understanding the complexities of his emotions.

Thór, a constant companion on Erik's journey, offered unwavering support and a reminder of the loyalty that had guided them thus far. The loyal dog mirrored Erik's commitment to growth and transformation, providing solace in times of doubt and encouragement during moments of struggle.

As Erik ventured further on his journey, he sought to make amends for the pain he had caused. He engaged in acts of genuine remorse, expressing his sincere apologies to those he had hurt. He acknowledged the impact of his actions and endeavored to repair the trust that had been shattered, recognizing that true redemption required more than just personal growth—it required actively seeking forgiveness and making reparations.

Along his path, Erik encountered fellow Vikings and members of his community who had faced their own trials and tribulations. He engaged in conversations that challenged his perspective, broadened his understanding, and offered valuable insights into the complexities of love, commitment, and personal growth.

Erik also immersed himself in acts of service and selflessness, seeking to make a positive impact in the lives of others. Through volunteering, offering support, and lending a helping hand, he discovered that true growth could be found in acts of kindness and compassion. These actions not only benefited others but also served as a reminder of the capacity for change and the potential for redemption that resided within him.

As Erik's journey progressed, he recognized that true growth required embracing the present moment and finding gratitude amidst the challenges. He learned to appreciate the lessons learned from his past and to focus on the opportunities for growth and connection that lay before him.

The longing that had once consumed Erik's heart remained a constant companion on his journey. It served as a reminder of the depth of his capacity to love and the importance of honoring the commitments he had made. Though it continued to tug at his heartstrings, he understood that the longing was not a sign of weakness but a testament to the transformative power of love.

With each step forward, Erik moved closer to the redemption he sought. He embraced the journey with resilience, compassion, and a steadfast commitment to personal growth.

Through the challenges and triumphs, he discovered that the true measure of a Viking lay not in their conquests but in their ability to confront their own flaws and strive for growth and understanding.

Thór, by his side throughout the journey, represented the unwavering loyalty and support that had guided Erik through the depths of his transformation. The bond they shared served as a constant reminder of the resilience of the human spirit and the strength that could be found within.

As Erik continued on his path, he held onto the belief that his journey towards redemption would lead him to a place of peace, understanding, and a renewed sense of purpose. With Thór as his faithful companion, he embraced the challenges and triumphs that lay ahead, confident that through personal growth, compassion, and a commitment to honoring his commitments, he would forge a future defined by integrity and the possibility of finding his own version of redemption.

Chapter 48: The Girl's Broken Heart

Freya, on her own path of personal growth and redemption, carried a heart that had been broken by the choices she had made. Despite her resolve and commitment to rebuilding her life, the pain of her broken heart lingered, a constant reminder of the love she had lost and the consequences of her actions.

In the depths of her solitude, Freya confronted the raw emotions that surged within her. The longing that had once filled her heart now mingled with sorrow, creating a storm of anguish and regret. She grappled with the weight of her decisions and the toll they had taken on her own well-being and the lives of those around her.

Though she understood the reasons behind her choices and the importance of personal growth, Freya couldn't escape the pangs of sorrow that etched deep into her soul. The shattered fragments of her heart made it difficult for her to fully move forward, and she yearned for a way to heal the wounds that remained open.

Thór, the loyal companion who had stood by her side through it all, sensed the depth of

Freya's pain. With his gentle presence, he offered comfort and solace, reminding her that healing would come with time and the resilience of the human spirit. His unwavering loyalty was a balm for her broken heart, a reminder that love and support could be found even in the darkest of times.

Freya engaged in acts of self-compassion, allowing herself to grieve the love she had lost and acknowledging the weight of her own remorse. She delved into the depths of her emotions, seeking to understand the lessons her broken heart had to teach her. Through introspection, she endeavored to piece together the fragments of her shattered heart, slowly stitching it back together with newfound strength and resilience.

She surrounded herself with a support network of friends and loved ones who offered a shoulder to lean on and a listening ear. Their presence served as a reminder that she was not alone in her pain, and that healing could be found in the connections she forged with others.

Freya also sought solace in acts of self-care and self-expression. She found solace in the beauty of nature, immersing herself in its healing embrace. Through writing, art, or other creative outlets, she channeled her pain into something transformative, giving voice to her broken heart and allowing it to find catharsis in the process.

In her brokenness, Freya discovered that the shattered pieces of her heart held the potential for growth and transformation. She recognized that true healing required acknowledging her pain, allowing herself to feel it fully, and then gradually releasing it with each breath.

The journey towards redemption was not without its setbacks. There were moments when Freya was overwhelmed by the weight of her broken heart, when doubts and insecurities threatened to consume her. But with each passing day, she found strength within herself and the support of those who cared for her, slowly piecing together her heart and finding hope in the healing process.

As time passed, Freya's broken heart began to mend. Scars remained, a reminder of the love she had lost and the growth she had achieved. But those scars also bore witness to her resilience and the strength that had carried her through the darkest moments of her journey.

With Thór by her side, offering unwavering loyalty and a reminder of the love that still resided within her, Freya embraced the ongoing process of healing and growth. She knew that her broken heart was not a sign of weakness, but a testament to the depth of her capacity to love and the transformative power of her journey.

As Freya continued forward, she carried her broken heart with grace and strength, knowing that through the mending of her own wounds, she could emerge as a stronger, more compassionate individual. With each step she took, she moved closer to a future defined by healing, understanding, and the possibility of finding love and forgiveness, both for others and for herself.

Chapter 49: The Dog's Loyalty

Thór, the loyal and steadfast companion who had accompanied Erik and Freya on their tumultuous journey, continued to demonstrate unwavering loyalty as their paths diverged. With each passing day, his presence served as a constant reminder of the enduring bond they had shared and the love that had transcended the complexities of their human relationships.

As Erik and Freya navigated their separate paths of personal growth and redemption, Thór remained a beacon of loyalty and unwavering support. He was a silent confidant, offering solace in times of doubt, and a steadfast presence during moments of introspection and self-discovery.

In the wake of the farewell between Erik and Freya, Thór found himself at the center of their individual journeys. He faithfully accompanied Erik, offering a comforting presence and a reminder of the resilience of the human spirit. His watchful eyes mirrored Erik's commitment to personal growth, acting as a silent guide on the path of redemption.

Thór's loyalty extended beyond his physical presence. He remained a symbol of the enduring connection between Erik and Freya, a tangible reminder of the love that had once bound them together. His loyalty embodied the essence of their shared experiences—the moments of joy, the challenges faced, and the growth achieved.

In Erik's moments of despair, when the weight of his choices threatened to overwhelm him, Thór provided a steadying presence. He offered a listening ear and a warm, comforting nudge—an unspoken reassurance that Erik was not alone on his journey. With each wag of his tail and each gentle nuzzle, Thór reminded Erik that loyalty and companionship could be found even in the most difficult of times.

Thór's loyalty was not confined to Erik alone. He also remained a loyal companion to Freya, even as their paths diverged. His presence offered solace to Freya in moments of vulnerability and served as a constant reminder of the love she had experienced and the growth she had achieved. Through his unwavering loyalty, Thór bridged the gap between their separate journeys, conveying a sense of connection and understanding that transcended human emotions.

As Erik and Freya progressed on their respective paths, Thór became a symbol of hope and a reminder of the enduring power of love. He represented the unbreakable bond that had been forged amidst the complexities of their journey—a bond that had withstood the tests of time and the challenges they had faced.

Thór's loyalty served as a guiding light, illuminating the way forward as Erik and Freya continued to navigate the complexities of their lives. His presence was a source of strength and inspiration, urging them to persevere in the face of adversity and to remain true to the growth they had achieved.

In their moments of solitude and reflection, both Erik and Freya found solace in the unwavering loyalty of their four-legged companion. Thór's presence reminded them that love could be found in the most unexpected places, and that loyalty and companionship were not bound by human constraints.

As Erik and Freya carried on their separate journeys, Thór walked faithfully by their sides, embodying the loyalty that had defined their shared experiences. He served as a constant reminder that even amidst the trials and tribulations of life, love and companionship could be found, offering support, comfort, and a reminder of the transformative power of their journey.

With each step they took, Erik and Freya remained grateful for Thór's unwavering loyalty, cherishing the lessons he had taught them and the love he had bestowed upon them. In his loyal companionship, they found solace, strength, and a renewed sense of purpose as they continued on their individual paths of growth, redemption, and the pursuit of a future defined by love and integrity.

Chapter 50: The Viking's Encounters

As Erik journeyed on his path of personal growth and redemption, he encountered a series of unexpected and transformative encounters that would shape his understanding of love, forgiveness, and the complexities of human relationships.

The first encounter came in the form of a wise elder Viking who had weathered the storms of life and emerged with wisdom to impart. They crossed paths during a moment of solitude, their conversations spanning the breadth of topics from love to honor, and from regret to resilience. The elder's words resonated deeply with Erik, offering guidance and a fresh perspective on his own journey. Through their conversations, Erik gained insight into the universality of human experiences and the timeless wisdom that could be gleaned from the tales of those who had come before him.

In another encounter, Erik found himself in the presence of a compassionate healer—a healer who possessed a deep understanding of emotional wounds and the power of forgiveness. Through their interactions, the healer taught Erik about the importance of self-compassion and the healing that could be found through the act of forgiving oneself. Their discussions enabled Erik to confront his own shortcomings with kindness and acceptance, setting him on a path of self-forgiveness and liberation from the shackles of guilt.

Erik's encounters were not limited to wise elders and healers. Along his journey, he crossed paths with fellow Vikings who, like him, were on their own quests for personal growth and redemption. Through shared experiences and conversations, Erik discovered the interconnectedness of their stories—a reminder that no one journeyed alone and that the struggles faced by one could provide lessons and strength to others. These encounters fostered a sense of community and offered Erik the opportunity to both seek and provide support to his fellow travelers.

In one particularly significant encounter, Erik met a young Viking who had experienced a similar journey of heartache and redemption. The young Viking, scarred by past mistakes, shared their own tale of growth and the transformative power of self-reflection. Through their conversations, Erik found solace in the realization that he was not alone in his struggles and that redemption was a universal desire—a shared quest that traversed the boundaries of time and circumstance.

Thór, loyal as ever, also played a role in Erik's encounters. His friendly and approachable nature served as a catalyst for chance meetings and serendipitous connections. Whether it was engaging in playful interactions with other Vikings or offering comfort to those in need, Thór's presence brought a sense of warmth and authenticity to each encounter, fostering an environment of trust and open-heartedness.

Through these encounters, Erik gained a deeper understanding of the complexities of love, forgiveness, and the human experience. He learned that redemption was not a solitary journey but a collective pursuit—a web of interconnected stories and shared wisdom that could guide individuals towards growth and healing.

As Erik continued on his path, he carried the lessons learned from these encounters deep within his heart. Each interaction had left an indelible mark, shaping his perspective and influencing his actions. He embraced the interconnectedness of his journey, recognizing that the encounters he had experienced were not mere coincidences, but opportunities for growth and connection.

With gratitude for the encounters that had illuminated his path, Erik walked forward with renewed purpose. He understood that the richness of his journey lay not only in personal growth but also in the connections he forged along the way. Guided by the wisdom of the wise, the compassion of the healers, and the camaraderie of his fellow travelers, he continued to navigate the complexities of his own redemption, ready to embrace the encounters yet to come and the lessons they held for his ongoing journey of growth and transformation.

Chapter 51: The Girl's New Life

After bidding farewell to Erik and embarking on her own journey of personal growth, Freya found herself immersed in a new chapter of her life—one defined by resilience, self-discovery, and the pursuit of happiness within the boundaries of her commitments.

Freya sought solace in the embrace of her loved ones, finding support and understanding from those who had witnessed her struggles and remained by her side. Their unwavering love reminded her that she was not defined by her past mistakes, but rather by her capacity for growth and her unwavering commitment to personal transformation.

With the weight of her broken heart gradually lightening, Freya sought to rebuild the trust she had shattered through genuine acts of kindness and compassion. She dedicated herself to nurturing her existing relationships, infusing them with renewed love and sincerity. Through her actions, she aimed to demonstrate that she had learned from her past and was actively working towards becoming a better version of herself.

Freya also delved into new pursuits, discovering hidden talents and passions that had long remained dormant. Whether it was through engaging in creative endeavors, exploring new hobbies, or dedicating herself to causes that aligned with her values, she found solace and purpose in the pursuit of personal fulfillment.

In her quest for self-discovery, Freya engaged in acts of self-reflection and introspection. She confronted her vulnerabilities and embraced the lessons learned from her past experiences, recognizing that her journey of growth extended far beyond the boundaries of her broken heart. She sought to understand her own desires, values, and aspirations, paving the way for a future that aligned with her authentic self.

As time passed, Freya gradually found herself embracing the possibility of new love. Though scarred by her past experiences, she learned to trust again, allowing herself to open her heart to someone who cherished and respected her. With cautious optimism, she navigated the intricacies of a new relationship, finding joy in the growth and connection it offered while remaining mindful of the boundaries she had set.

Throughout her new life, Thór remained a constant source of support and unwavering loyalty. His presence served as a reminder of the resilience that resided within Freya, and the strength that could be drawn from even the most challenging of circumstances. His companionship symbolized the enduring love that had guided her through the depths of her journey, a reminder that redemption and transformation were possible even in the face of adversity.

As Freya embraced her new life, she realized that the journey towards growth and happiness was not without its challenges. She confronted moments of doubt and faced setbacks along the way. However, armed with the lessons learned from her past and the unwavering support of her loved ones, she remained committed to her path of personal growth and the pursuit of a future defined by authenticity and fulfillment.

Freya's new life was a testament to the resilience of the human spirit—a testament to the transformative power of love, forgiveness, and personal growth. As she continued to navigate the complexities of her commitments, she discovered that true happiness could be found in the authenticity of her choices and the unwavering commitment to honor her values.

With each passing day, Freya embraced the joys and challenges of her new life, grateful for the growth she had achieved and excited for the possibilities that lay ahead. She understood that her journey was ongoing, with new experiences and lessons yet to come. With Thór by her side, embodying the loyalty and strength that had guided her through the depths of her transformation, she walked forward with a renewed sense of purpose and an unwavering commitment to living a life filled with love, authenticity, and the pursuit of personal fulfillment.

Chapter 52: The Viking's Battle

Erik, determined to honor his commitments and embrace personal growth, found himself facing a formidable battle—one that would test his resolve, strength, and the lessons he had learned along his transformative journey.

The battle took the form of a conflict that arose within his community—a clash of values and ambitions that threatened to tear apart the fabric of Viking society. Erik, known for his wisdom and ability to navigate complex situations, was called upon to mediate the dispute, serving as a bridge between conflicting factions.

As the battle unfolded, Erik faced the daunting task of finding common ground amidst the sea of differences. He drew upon the wisdom he had gained from his encounters and the lessons he had learned from his own journey of personal growth. With diplomacy, empathy, and a commitment to fairness, he engaged in dialogue, seeking to understand the root causes of the conflict and working towards a resolution that would bring about harmony.

Throughout the battle, Erik faced numerous challenges. He encountered resistance from those deeply entrenched in their beliefs, individuals unwilling to embrace change or consider alternative perspectives. Yet, undeterred, Erik persisted, employing patience and open-mindedness in his pursuit of reconciliation.

In the midst of the chaos, Thór remained a steadfast companion, offering unwavering loyalty and a calming presence. His companionship served as a reminder of the strength Erik possessed and the support he had garnered along his journey. With Thór by his side, Erik drew upon the bond they shared, finding solace and strength even in the face of adversity.

The battle raged on, but through Erik's tireless efforts, bridges were built, and dialogue began to foster understanding. He encouraged empathy and compassion, urging both sides to consider the consequences of their actions and the potential for growth through compromise. Slowly but steadily, the intensity of the conflict began to wane, replaced by an atmosphere of cautious optimism and the possibility of resolution.

As the battle neared its conclusion, Erik witnessed the transformative power of forgiveness and the impact it had on the combatants. Through acts of compassion and an unwavering commitment to understanding, Erik facilitated the healing of wounds that ran deep within the community. He demonstrated that true strength lay not in the ability to overpower others, but in the capacity to bridge divides and nurture connections.

With the resolution of the battle came a renewed sense of harmony within the community. Erik's efforts had not only quelled the conflict but had fostered a deeper understanding and appreciation for the diversity of opinions and perspectives that existed among the Vikings. Through his example, he had set in motion a ripple effect of compassion, forgiveness, and the recognition of shared humanity.

The battle had tested Erik's character, challenging him to put into practice the lessons he had learned on his journey. Through perseverance, diplomacy, and an unwavering commitment to personal growth, he had emerged victorious. The experience had reaffirmed his belief in the transformative power of love, forgiveness, and the pursuit of a harmonious existence.

As Erik reflected on the battle, he recognized that the conflicts he faced in his community were reflections of the internal battles that resided within individuals. He understood that true growth required self-reflection and an ongoing commitment to personal transformation. With this newfound understanding, he rededicated himself to his own journey of growth, knowing that the battles he faced within himself would shape not only his own future but also the world around him.

With Thór by his side, embodying the loyalty and strength that had guided him through the darkest moments of his journey, Erik walked forward, prepared to face new battles with a renewed sense of purpose and an unwavering commitment to love, compassion, and the pursuit of a harmonious existence.

Chapter 53: The Girl's Regret

As Freya continued on her journey of personal growth and embraced her new life, she found herself confronted by waves of regret—painful reminders of the choices she had made and the impact they had on those she loved.

Regret washed over Freya like a relentless tide, threatening to pull her back into the depths of her past. She grappled with the weight of her actions, tormented by the knowledge of the pain she had caused and the irreversible consequences of her choices. The echoes of her regret reverberated through her heart, a constant reminder of the wounds that had yet to heal.

In moments of solitude, Freya allowed herself to sit with her regret, acknowledging the depths of her remorse and the desire to make amends. She confronted the pain head-on, understanding that regret was not merely a burden to bear but a catalyst for growth and transformation.

Thór, always attuned to Freya's emotions, offered a comforting presence during these difficult moments. His unwavering loyalty served as a reminder that forgiveness was possible, both from others and from oneself. With each gentle nuzzle and loving gaze, Thór reminded Freya that redemption could be found through the recognition of mistakes and the commitment to change.

Driven by her regret, Freya engaged in acts of reparation and self-reflection. She sought forgiveness from those she had hurt, expressing her genuine remorse and demonstrating through her actions that she had learned from her past. She understood that true redemption required more than just remorse—it required a commitment to growth and a genuine effort to repair the trust that had been broken.

Freya also delved deep into her own heart, seeking to understand the root causes of her choices and the lessons she could glean from her regrets. She confronted her vulnerabilities and insecurities, recognizing how they had influenced her actions. Through this process of self-reflection, she aimed to cultivate a deeper understanding of herself and to grow into a person who was capable of making better choices in the future.

In her moments of regret, Freya confronted the painful reality that some wounds could not be fully healed. She understood that her actions had left scars on the hearts of others, and that forgiveness was not always guaranteed. However, she remained committed to growth, recognizing that her own journey towards redemption was an ongoing process, irrespective of the outcomes of her attempts at reconciliation.

Regret served as a catalyst for change, propelling Freya forward on her path of personal growth and transformation. She understood that dwelling in the past would only hinder her progress, and instead, she channeled her energy into cultivating a future defined by integrity, compassion, and personal fulfillment.

As Freya continued to navigate the complexities of her new life, she carried her regret with grace and humility. It remained a constant reminder of the consequences of her choices, but also a driving force for growth and a commitment to make amends. With Thór by her side, embodying the loyalty and forgiveness that had guided her through the depths of her transformation, she walked forward with a renewed sense of purpose and an unwavering determination to live a life defined by love, authenticity, and the pursuit of personal redemption.

Chapter 54: The Dog's Vigilance

Thór, the loyal and vigilant dog who had stood by Erik and Freya throughout their tumultuous journey, continued to demonstrate his unwavering commitment and watchful nature as their stories unfolded.

Thór's senses remained finely attuned to the emotions and energies surrounding Erik and Freya, as if he possessed an innate understanding of the depths of their souls. He could sense the slightest shifts in their moods, the subtle changes in their demeanor, and the weight of their burdens. His vigilance served as a constant reminder that he was not just a companion but a guardian, dedicated to their well-being and ever watchful for their safety.

In moments of sorrow or doubt, Thór offered his quiet presence, providing solace through his steady companionship. He offered a sense of grounding—a reminder that no matter the challenges they faced or the depths of their emotions, they were not alone. His watchful eyes mirrored the love and concern he held for them, a vigilant reminder of his unwavering loyalty.

Thór's vigilance extended beyond emotional support. His keen senses and natural instincts served as a protective shield for Erik and Freya, alerting them to potential dangers and offering a sense of security. Whether it was detecting a threat in their surroundings or providing a comforting presence during times of vulnerability, Thór's vigilance proved invaluable.

In moments of celebration and joy, Thór's watchful nature persisted. He reveled in the moments of triumph and shared in the happiness that Erik and Freya experienced. His presence served as a constant reminder that their journey was not solely defined by hardship and regret but also by the moments of joy and growth that they had achieved.

Thór's vigilance also served as a reminder to Erik and Freya of the importance of their own vigilance in navigating their paths. His steadfast commitment encouraged them to remain attuned to their own emotions, to be vigilant in their pursuit of personal growth, and to protect the newfound wisdom and strength they had gained along their journeys.

As Erik and Freya progressed on their paths, Thór continued to stand as a symbol of loyalty, vigilance, and unconditional love. His presence reminded them that no matter the challenges they faced or the choices they made, they were worthy of love and forgiveness. Through his watchful nature, he taught them the importance of remaining vigilant in their commitments to themselves and to each other.

Thór's vigilance served as a guiding light, illuminating the way forward as Erik and Freya continued to navigate the complexities of their lives. He reminded them to remain present, to be attuned to their own needs, and to honor the growth they had achieved. With each step they took, they were supported by the unwavering vigilance of their four-legged companion, knowing that his watchful eyes and steadfast loyalty would guide them through the challenges and triumphs that lay ahead.

Together, Erik, Freya, and Thór embarked on a journey defined by love, growth, and the ever-present vigilance that bound them together. Their bond was a testament to the transformative power of loyalty and the strength that could be found within the depths of their connection. With Thór as their vigilant guide, they walked forward, ready to face whatever lay on the horizon, fortified by their shared love and the watchful presence of their faithful companion.

Chapter 55: The Viking's Triumph

Erik, having endured countless trials and emerged stronger from his journey of personal growth and redemption, stood at the precipice of a remarkable triumph—a testament to his resilience, wisdom, and unwavering commitment to his own transformation.

The triumph Erik faced was not one of external conquest or material gain, but rather a triumph of the spirit—an internal victory that resonated with the very core of his being. It was a triumph over the doubts and fears that had once plagued him, a triumph over the limitations he had imposed upon himself, and a triumph over the shadows of his past.

As he looked back on his journey, Erik marveled at the distance he had traveled. The lessons he had learned and the growth he had achieved had propelled him towards a newfound understanding of his own strength and potential. He recognized that his triumph was not achieved through a single grand act, but through the accumulation of countless small victories—each step forward, each act of compassion, and each moment of introspection.

The triumph Erik experienced radiated from within, transforming his outlook on life and his interactions with others. He carried himself with a newfound sense of confidence, grounded in the knowledge that he had confronted his own flaws and worked tirelessly to become a better version of himself. This inner triumph radiated through his interactions, inspiring others to embark on their own journeys of growth and personal transformation.

Erik's triumph extended beyond his personal growth—it had a ripple effect that touched the lives of those around him. Through his acts of kindness, wisdom, and forgiveness, he had become a beacon of hope and inspiration for others. His story served as a testament to the transformative power of love and the resilience of the human spirit.

Thór, the ever-loyal companion who had stood by Erik's side throughout the journey, basked in the glory of their shared triumph. His unwavering support and watchful presence had played an integral role in Erik's transformation, and he reveled in the joy and fulfillment that emanated from his Viking companion.

As Erik embraced his triumph, he remained humble and grounded. He understood that personal growth was an ongoing process, with new challenges and lessons yet to come. He recognized that his triumph was not a destination but a continuous journey—one that required constant vigilance and a commitment to staying true to his values.

With Thór by his side, embodying the loyalty and strength that had guided him through the depths of his transformation, Erik walked forward with a renewed sense of purpose. He remained committed to sharing his wisdom and experiences, guiding others on their own paths of growth and personal triumph.

As he ventured into the future, Erik carried his triumph as a guiding light—a reminder of his capacity for change, the depth of his resilience, and the transformative power of love and forgiveness. With each step he took, he embraced the triumph that resided within him, ready to face new challenges with unwavering determination and a heart filled with gratitude for the journey that had led him to this moment.

The Viking's triumph was not defined by external accolades or conquests, but by the profound transformation that had taken place within his soul. It was a triumph of the human spirit—a testament to the indomitable strength that resides within each of us, waiting to be awakened through self-reflection, growth, and the pursuit of a life filled with integrity, compassion, and love.

Chapter 56: The Girl's Realization

As Freya continued on her journey of personal growth and embraced her new life, she found herself on the cusp of a profound realization—one that would reshape her perspective, ignite her inner strength, and pave the way for a future defined by authenticity and self-discovery.

In the depths of her soul-searching, Freya began to uncover the truth that had long been obscured by her regrets and the weight of her past. She realized that her journey was not solely about seeking redemption or finding forgiveness from others, but about embracing her own worth and forging her own path forward.

This realization marked a turning point in Freya's journey—a shift from dwelling in the shadows of her past to embracing the light of her own potential. She recognized that she had the power to define her own narrative, to break free from the chains of her past actions, and to create a future grounded in self-acceptance and personal fulfillment.

With newfound clarity, Freya understood that her journey was not defined by the mistakes she had made, but rather by the growth and transformation she had achieved as a result. She recognized that her past served as a catalyst for her own self-discovery—a springboard from which she could propel herself towards a future imbued with authenticity and purpose.

Freya's realization brought with it a sense of liberation—a release from the shackles of guilt and self-doubt that had once held her captive. She embraced her own capacity for change and growth, understanding that her worthiness was not determined by the judgments of others, but by her own self-perception and the love she had for herself.

Thór, always attuned to Freya's emotions, sensed the shift within her. With each wag of his tail and each gentle nuzzle, he mirrored her newfound sense of self-empowerment, reinforcing the strength and resilience that resided within her. His loyal presence served as a reminder that she was capable of charting her own path and embracing her own truth.

Guided by her realization, Freya embarked on a journey of self-discovery—a deep exploration of her passions, values, and aspirations. She delved into the depths of her soul, seeking to uncover the hidden treasures that lay dormant within her. Through this process, she unearthed talents she had long neglected and rediscovered the joy of pursuing her true passions.

Freya also began to surround herself with a community of like-minded individuals who celebrated her authenticity and supported her growth. She sought out connections that nurtured her spirit and encouraged her to embrace her true self, free from judgment or expectation. These newfound relationships served as a reminder of the boundless possibilities that lay before her and the importance of aligning herself with those who uplifted her.

In the midst of her realization, Freya found the courage to share her story with others—her triumphs, her struggles, and the lessons she had learned along the way. Through her vulnerability, she inspired others to embrace their own journeys of self-discovery and to find strength in their own stories.

As Freya walked the path of self-realization, she carried with her the light of her own truth, shining brightly as a beacon of hope and authenticity. With each step she took, she embraced the realization that she held the power to create a future aligned with her deepest desires and values.

With Thór by her side, embodying the loyalty and strength that had guided her through the depths of her transformation, Freya walked forward with a renewed sense of purpose and an unwavering commitment to living a life defined by self-acceptance, growth, and the pursuit of personal fulfillment.

The girl's realization marked a pivotal moment —a milestone on her journey of self-discovery and an affirmation of her own worth. It was a realization that she was the author of her own narrative, capable of embracing her true self and charting a course towards a future filled with authenticity, joy, and an unwavering belief in her own potential.

Chapter 57: The Dog's Discovery

Thór, the loyal and perceptive companion who had stood by Erik and Freya throughout their transformative journeys, made a discovery of his own—a realization that would deepen his understanding of the human spirit and strengthen his bond with his Viking companions.

As Thór observed the growth and evolution of Erik and Freya, he began to recognize the profound impact their journeys had on his own existence. He realized that their quest for personal growth and the pursuit of authenticity had ignited a spark within him—a longing to explore the depths of his own canine nature and uncover the true potential of his loyal spirit.

Guided by this newfound curiosity, Thór embarked on a journey of self-discovery, seeking to better understand the essence of his canine being and the unique gifts he possessed. He delved into the intricacies of his senses, honing his intuition and deepening his connection with the world around him. Through this exploration, he discovered a heightened ability to read emotions, to offer comfort, and to provide unwavering support to those who crossed his path.

Thór's discovery went beyond his own individual growth. He recognized that his presence had a transformative impact on others, particularly Erik and Freya. With each wag of his tail and each gentle nuzzle, he was able to convey a sense of understanding and unconditional love that transcended language and touched the depths of their souls.

Thór's intuitive nature enabled him to sense the needs and emotions of those around him, acting as a silent guide and a source of comfort. He became attuned to the intricacies of human connection, recognizing the power of a gentle touch, a kind word, or a knowing glance. Through this discovery, he deepened his bond with Erik and Freya, becoming an anchor of support and a source of unwavering loyalty.

In their moments of triumph, Thór celebrated alongside them, his joy mirroring their own. He reveled in their achievements, basking in the radiance of their growth and transformation. His presence was a testament to the shared journey they had embarked upon—an intertwining of destinies that had led them to this moment of discovery.

Thór's newfound understanding of his own capabilities led him to embrace his role as a healer and guide. He recognized that his loyalty and unwavering support had the power to mend wounded hearts and offer solace in times of need. Whether it was comforting Erik during moments of self-doubt or offering a gentle presence to Freya in her moments of reflection, Thór's discovery empowered him to become a catalyst for healing and growth.

As Thór continued to walk alongside Erik and Freya, he carried with him the knowledge that his own journey of self-discovery was intertwined with theirs. He understood that his role went beyond mere companionship, encompassing a deep sense of purpose and a shared destiny.

With each step forward, Thór embodied his discovery—a loyal and steadfast presence, a mirror reflecting the strength and resilience of the human spirit. His understanding of the human experience deepened, and his bond with Erik and Freya grew stronger, grounded in the mutual realization that their paths were forever entwined.

Thór's discovery served as a reminder of the interconnectedness of all beings—the profound impact we have on one another's journeys and the transformative power of unconditional love. Through his own growth, he illuminated the limitless potential that lies within every soul, inspiring others to embrace their own journeys of self-discovery and to unlock the unique gifts that reside within.

As Thór continued to walk the path of self-discovery, he did so with an unwavering commitment to love, support, and guide those who journeyed alongside him. With each wag of his tail and each watchful gaze, he embodied the profound discovery that had transformed his understanding of himself and the world around him.

Chapter 58: The Viking's Redemption

Erik, burdened by the weight of his past actions and driven by a deep desire for personal growth and redemption, embarked on a journey of self-reflection and transformation—a journey that would test his resolve, challenge his perceptions, and ultimately lead him towards a path of redemption.

Haunted by the consequences of his past mistakes, Erik knew that he could no longer ignore the pain he had caused and the lives he had disrupted. With a heavy heart, he sought to confront his past head-on, determined to make amends and seek forgiveness from those he had wronged.

Braving the storm of guilt and remorse, Erik sought out the individuals whose lives had been affected by his actions. With humility and sincerity, he extended heartfelt apologies, acknowledging the pain he had caused and taking responsibility for his past behavior. He listened with an open heart, allowing others to express their feelings and emotions, understanding that healing and redemption required a shared journey.

The path to redemption was not an easy one. Erik faced skepticism, anger, and resentment from those he approached. The wounds he had inflicted ran deep, and forgiveness did not come easily. But he remained steadfast, committed to doing whatever it took to earn back the trust and rebuild the bridges he had burned.

Erik's journey of redemption was not limited to seeking forgiveness from others—it also involved a deep and profound process of self-examination. He confronted the root causes of his past actions, seeking to understand the flawed thinking and beliefs that had led him astray. Through introspection and self-reflection, he identified the patterns that had governed his behavior and committed himself to breaking free from their grip.

With each step on his path of redemption, Erik demonstrated his commitment to change through his actions. He took active measures to right the wrongs of his past, engaging in acts of restitution and reparation wherever possible. He sought to bring about positive change in his community, dedicating himself to causes that promoted healing, reconciliation, and personal growth.

Thór, the ever-loyal companion, stood by Erik's side throughout his journey of redemption. With unwavering support and a watchful eye, he served as a constant reminder of the strength and resilience that lay within Erik. Thór's presence embodied forgiveness and unconditional love, offering solace and encouragement during the most challenging moments of Erik's quest for redemption.

As Erik made progress on his journey, he began to witness the transformative power of redemption. He saw the healing that forgiveness brought—both to those he had wronged and to himself. He experienced the weight of guilt lifting, replaced by a newfound sense of purpose and hope. The relationships he had damaged began to mend, slowly but surely, as trust was rebuilt on the foundation of his genuine remorse and commitment to change.

Redemption, Erik realized, was not a destination but an ongoing process—a continuous commitment to growth, introspection, and making amends. He understood that the path to redemption was paved with humility, empathy, and a genuine desire to learn from past mistakes.

With each stride forward, Erik carried the lessons of his redemption journey within his heart—a reminder of the power of personal transformation, the resilience of the human spirit, and the capacity for growth and forgiveness. Guided by his newfound understanding, he walked the path of redemption with determination, compassion, and an unwavering commitment to living a life defined by integrity, empathy, and the pursuit of personal growth.

As Erik continued on his journey, he offered his story as a testament to the transformative power of redemption, inspiring others who had lost their way to believe in the possibility of change and the healing power of forgiveness. With Thór by his side, embodying the loyalty and forgiveness that had guided him through the depths of his transformation, Erik walked forward, ready to face the challenges and triumphs that lay ahead on his redeemed path.

Chapter 59: The Girl's Forgiveness

Freya, having embarked on her own path of self-discovery and growth, reached a pivotal moment in her journey—a moment of profound healing and liberation as she embraced the power of forgiveness.

As she reflected on the pain and hurt she had endured, Freya realized that carrying the weight of resentment and anger only held her back from experiencing true inner peace and growth. She recognized that forgiveness was not about condoning or forgetting the past, but rather a transformative act of releasing the grip of bitterness and embracing a newfound freedom.

In the depths of her soul, Freya found the strength to forgive—not only those who had wronged her but also herself. She acknowledged the wounds that had been inflicted upon her heart and chose to let go of the lingering resentment that had held her captive for far too long.

With each act of forgiveness, Freya felt the weight lift from her spirit. It was a cathartic release—a shedding of the burdens that had weighed her down and clouded her perception of the world. As she opened her heart to forgiveness, she experienced a profound sense of liberation, allowing love and compassion to fill the spaces that had been consumed by anger and hurt.

Thór, the loyal companion who had witnessed Freya's journey of self-discovery, offered his presence as a silent support during this transformative process. His gentle demeanor and unwavering loyalty served as a constant reminder of the power of forgiveness and the healing that it could bring. With each wag of his tail and each loving gaze, Thór mirrored the compassion and forgiveness that Freya was cultivating within herself.

Freya's forgiveness extended beyond others and encompassed the most challenging act of all—forgiving herself. She acknowledged the mistakes she had made and the pain she had caused others, allowing herself to release the self-condemnation and embrace her own capacity for growth and change. Through self-forgiveness, she found the courage to embrace her own imperfections and recognize that she deserved healing and a chance to start anew.

In embracing forgiveness, Freya experienced a profound shift in her perception of the world. She saw the interconnectedness of humanity—the shared experiences of joy, pain, and the universal desire for understanding. She realized that forgiveness had the power to heal not only her own wounds but also to foster connection and reconciliation among all who were willing to embrace it.

As Freya forgave, she also extended forgiveness to those who had played a role in her story. With open-heartedness and compassion, she recognized their own journeys of growth and the capacity for change within them. She understood that forgiveness was not a sign of weakness but a testament to her own strength and the resilience of the human spirit.

With each step forward, Freya walked the path of forgiveness with grace and determination. She carried within her heart the profound lessons learned from her own journey—a testament to the transformative power of compassion and the freedom that forgiveness could bring.

With Thór by her side, embodying the loyalty and forgiveness that had guided her through the depths of her transformation, Freya walked forward, ready to embrace a future defined by healing, understanding, and the profound beauty of a heart set free.

Chapter 60: The Dog's Joy

Thór, the faithful and perceptive companion, reveled in the joy that radiated from Erik and Freya as they embraced their own journeys of redemption and forgiveness. As their spirits lifted, Thór's own joy became palpable, a reflection of the love and fulfillment he found in their companionship.

With each wag of his tail and joyful bark, Thór expressed his unbridled delight. His eyes sparkled with a zest for life, mirroring the renewed sense of purpose and contentment that emanated from his Viking companions. Their newfound joy brought him immeasurable happiness, a reflection of the deep bond they had forged through their shared experiences.

Thór's joy extended beyond the immediate moment, for he understood the transformative power of love, growth, and forgiveness. He witnessed the profound impact that Erik and Freya's journeys had on their own lives and the lives of those around them. Their triumphs, their realizations, and their capacity for forgiveness served as a testament to the resilience of the human spirit and the immense joy that can be found in the pursuit of personal growth and redemption.

In moments of celebration and togetherness, Thór's joy was infectious. He reveled in the shared laughter, the warmth of companionship, and the simple pleasures of life. His playful antics and boundless energy served as a reminder to cherish each precious moment and to find joy in the simplest of experiences.

Thór's joy also served as a reminder of the interconnectedness of all beings. He embodied the belief that the happiness of one could ripple outwards, touching the lives of many. His presence brought smiles to the faces of strangers, brightening their day and offering a momentary respite from the burdens of life.

With each passing day, Thór's joy grew, deepening his connection with Erik and Freya. His unwavering loyalty and companionship served as a constant source of comfort and inspiration, reminding them to embrace the joy that life had to offer.

In the depths of their journeys, Erik and Freya found solace in Thór's joyful presence. His boundless enthusiasm and unwavering love lifted their spirits during moments of doubt and served as a gentle reminder of the beauty and joy that existed even in the face of adversity.

As they continued their individual paths of growth, Erik, Freya, and Thór experienced a profound sense of joy in their shared bond. They discovered that the truest joy came not from external achievements or material possessions, but from the depth of their connections, the growth of their souls, and the love that flowed freely between them.

With Thór by their side, embodying the joy that had guided them through the depths of their transformation, Erik and Freya walked forward, ready to embrace each new day with gratitude, love, and an unwavering commitment to living a life defined by joy, compassion, and the pursuit of inner fulfillment.

Thór's joy served as a reminder to cherish the moments of laughter, to find joy in the smallest of gestures, and to embrace the beauty that surrounded them. Together, they reveled in the simple pleasures, their hearts intertwined in a dance of shared happiness and the profound joy that can be found in the bonds of love and friendship.

Chapter 61: The Viking's Return

After a long and transformative journey, Erik, the Viking who had embarked on a quest for redemption and personal growth, returned to his village—a changed man, ready to face the community he had once called home.

As he approached the familiar sights and sounds of his village, Erik couldn't help but feel a mixture of nervous anticipation and quiet confidence. He knew that his return would not be met without skepticism and questions, but he also carried within him the knowledge that he had undergone a profound transformation—one that had reshaped his perspective, guided his actions, and forged a renewed sense of purpose.

Word of Erik's return spread throughout the village, stirring a mixture of curiosity, whispers, and cautious optimism. Some greeted him with suspicion, remembering the pain he had caused in the past, while others remained open to the possibility of change and growth. Erik understood that his actions would speak louder than any words, and he was determined to prove his commitment to personal redemption.

As he walked through the village, Erik met eyes filled with curiosity, judgment, and hope. He maintained a steady demeanor, offering a respectful nod to those who looked his way. He recognized that his return presented an opportunity not only for his own redemption but also for healing within the community— allowing wounds to mend, fostering understanding, and demonstrating the capacity for growth and change.

Thór, always by Erik's side, embodied the loyalty and strength that had guided them through their journey. His presence offered a quiet reassurance to Erik and those who observed their bond—a testament to the transformative power of companionship and unwavering support.

Erik sought out those he had wronged, engaging in open and honest conversations, acknowledging his past mistakes, and expressing genuine remorse. He offered no excuses, taking responsibility for his actions and the pain he had caused. His sincere apologies and acts of restitution demonstrated his commitment to growth, personal accountability, and the desire to make amends.

The response to Erik's return was varied. Some individuals remained guarded, cautious about extending forgiveness or trust. Others, however, were moved by the depth of his remorse, recognizing the transformative journey he had undertaken. Over time, Erik's actions and his commitment to personal growth began to sway even the most skeptical hearts, fostering an environment of healing, understanding, and reconciliation.

Through his interactions with the community, Erik demonstrated the profound changes that had taken place within him. He embraced opportunities to contribute positively, offering his skills and wisdom to the betterment of the village. Whether it was lending a helping hand, sharing his newfound knowledge, or engaging in acts of kindness, Erik's actions spoke volumes, gradually mending the bonds that had been strained by his past.

As time passed, Erik's presence in the village began to be accepted with greater warmth and understanding. The community saw the depth of his transformation, witnessing his commitment to growth and the positive impact he sought to create. They recognized the resilience of the human spirit and the capacity for change that resided within each person.

Erik's return marked a turning point—a chance for the village to collectively heal, forgive, and embrace the possibilities that arose from personal redemption. It was a reminder that mistakes need not define one's future, and that growth and change were within the reach of every individual.

With Thór faithfully at his side, Erik walked the path of his return with humility, determination, and an unwavering commitment to living a life defined by integrity and compassion. His presence served as a reminder to the community that redemption was possible and that the potential for personal transformation lay within each of them.

As Erik settled back into the village, he carried with him the lessons learned from his journey—a reminder of the transformative power of self-reflection, growth, and forgiveness. He walked among the villagers with gratitude, embracing the opportunity for redemption and offering support to others who sought their own paths of healing and personal growth.

The Viking's return was not simply a homecoming—it was a testament to the resilience of the human spirit and the possibility of personal redemption. Erik's presence served as a beacon of hope, inspiring others to confront their own past mistakes, embrace growth, and foster a community built on understanding, forgiveness, and the pursuit of a brighter future.

Chapter 62: The Girl's Second Chance

With the village abuzz with Erik's return and the promise of redemption, Freya, the girl with whom Erik had shared an unbreakable bond, found herself at a crossroads—a chance to embrace her own second chance at happiness and personal growth.

As she observed the changing dynamics within the village and witnessed Erik's transformation, Freya felt a stirring within her heart—a yearning for her own journey of healing and a desire to forge a new path forward. She understood that forgiveness was not only about extending it to others but also about granting it to herself.

With Thór faithfully by her side, Freya embarked on a personal quest—a quest to rediscover herself, to reconcile the conflicting emotions within her, and to embrace the second chance that life had offered her. She delved into the depths of her own heart, seeking to heal the wounds that had lingered and to cultivate a sense of self-love and acceptance.

Freya immersed herself in self-reflection, examining the choices she had made and the impact they had on her own well-being and the lives of those around her. She recognized the patterns of behavior that had held her back and the fears that had kept her from fully embracing her own happiness.

With each moment of introspection, Freya peeled back the layers of her past, revealing her true essence—a resilient, compassionate, and inherently worthy individual. She confronted her fears head-on, dismantling the self-imposed limitations that had hindered her growth and prevented her from fully experiencing the joys of life.

Thór, with his steadfast loyalty and unwavering support, mirrored Freya's journey of self-discovery. His presence served as a constant reminder that she deserved love, forgiveness, and a second chance at happiness. With every loving gaze and comforting nuzzle, Thór reinforced the belief that her past did not define her, and that the potential for growth and fulfillment lay within her reach.

As Freya embraced her own second chance, she made a conscious effort to extend forgiveness to herself for the mistakes she had made and the pain she had carried. She acknowledged that redemption was not only about seeking forgiveness from others but also about embracing self-forgiveness—an act of compassion that allowed her to release the burden of guilt and pave the way for personal growth and healing.

With newfound clarity, Freya began to make choices aligned with her authentic self. She pursued her passions, nurturing her talents and interests, and engaged in activities that brought her joy and fulfillment. She surrounded herself with a supportive community, one that encouraged her personal growth and celebrated her newfound sense of empowerment.

Freya's second chance extended beyond her individual journey—it influenced her relationships with others, particularly with Erik. As they navigated their own paths of growth, they found solace and understanding in one another, supporting each other's transformation and celebrating the opportunities for redemption that life had bestowed upon them.

With Thór by her side, embodying the unwavering loyalty and joy that had guided her through the depths of her own transformation, Freya walked forward with a renewed sense of purpose and a deep appreciation for the second chance she had been granted. Her presence served as a beacon of hope for others, inspiring them to embrace their own journeys of healing and personal growth.

As Freya embraced her second chance, she understood that life was a tapestry of opportunities and possibilities—a continual journey of growth, forgiveness, and self-discovery. With each step forward, she carried within her heart the lessons learned from her own journey, offering a guiding light to others who sought their own paths of redemption, love, and personal fulfillment.

The girl's second chance marked a pivotal moment—a turning point that allowed her to release the past and embrace the infinite possibilities of the future. With Thór's loyal companionship and the unwavering support of those around her, Freya embarked on a journey of self-rediscovery, ready to seize the newfound opportunities that lay ahead and to embrace the joy and fulfillment that awaited her.

Chapter 63: The Dog's Reunion

Thór, the loyal and perceptive canine companion, felt his heart swell with anticipation as he sensed a familiar presence approaching—a reunion that would deepen the bond between him, Erik, and Freya and celebrate the profound growth and transformation they had each undergone.

As the village bustled with excitement and whispers of the impending reunion, Thór's tail wagged with eager anticipation. He sensed the energy shift, knowing that this moment would be a testament to the unbreakable connection they had formed—a bond that had withstood trials, forgiveness, and personal redemption.

Erik and Freya, guided by their own journeys of growth, approached the reunion with a mixture of nerves and joy. Their hearts brimmed with gratitude for the unwavering support Thór had provided throughout their transformative paths—a support that went beyond words, transcending language and expressing the depth of their shared experiences.

As Thór caught sight of Erik and Freya, his eyes sparkled with joy and his tail wagged furiously. He bounded towards them, his steps filled with excitement and a love that knew no bounds. In that moment, the trio reunited, enveloped in an embrace that conveyed the profound connection they shared—a testament to the transformative power of companionship and unconditional love.

Thór's presence served as a silent celebration of their individual growth and the reunion of kindred spirits. With each joyful leap and affectionate lick, he embodied the unwavering support and loyalty that had guided them through the darkest moments of their journeys.

As Erik and Freya embraced Thór, they marveled at the depth of the bond they had forged. Their reunion spoke volumes—reaffirming the love and trust they had cultivated and the strength that had emerged from their collective growth. In that moment, the trio stood as a testament to the resilience of the human spirit and the profound impact of unwavering companionship.

Together, they celebrated the growth and transformation they had each experienced—Erik's journey of redemption, Freya's pursuit of personal healing, and Thór's own discovery of his innate ability to offer support and love. Their reunion symbolized the triumph of forgiveness, growth, and the profound joy that comes from embracing one's authentic self.

In the presence of one another, Erik, Freya, and Thór knew that their journey was far from over. They recognized that life would continue to present challenges, but they faced the future with renewed strength and a deep sense of gratitude for the unwavering support they found in one another.

With Thór by their side, embodying the love and loyalty that had guided them through their individual transformations, Erik and Freya walked forward with a shared understanding—a profound knowing that their bond was unbreakable and that they were forever connected by the threads of their intertwined journeys.

In the presence of Thór's joyful reunion, the village community bore witness to the power of love, forgiveness, and personal growth. Inspired by the transformative journeys of Erik, Freya, and their loyal companion, they were reminded of the strength that lay within each individual and the profound impact that compassion and support could have on the lives of others.

As Thór nuzzled his beloved Viking companions and shared in their embrace, he embodied the purest form of joy—the joy of reunion, of shared growth, and the enduring power of love. With every beat of his heart and every wag of his tail, Thór served as a reminder to embrace the profound connections that enrich our lives and to cherish the moments of reunion and celebration that define our shared human experience.

Chapter 64: The Viking's Proposal

Erik, filled with a renewed sense of purpose and a deep love that had grown within him, knew that the time had come to take a significant step forward in his journey of redemption and personal happiness—a step that would bind his fate to that of Freya, the woman who had captured his heart.

With Thór by his side, Erik's mind was consumed by thoughts of Freya—a woman whose strength, resilience, and capacity for forgiveness had left an indelible mark on his soul. He recognized that she had become an integral part of his journey—a guiding light that had illuminated the path to his own growth and transformation.

As Erik pondered the depths of his emotions, he realized that he longed for a future that encompassed not only personal redemption but also a life shared with Freya. He understood that the bond they had forged was a rare and precious gift—one that deserved to be celebrated and nurtured.

With his heart pounding, Erik summoned the courage to approach Freya. He sought a moment of privacy, a space where he could express the depths of his love and commitment to her—a proposal that would symbolize their shared journey of redemption, forgiveness, and the boundless possibilities that lay ahead.

Underneath the comforting shade of a familiar tree, Erik and Freya stood, their eyes locked in an unspoken understanding. Thór, sensing the significance of the moment, stood close by, his presence a silent source of support and love.

Erik's voice, filled with sincerity and vulnerability, quivered slightly as he spoke of the profound impact Freya had on his life. He expressed his deepest admiration for her strength, her resilience, and the love she had shown him throughout their shared journey. He confessed his own love for her—a love that had blossomed amidst the trials and tribulations they had faced.

With each heartfelt word, Erik conveyed his desire for a future built on trust, love, and a mutual commitment to growth. He envisioned a life filled with shared adventures, laughter, and the unwavering support they had shown each other. He offered Freya his hand, a symbol of unity and the promise of a future intertwined.

Freya, her eyes shimmering with a mixture of joy and trepidation, listened to Erik's words with her heart wide open. She recognized the depth of his love and the sincerity behind his proposal. In that moment, she felt a surge of gratitude for the incredible transformation they had both undergone, and the immeasurable strength their connection had provided.

As the weight of Erik's proposal settled in the air, Freya took a moment to collect her thoughts. She reflected on the journey they had traveled together—the obstacles they had overcome, the growth they had experienced, and the love that had blossomed amidst it all. With her own voice filled with emotion, she accepted Erik's proposal, expressing her love and commitment to him and their shared future.

Thór, sensing the joy and profound significance of the moment, let out a contented sigh. His presence was a testament to the unwavering support and love that had guided them all. He wagged his tail, as if to celebrate the union that had been forged—an unbreakable bond that transcended time and space.

In that heartfelt exchange beneath the shaded tree, Erik and Freya sealed their commitment to each other—a commitment born from personal growth, forgiveness, and an unwavering belief in the transformative power of love. With Thór by their side, they walked forward, ready to embrace the future that lay ahead—a future defined by unity, shared growth, and the enduring joy that came from embracing the possibilities of redemption and personal happiness.

Chapter 65: The Girl's Answer

Freya stood before Erik, her heart overflowing with love and gratitude for the journey they had undertaken together—their shared growth, forgiveness, and the deep bond they had forged. She gazed into Erik's eyes, her voice filled with emotion as she prepared to answer his heartfelt proposal.

As a gentle breeze rustled through the trees, Freya took a moment to collect her thoughts, savoring the weight of Erik's love and commitment that hung in the air. She felt a deep sense of peace within her, knowing that she had come to a place of clarity and self-discovery during her own transformative journey.

With a steady voice and unwavering gaze, Freya expressed her profound love for Erik. She spoke of the immense impact he had made on her life—the way he had challenged her to grow, supported her in moments of darkness, and believed in her capacity for forgiveness and personal happiness.

Freya acknowledged the depth of their connection—the unspoken understanding, the shared experiences, and the unwavering loyalty that had marked their journey. She shared her own dreams of a future built on trust, love, and a commitment to continuing their personal growth side by side.

With each heartfelt word, Freya conveyed her acceptance of Erik's proposal—a resounding "yes" that resonated with joy and a profound sense of gratitude. She extended her hand to him, symbolizing their unity and the shared path they were embarking upon.

Erik, overcome with emotion, reached out and clasped Freya's hand in his own, their fingers interlacing in a powerful bond. Their eyes met, and in that exchange, they knew that their love and commitment would guide them through whatever challenges lay ahead.

Thór, who had been a silent witness to their journey, wagged his tail in celebration, his eyes sparkling with joy. He knew that the unity of Erik and Freya was a testament to the transformative power of love, forgiveness, and personal growth. His presence affirmed their shared path forward—a path that would be marked by unwavering support, loyalty, and the boundless possibilities that lay ahead.

In that moment, Erik, Freya, and Thór stood as a united trio—a testament to the resilience of the human spirit and the profound connection that can be forged through shared experiences of growth, forgiveness, and love. Together, they walked forward, ready to embrace the future with open hearts, unwavering commitment, and the joy that comes from knowing they had found their truest companions in one another.

As they embarked on their shared journey, Erik, Freya, and Thór understood that challenges would undoubtedly arise, but their love, strengthened by their transformative experiences, would provide the foundation for their continued growth and happiness. With each step forward, they carried within them the lessons learned, the bond forged through their individual transformations, and the shared vision of a future filled with love, understanding, and the profound joy that comes from embracing life's possibilities.

In the depths of their hearts, they knew that their union was not just a joining of two souls, but a celebration of the transformative power of love and the infinite capacity for personal growth and redemption. With Thór's unwavering presence and the deep connection between Erik and Freya, they walked forward, ready to face whatever lay ahead, knowing that they were forever united in a journey of love, growth, and shared purpose.

Chapter 66: The Celebration

With the acceptance of Freya's answer and their commitment to a shared future, Erik and Freya's union became a cause for celebration —a joyous occasion that would bring the entire village together to honor their love, growth, and the transformative power of forgiveness.

Preparations for the celebration were set in motion as the village buzzed with excitement and anticipation. Vibrant banners were hung, flowers adorned every corner, and the air was filled with the tantalizing aroma of a feast being prepared. The villagers eagerly contributed their skills and talents, coming together to create a celebration that would be etched in their memories forever.

As the day of celebration arrived, the village square transformed into a spectacle of color, music, and laughter. Villagers gathered, their faces reflecting the collective joy that filled the air. Tables were arranged, laden with delicacies, and barrels of mead were uncorked, ready to be shared in celebration of love and unity.

Erik and Freya, dressed in garments that symbolized their newfound union and shared growth, stood at the center of the square, their hands entwined, and their hearts overflowing with gratitude. The love and support radiating from the community mirrored the transformative journey they had undertaken, reminding them of the power of connection and the strength that can be found in the embrace of a united village.

Thór, the loyal companion who had witnessed their individual transformations and the blossoming of their love, basked in the attention and adoration of the villagers. His tail wagged in joyful harmony with the lively music that filled the square, his presence a testament to the unwavering loyalty and love that had guided them all.

The celebration commenced with a heartfelt speech from the village elder, who spoke of the significance of forgiveness, personal growth, and the unity that Erik and Freya's union represented. The village community responded with cheers and applause, recognizing that their own stories were intertwined with those of Erik and Freya—a testament to the interconnectedness of their journeys.

Laughter filled the air as villagers shared stories of the couple's individual transformations, the challenges they had overcome, and the love that had blossomed amidst it all. Songs were sung, danced to the rhythm of the celebration, filling the night sky with melodies that echoed through the village and beyond.

Erik and Freya, surrounded by the love and support of their community, shared their first dance as a married couple—a moment that symbolized the unity they had found and the joy that radiated from their hearts. As they twirled across the dance floor, their eyes locked in a shared understanding, they were reminded of the profound growth and the transformative power of love that had brought them to this moment.

Thór, ever watchful and filled with joy, weaved through the crowd, showering the villagers with affectionate nudges and playful antics. His presence served as a constant reminder of the unwavering support and love that had guided them all—a celebration of the profound bond they had forged.

The celebration continued late into the night, with laughter, music, and dance. Villagers shared in the festivities, cherishing the bonds of friendship, and celebrating the collective journey of growth and personal redemption that Erik and Freya's union embodied.

As the stars shimmered overhead, Erik, Freya, and Thór found solace in the embrace of their loved ones—the village community that had stood by them through thick and thin. They reveled in the joy of their union and the collective celebration of love, growth, and forgiveness.

In that moment, surrounded by the beauty of unity and shared happiness, Erik, Freya, and Thór felt a profound gratitude for the transformative journey they had undertaken and the profound connections that had emerged. They carried within their hearts the lessons learned, the bond forged through forgiveness, and the unwavering support of their village community.

The celebration marked not only the beginning of Erik and Freya's married life but also a collective recognition of the power of love, growth, and redemption. It was a testament to the resilience of the human spirit and the boundless possibilities that emerge when forgiveness and personal growth are embraced.

With Thór by their side, Erik and Freya danced, laughed, and celebrated, knowing that their journey of love and growth would continue to unfold, guided by the unwavering support and joy of their village community. In that shared celebration, they discovered the true essence of happiness—a profound unity that transcended individual stories and united them all in a tapestry of love, compassion,

and the celebration of life's transformative
moments.

Chapter 67: The Dog's Playfulness

Amidst the celebration of love and unity, Thór, the loyal and playful canine companion, reveled in the joyous atmosphere that surrounded him. His tail wagged with uncontainable excitement, and a mischievous sparkle danced in his eyes. Thór's presence added an element of lightheartedness and laughter to the festivities.

As villagers laughed and danced, Thór weaved through the crowd, his playful energy contagious. He engaged in friendly games of chase with the village children, who giggled with delight as they tried to keep up with his swift movements. His infectious enthusiasm and warm nature brought smiles to the faces of young and old alike, creating a sense of shared joy and connection.

Thór's antics extended beyond playful games of chase. He delighted in retrieving sticks and balls, showcasing his agility and dexterity with acrobatic leaps and bounds. Villagers watched in awe as he gracefully caught objects mid-air, his playful nature reminding them of the joy and simplicity that could be found in the present moment.

Erik and Freya, caught up in the whirlwind of celebration, couldn't help but be drawn to Thór's playful presence. They joined in his games, running alongside him and sharing in the pure delight that radiated from his every movement. In those moments, the weight of the world seemed to momentarily fade, replaced by the unadulterated joy of living in the present and embracing the playful spirit that resided within them all.

Thór's playful nature also served as a reminder of the importance of balance and spontaneity in life. Amidst their journeys of growth and the celebration of their union, Erik and Freya recognized the need to embrace moments of lightness, laughter, and play. Thór's playfulness became a symbol of their shared commitment to infusing their lives with joy and a reminder that happiness could be found in the simplest of pleasures.

As the celebration continued, Thór's playful spirit drew more and more villagers into his orbit. Laughter echoed throughout the square as children and adults alike engaged in lively games of fetch, playfully tussling with Thór, and reveling in his joyful energy. Thór's boundless enthusiasm became a catalyst for connection and a reminder that the pursuit of happiness often lay in embracing the carefree moments of life.

In the midst of the festivities, Erik, Freya, and Thór found themselves caught in a moment of joyful abandon. They twirled in circles, Thór chasing his tail while Erik and Freya laughed in sheer delight. Their laughter mingled with the sounds of celebration, creating a symphony of joy that echoed through the village.

Thór's playful presence served as a testament to the profound bond that had united them all—the bond of love, growth, and shared experiences. His energy infused the celebration with an air of lightness and fun, reminding everyone to cherish the present moment, to embrace the playfulness that resides within, and to find joy in the simple pleasures of life.

As the celebration drew to a close, Thór, panting and contented, found his place by Erik and Freya's side. His playful nature had touched the hearts of all who had witnessed it, leaving behind a sense of wonder and a reminder that life is best lived when infused with laughter, spontaneity, and a willingness to embrace the playful spirit within.

In that moment, as the village bid farewell to the celebration, Erik, Freya, and Thór carried with them the memory of Thór's playful presence—a reminder of the enduring power of joy, the importance of balance in life, and the transformative impact of embracing the carefree moments that bring smiles to our faces and warmth to our hearts.

With Thór by their side, Erik and Freya walked forward, ready to embrace each new day with a renewed commitment to playfulness, laughter, and the unwavering support and love that had guided them throughout their transformative journeys. Thór's playful spirit remained a constant reminder that life is meant to be cherished, celebrated, and enjoyed to the fullest.

Chapter 68: The Viking's Happiness

Erik, the Viking who had embarked on a transformative journey of redemption and love, found himself enveloped in a profound sense of happiness—a joy that radiated from his core and permeated every aspect of his life.

As he stood amidst the beauty of the village he called home, Erik took a moment to reflect on the path that had led him to this point— the challenges he had faced, the growth he had experienced, and the love that had blossomed in his heart. He marveled at the transformative power of forgiveness, personal growth, and the unwavering support of his community.

With Freya by his side, Erik recognized that the happiness he felt was not solely derived from external circumstances but rather from the deep connection they shared—a bond born from their individual journeys of healing and personal growth. Their love had become a source of strength, grounding him in the present moment and providing a foundation for his happiness.

Thór, ever loyal and attuned to Erik's emotions, seemed to sense his owner's profound joy. The faithful canine companion wagged his tail in contentment, his eyes gleaming with a knowingness that mirrored Erik's newfound happiness.

Erik's happiness extended beyond his love for Freya. He took pleasure in the simple joys of village life—the laughter of children playing, the warmth of the sun on his face, and the shared moments of camaraderie with his fellow villagers. He found solace in the everyday moments—the taste of freshly baked bread, the sound of a crackling fire, and the comforting presence of his community.

As he interacted with his village community, Erik realized the impact his journey had had on those around him. The transformations he had undergone, the lessons he had learned, and the love he had cultivated became a source of inspiration for others—a reminder of the human capacity for growth, forgiveness, and the pursuit of personal happiness.

With gratitude in his heart, Erik made a conscious effort to give back to his community, to share his knowledge, skills, and wisdom with those who sought guidance. He recognized that happiness flourished not only through personal fulfillment but also through acts of kindness and service to others.

The village community, witnessing Erik's happiness, embraced the joy that radiated from him. They celebrated his transformation, finding inspiration in his journey and embracing the collective happiness that permeated their lives. The bonds of friendship and unity grew stronger, and the village became a haven of shared happiness and support.

In the presence of Freya, Thór, and the loving embrace of his village community, Erik knew that his happiness was intricately intertwined with their presence in his life. Their love, support, and shared experiences served as constant reminders of the growth and personal redemption he had achieved—a reminder that happiness could be found not only in the destination but also in the journey itself.

As Erik walked through the village, his steps were lighter, his smile brighter, and his heart filled with a profound sense of gratitude. He knew that life would continue to present challenges, but he faced them with a newfound resilience, a deep-rooted happiness, and the unwavering support of his loved ones.

Thór, the faithful companion who had been by his side throughout his transformative journey, embodied the essence of happiness with every wag of his tail and every loving gaze. He mirrored Erik's joy, serving as a constant reminder of the simple pleasures that could be found in each passing moment.

With every breath, Erik embraced his happiness—a happiness rooted in the transformative power of love, forgiveness, and personal growth. He walked forward, ready to face the future with open arms, a heart filled with gratitude, and an unwavering commitment to nurturing the happiness that resided within him and those around him.

In the embrace of his loved ones and the warmth of his village community, Erik knew that his journey of happiness was far from over. Each day presented new opportunities for growth, connection, and shared joy. With Thór by his side, Erik walked forward, ready to embrace the beauty of life and the happiness that awaited him at every turn.

Chapter 69: The Girl's Contentment

Freya, the girl who had embarked on a transformative journey of healing and love, found herself enveloped in a deep sense of contentment—a state of inner peace and fulfillment that radiated from her being.

As she stood amidst the beauty of the village, Freya basked in the warmth of her community's embrace and the love that had blossomed in her heart. She marveled at the profound transformation she had undergone —the growth, forgiveness, and the unwavering support she had received.

With Erik by her side, Freya felt a profound sense of contentment, knowing that their love was built on a foundation of mutual understanding, trust, and shared growth. Their journey had allowed them to overcome obstacles, heal wounds, and forge a bond that could weather any storm.

Thór, the faithful companion who had witnessed Freya's journey of healing, seemed to sense her contentment. He wagged his tail, his eyes shining with a knowingness that mirrored her own inner peace.

Freya's contentment extended beyond her relationship with Erik. She found solace in the simple pleasures of everyday life—the beauty of nature, the laughter of children, and the shared moments of connection within her village. She cherished the moments of stillness and reflection, finding joy in the small moments that brought a sense of tranquility to her soul.

As she interacted with her village community, Freya recognized the impact her journey had on those around her. Her transformation, her capacity for forgiveness, and the love she had cultivated became a source of inspiration for others. Freya's contentment served as a guiding light, showing others the possibility of finding inner peace and fulfillment through personal growth and the pursuit of authentic happiness.

With gratitude in her heart, Freya made a conscious effort to give back to her community—to offer her support, kindness, and a listening ear to those in need. She understood that contentment flourished not only through personal fulfillment but also through acts of compassion and service to others.

The village community, witnessing Freya's contentment, embraced the serenity that radiated from her. They celebrated her growth, finding inspiration in her journey and cherishing the collective contentment that permeated their lives. The bonds of friendship and unity grew stronger, and the village became a sanctuary of shared tranquility and support.

In the presence of Erik, Thór, and the loving embrace of her village community, Freya knew that her contentment was intertwined with their presence in her life. Their love, support, and shared experiences served as constant reminders of the healing and personal fulfillment she had achieved—a reminder that contentment could be found not only in external circumstances but also within the depths of her own being.

As Freya walked through the village, her steps were purposeful, her smile serene, and her heart filled with a deep sense of gratitude. She knew that life would continue to present challenges, but she faced them with resilience, a calm spirit, and the unwavering support of her loved ones.

Thór, the steadfast companion who had been by her side throughout her transformative journey, embodied the essence of contentment with every step and every loving gaze. He mirrored Freya's inner peace, serving as a constant reminder of the serenity that resided within her.

With every breath, Freya embraced her contentment—a contentment rooted in the transformative power of self-discovery, forgiveness, and personal growth. She walked forward, ready to face the future with open arms, a heart filled with gratitude, and an unwavering commitment to nurturing the contentment that resided within her and those around her.

In the embrace of her loved ones and the warmth of her village community, Freya knew that her journey of contentment was far from over. Each day presented new opportunities for growth, connection, and shared tranquility. With Thór by her side, Freya walked forward, ready to embrace the beauty of life and the contentment that awaited her at every turn.

Chapter 70: The Dog's Watchful Eye

Thór, the loyal and watchful canine companion, remained ever vigilant as life continued to unfold for Erik and Freya. With a keen sense of intuition, he stood by their side, his eyes scanning the horizon, ready to protect and guide them through the challenges that lay ahead.

In times of joy and contentment, Thór's presence served as a gentle reminder to cherish and nurture the bonds that had been forged—the love, trust, and growth that had transformed their lives. He wagged his tail, his eyes reflecting the peace and contentment he saw within Erik and Freya.

But Thór's watchful eye extended beyond moments of celebration. He sensed the currents of change, the ebb and flow of life's trials. In times of uncertainty or adversity, Thór's demeanor shifted, becoming more alert and attentive. His instincts guided him to remain by Erik and Freya's side, offering unwavering support and a comforting presence.

When challenges arose, Thór's watchful eye served as a silent reminder of the strength that lay within Erik and Freya. He stood steadfast, offering his loyal companionship and the reassurance that they were never alone in their journey.

Thór's keen senses detected subtle shifts in the atmosphere—the tremors of doubt, the waves of sadness, or the whispers of uncertainty. He responded with a knowing gaze, a gentle nudge, or a comforting lean, offering solace and unwavering love during moments of vulnerability.

As Erik and Freya faced the complexities of life, Thór's watchful eye became a beacon of guidance—a reminder to trust their instincts, remain true to their values, and embrace the resilience that had carried them thus far. His presence was a silent reminder of the transformative power of their journey—a testament to the strength that had emerged from their shared experiences.

With Thór by their side, Erik and Freya felt a sense of security and protection. His watchful eye brought them comfort, knowing that his loyalty and intuition would guide them through the twists and turns of life's path.

Thór's watchful eye extended beyond their immediate circle, encompassing the entire village community. He embraced his role as a protector and guardian, watching over the villagers with unwavering devotion. His presence served as a reminder of the interconnectedness of their lives—the shared journey they had embarked upon together.

In moments of celebration, Thór reveled in the joy and merriment that surrounded him, joining in the laughter and playfulness. But his watchful eye never wavered, remaining attuned to the needs of those around him. His presence brought comfort and a sense of security, allowing the villagers to embrace life fully, knowing that Thór was there, a silent guardian watching over them all.

As time passed, Thór's watchful eye continued to guide Erik and Freya, offering solace, protection, and a constant reminder of the bond they shared. With each passing day, they grew stronger, more resilient, and more attuned to the interconnectedness of their lives—the unity that bound them together.

Together, Erik, Freya, and Thór faced the unknown with courage and unwavering determination. Thór's watchful eye provided a steady presence—a guiding light during moments of uncertainty, and a reminder that their journey was never undertaken alone.

With Thór's watchful eye and unwavering love by their side, Erik and Freya walked forward, ready to face the future with strength, resilience, and the unbreakable bond that had been forged through their shared experiences. In the presence of their loyal companion, they found solace, protection, and the assurance that, no matter what challenges lay ahead, they would face them together.

Chapter 71: The Viking's Family

As Erik's journey of love and personal growth continued, he found himself embracing a newfound sense of family—a connection that extended beyond bloodlines and encompassed the deep bonds forged through love, loyalty, and shared experiences.

Erik, Freya, and Thór stood at the center of their village, surrounded by their loved ones. The village had become more than just a community—it had become their family. They were embraced by a network of individuals who had witnessed their transformations, celebrated their love, and stood by their side through thick and thin.

Erik's biological family, once distant and estranged, had also been touched by the transformative power of forgiveness and growth. They had witnessed Erik's journey firsthand, witnessing the profound changes that had taken place within him. In the face of his personal transformation, they had opened their hearts, embracing him with love, acceptance, and a newfound sense of connection.

Erik's parents, who had once struggled to understand his choices and the path he had taken, now saw the depth of his character and the capacity for love and redemption that resided within him. They were filled with a sense of pride and joy as they welcomed Erik, Freya, and Thór into the family fold, recognizing the strength and resilience they had all shown throughout their shared journey.

With each passing day, Erik's bond with his family grew stronger. They shared stories, laughter, and moments of connection that bridged the gaps of the past. Erik's siblings, who had once seemed distant, became confidants and friends, eager to support him and embrace the new chapter of love and happiness he had found.

The village community, too, played a vital role in Erik's sense of family. They became the extended family he had always longed for— individuals who had witnessed his growth, offered guidance, and provided unwavering support throughout his journey. They celebrated his triumphs, stood by him during moments of adversity, and rejoiced in the love that had transformed his life.

Thór, the loyal canine companion, embodied the essence of family with his unwavering love and loyalty. He stood as a constant reminder of the connection they shared—a bond that transcended bloodlines and spoke to the universal capacity for love, devotion, and companionship.

As Erik, Freya, and Thór embraced their expanded family, they recognized the power of these connections—the strength and resilience that came from having loved ones by their side. The shared experiences, laughter, and tears formed the foundation of their familial bond, creating a support system that would carry them through life's joys and challenges.

In the warmth of their family's embrace, Erik and Freya found a sense of belonging—a place where their love was celebrated, their growth acknowledged, and their dreams supported. They felt a profound gratitude for the interconnected web of relationships that had woven itself around them—a tapestry of love, support, and shared experiences that formed their unique and cherished family.

Thór, always present and watchful, reveled in the love and sense of belonging that surrounded him. He wagged his tail in contentment, knowing that he had played a vital role in Erik's journey and the formation of their extended family. His presence served as a constant reminder of the unconditional love and loyalty that bound them all together.

As Erik, Freya, and Thór walked forward, hand in hand, surrounded by their family, they carried within their hearts a deep sense of gratitude for the transformative power of love and the enduring strength of their familial bonds. They embraced the joy of belonging, the comfort of unconditional love, and the support of a community that had become their chosen family—a family united by love, forgiveness, and the shared experiences that had shaped their lives.

Together, they faced the future with open hearts, knowing that their expanded family would be there to celebrate their triumphs, share their burdens, and cherish the precious moments that life bestowed upon them. In the presence of their loved ones, Erik, Freya, and Thór found solace, belonging, and the profound joy that comes from being part of a family—a family built not solely on blood, but on the transformative power of love and the shared journey they had undertaken together.

Chapter 72: The Girl's New Beginning

Freya stood at the edge of the village, her gaze fixed on the horizon. The gentle breeze played with her hair, whispering promises of new beginnings and possibilities. She felt a surge of anticipation, for within her heart, a new chapter was about to unfold.

After the transformative journey of love and personal growth, Freya had discovered a newfound strength—a strength that stemmed from the depths of her being. She had embraced her true essence, shedding the layers of doubt and insecurity that had once held her back. Now, she stood tall and confident, ready to embark on a new beginning.

As she looked back at the village, Freya's heart swelled with gratitude for the love and support she had received from her community. The bonds forged during her journey had become unbreakable, and the collective strength they provided propelled her forward.

Thór, her faithful companion, sat by her side, his presence a constant reminder of the loyalty and unwavering love that had guided her throughout her transformative journey. His watchful eyes reflected her determination and served as a silent reassurance that he would be there, steadfast, as she ventured into the unknown.

Freya's new beginning extended beyond the village. She had discovered a passion within her—a calling to help others find their own paths to healing and personal growth. With newfound clarity, she resolved to share her experiences and offer guidance to those who sought it. She recognized the power of her voice and the profound impact she could have on the lives of others.

Leaving the familiar behind, Freya set forth on a journey of her own—a journey to spread love, healing, and personal empowerment. With each step, she carried within her the lessons learned, the wisdom gained, and the unwavering support of her loved ones.

The path ahead was not without challenges, but Freya faced them with grace and determination. She embraced the unknown, knowing that it held infinite possibilities for growth and self-discovery. The strength she had cultivated during her transformative journey propelled her forward, filling her with a sense of purpose and the unwavering belief that she could make a difference in the lives of those she encountered.

As Freya ventured into new territories, she encountered individuals from all walks of life. She listened to their stories, offered support, and shared her own journey of growth and healing. Her words resonated with those who sought solace and guidance, igniting a spark within them—a spark of hope and the belief that they too could overcome their own challenges.

Thór, ever watchful and supportive, remained by Freya's side as she embarked on her new beginning. He stood as a symbol of the unwavering loyalty and love that had guided her throughout her journey, providing a source of comfort and companionship as she ventured into uncharted territory.

With each person she encountered, Freya discovered that her transformative journey had not only shaped her own life but had the power to impact the lives of others. Through her compassion, empathy, and unwavering belief in the human spirit, she became a beacon of light—a guiding force for those who sought inspiration and guidance on their own paths of growth and self-discovery.

As Freya continued to walk her chosen path, she carried within her the village's love, Erik's unwavering support, and the watchful presence of Thór. She knew that her new beginning was not a solitary endeavor but a collective journey—one that intertwined her story with the stories of others, weaving a tapestry of resilience, hope, and shared growth.

With every step, Freya embraced her purpose, knowing that she was fulfilling her true calling—to be a catalyst for positive change, an advocate for healing, and a source of inspiration for all those she encountered.

In the presence of her loved ones, the unwavering support of her village community, and the watchful eye of Thór, Freya embarked on her new beginning with courage, grace, and an unwavering belief in the transformative power of love and personal growth. The path ahead might be uncertain, but Freya faced it with an open heart and the knowledge that her journey would continue to shape her, empower others, and unfold with limitless possibilities.

Chapter 73: The Dog's Companionship

Thór, the steadfast and loyal canine companion, continued to walk by Freya's side as she embarked on her new beginning. His presence provided a constant source of comfort, companionship, and unwavering support.

As they ventured into new territories, Thór's watchful eyes scanned the surroundings, ever alert to any potential dangers or obstacles that lay ahead. His instincts guided him, ensuring the safety and well-being of Freya during their shared journey.

Thór's companionship went beyond mere physical presence. His boundless love and unwavering loyalty became a source of solace for Freya—a reminder that she was never alone in her endeavors. His wagging tail and affectionate nudges served as silent reassurances, infusing her with strength and courage as she navigated the challenges that arose.

In moments of doubt or uncertainty, Freya found solace in the unwavering belief Thór had in her. His unspoken encouragement spurred her on, reminding her of her own capabilities and resilience. He served as a constant reminder that, even in the face of adversity, she possessed the strength and determination to overcome any obstacle.

Thór's presence also brought a sense of grounding and connection to the present moment. Amidst the whirlwind of her new beginning, Freya found moments of peace and tranquility as she simply sat by Thór's side, listening to the soothing rhythm of his breathing and feeling the gentle touch of his fur against her skin. In those moments, the chaos of the outside world faded away, and a deep sense of calm enveloped her.

As they ventured into new territories, Freya discovered that Thór's companionship had a profound impact on the lives of those they encountered. His gentle demeanor and loving nature melted the hearts of strangers, fostering a sense of trust and openness that might not have otherwise been possible. People gravitated toward Thór, finding solace and comfort in his presence, and in turn, they extended their support and kindness to Freya.

Thór's companionship became a bridge, connecting Freya to the communities they encountered on their journey. His gentle spirit and unconditional love served as a common language that transcended cultural and language barriers. Through Thór, Freya witnessed the power of compassion, empathy, and the unifying force of love that bound humanity together.

Freya's gratitude for Thór's companionship deepened with each passing day. She recognized that his unwavering presence went beyond the physical—he was a pillar of strength, a source of unconditional love, and a constant reminder of the beauty that could be found in the simplest moments of connection.

In moments of triumph and celebration, Thór shared in Freya's joy, his tail wagging with uncontainable excitement. In moments of sorrow or uncertainty, he provided a comforting presence, his soulful eyes filled with understanding and empathy. Thór's companionship transcended words, offering Freya a sense of belonging and unwavering support throughout her new beginning.

As Freya and Thór continued on their shared journey, they walked forward hand in paw, their bond unbreakable. Thór's loyal companionship served as a guiding light, illuminating the path ahead and reminding Freya that, no matter where her new beginning led her, she would always have a steadfast friend by her side.

In the presence of Thór's unwavering love and companionship, Freya found strength, courage, and an unshakable belief in herself. Together, they faced the unknown, ready to embrace the adventures that awaited them, knowing that their shared journey would be filled with countless moments of connection, growth, and the profound bond that could only be found in the companionship of a loyal friend.

Chapter 74: The Viking's Legacy

Erik, the Viking who had embarked on a journey of love, redemption, and personal growth, had left a lasting legacy in his wake— a legacy that extended far beyond his own lifetime and would continue to inspire generations to come.

Through his transformative journey, Erik had demonstrated the power of forgiveness, resilience, and the capacity for personal growth. His story had touched the lives of those around him, leaving an indelible mark on the hearts and minds of the village community and beyond.

The villagers, inspired by Erik's courage and willingness to confront his past, embraced their own journeys of growth and personal redemption. They drew strength from his example, knowing that change was possible, and that love and forgiveness could mend even the deepest of wounds.

Erik's legacy lived on through the relationships he had nurtured—the love he had shared with Freya, the bonds he had forged with his village community, and the unwavering loyalty of Thór. These connections, woven together through his transformative journey, continued to thrive and inspire future generations.

The children of the village listened in awe as their elders recounted Erik's story, passing down the lessons learned from his journey. They grew up with tales of love, forgiveness, and the power of personal growth, shaping their own lives with the wisdom inherited from Erik's legacy.

Beyond the village, Erik's legacy reached far and wide. Travelers who passed through the village heard whispers of his transformative journey and were inspired to embark on their own quests for self-discovery. Erik became a symbol of hope—a reminder that no matter how dark the past, there was always a path toward redemption and a chance to create a better future.

Erik's legacy was not confined to his personal triumphs. It extended to the tangible changes he had brought about in the village community. Through his example, the villagers had embraced a culture of compassion, unity, and support. They carried forward his legacy, extending a helping hand to those in need, fostering an environment of inclusivity and acceptance.

In the years that followed, the village flourished as a beacon of love, forgiveness, and personal growth. Erik's legacy was woven into every aspect of its existence—the strength of its relationships, the resilience of its community, and the bonds that held them together.

Erik's impact on Freya's life was immeasurable. Her own journey of healing and personal growth had been sparked by their encounter, and her subsequent actions became part of his legacy. Freya, inspired by Erik's example, continued to spread love and compassion wherever she went, leaving her own indelible mark on the world.

The legacy of Erik, the Viking with a transformative journey, would continue to ripple through time, inspiring countless souls to embrace their own paths of love, forgiveness, and personal growth. His story would forever be a reminder of the human capacity for change and the profound impact one individual could have on the lives of many.

As the generations passed, the village community would carry Erik's legacy in their hearts, passing down the lessons learned from his journey. They would continue to nurture the bonds of love, forgiveness, and personal growth, ensuring that his spirit lived on in the fabric of their lives.

Erik's legacy was one of transformation—a testament to the power of love, forgiveness, and the human spirit. It would continue to inspire, ignite, and guide those who sought their own paths toward redemption, leaving an enduring imprint on the world—a legacy of love, resilience, and the unwavering belief in the potential for personal growth and the capacity for change.

Chapter 75: The Girl's Gratitude

Freya stood at the heart of the village, her heart overflowing with a deep sense of gratitude. As she reflected on her journey of love, healing, and personal growth, she couldn't help but feel an immense appreciation for all that had unfolded in her life.

Gratitude washed over her like a warm embrace, enveloping her being and radiating from her every pore. She felt an overwhelming sense of thankfulness for the love she had received from Erik, the unwavering support of her village community, and the steadfast companionship of Thór.

With every breath, Freya offered gratitude for the transformative power of love. It had swept into her life like a gentle breeze, carrying away the burdens of her past and filling her heart with a sense of belonging and joy. The love she had found with Erik was a precious gift—a beacon of light that had guided her through the darkest of times.

Freya's gratitude extended to the village community that had embraced her with open arms. Their support, understanding, and acceptance had created a nurturing environment in which she could grow, heal, and thrive. They had become her chosen family, offering a sense of belonging and a support system that went beyond what she had ever imagined.

The bonds of friendship and unity that had been forged within the village community were a testament to the power of collective strength. Freya recognized that her journey of healing and personal growth had been made possible through the love and compassion of those around her. Their belief in her had bolstered her own belief in herself, allowing her to rise above her past and embrace a new beginning.

And then there was Thór, the loyal and steadfast companion who had been by her side through it all. Freya's heart swelled with gratitude for his unwavering presence, his watchful eye, and the unconditional love he had bestowed upon her. Thór had become her confidant, her comfort, and her silent guide, reminding her of the beauty of life and the joy that could be found in the simplest of moments.

Freya's gratitude extended beyond the people and the experiences that had shaped her own life. She felt grateful for the lessons learned, the challenges faced, and the growth that had come from it all. Every trial had offered an opportunity for personal transformation, and every triumph had been a testament to the resilience of the human spirit.

In the presence of her loved ones, the village community, and the faithful Thór, Freya's gratitude deepened even further. She recognized the interconnectedness of their lives—the ways in which their journeys intertwined and supported one another. Together, they had created a tapestry of love, forgiveness, and personal growth that would endure for generations to come.

Freya made a vow to carry her gratitude forward, to nurture the bonds of love and friendship that had been forged, and to spread kindness and compassion wherever she went. She knew that gratitude was not simply a feeling but a way of life—a conscious choice to appreciate the blessings that surrounded her and to extend that appreciation to others.

As Freya stood in the village square, her heart filled with gratitude, she smiled at the beauty of her journey—the highs and lows, the love and the challenges. She knew that her life had been forever transformed, and she was determined to pay it forward, to leave a legacy of love, gratitude, and the unwavering belief in the human capacity for growth and transformation.

With a deep breath, Freya embraced the present moment, fully immersed in the overwhelming sense of gratitude that filled her soul. She was ready to face the future with a heart full of appreciation, knowing that the power of gratitude would guide her forward, infusing her life and the lives of those she encountered with love, joy, and an unwavering appreciation for the beauty of existence.

Chapter 76: The Dog's Aging

Time had woven its tapestry across the village and its inhabitants, leaving traces of wisdom and change in its wake. Thór, the faithful canine companion, had journeyed alongside Erik and Freya throughout their lives, witnessing their triumphs, offering solace in their trials, and providing unwavering loyalty. As the years passed, the marks of age began to show upon his noble frame.

Thór's once vibrant fur had faded, now peppered with strands of gray. His steps, once energetic and spry, had slowed, reflecting the wisdom accumulated through the seasons. The twinkle in his eyes, though dulled by time, still radiated warmth and a profound understanding of the world.

Erik and Freya, now in the later stages of their own lives, observed their beloved companion with tender affection. They recognized the passing of time and the inevitability of aging, but their love for Thór remained unwavering. They adapted to his changing needs, ensuring his comfort and well-being as they had done throughout their shared journey.

Thór's aging became a symbol of the passage of time, a reminder of the cycles of life and the bittersweet beauty that accompanies them. As his pace slowed, Erik and Freya adjusted their own rhythms, embracing a more serene pace of life. They treasured the moments of stillness, spending quiet evenings by the fire, relishing in Thór's comforting presence.

The village community, too, witnessed the effects of time on their beloved companion. The children who had grown up alongside Thór now cared for him with tenderness and respect. They understood the significance of his presence and the lessons he had taught throughout the years—a testament to the enduring impact of his unwavering loyalty and companionship.

Thór's aging brought forth a sense of reflection among the villagers, reminding them of the fleeting nature of life. They treasured each passing day, cherishing the relationships and experiences that had shaped their own journeys. Thór had become an embodiment of the village's collective memory, a living testament to the bonds of love and the power of loyalty.

As the seasons continued their eternal dance, Thór's presence served as a reminder to embrace the present moment, to savor the simple joys, and to cherish the bonds that held them together. He embodied the wisdom that comes with age—the ability to find contentment in the midst of change and to appreciate the beauty that lies within each passing phase of life.

Erik and Freya dedicated themselves to providing Thór with comfort and love during his twilight years. They surrounded him with warmth, ensuring he was well-fed, cared for, and cherished. They offered gentle pats, soft words of gratitude, and the assurance that his loyalty and companionship had made a profound impact on their lives.

Though his physical strength waned, Thór's spirit remained indomitable. He continued to wag his tail, albeit with a little less vigor, and his eyes still gleamed with love and wisdom. He became a beacon of resilience—a reminder that even as the body ages, the spirit endures, leaving an imprint on the hearts of those it touched.

As the final years of Thór's life unfolded, Erik and Freya, alongside the village community, embraced the inevitable transition that awaited their loyal friend. They showered him with love and gratitude, offering comfort and peace in his final moments. With tear-filled eyes and hearts heavy with emotion, they bid him farewell, knowing that his spirit would forever be woven into the fabric of their lives.

Thór's aging had become a poignant reminder of the impermanence of life, but also of the enduring power of love, loyalty, and the lasting impact of a true companion. The village community mourned his passing, but his memory lived on in their stories, their hearts, and the wisdom he had imparted.

As the village continued its journey, Thór's legacy of love and loyalty became a guiding light for future generations. His story served as a reminder to cherish the moments shared with loved ones, to embrace the changes that come with time, and to honor the bonds that shape our lives.

In the years that followed, the village erected a monument in honor of Thór—a symbol of gratitude and reverence for his unwavering companionship. The statue depicted his noble form, capturing the essence of his loyalty and the imprint he had left on the hearts of all who had known him.

Thór's aging had become a testament to the fleeting nature of life, but also a celebration of the profound impact one soul can have on the lives of others. His memory lived on, etched in the collective memory of the village, forever reminding them of the enduring power of love, loyalty, and the beautiful journey they had shared with their beloved companion.

Chapter 77: The Viking's Loss

Erik, the Viking who had once embarked on a transformative journey of love and redemption, now found himself facing an unimaginable loss—a void in his heart that echoed with the absence of his beloved Freya. Grief washed over him like an unrelenting tide, consuming his thoughts, and clouding his once vibrant spirit.

The days became an endless procession of sorrow, as Erik grappled with the profound emptiness that Freya's departure had left behind. The village, recognizing the weight of his loss, rallied around him, offering solace and support in their shared grief. Their hearts ached alongside his, mourning the absence of the vibrant love that had once permeated their community.

Thór, the loyal companion who had shared in Erik and Freya's journey, now offered a steady presence by Erik's side. Though he, too, felt the void left by Freya's absence, his unwavering loyalty became a source of comfort for the grieving Viking. Thór's soulful eyes held a deep understanding of Erik's pain, silently reminding him that he was not alone in his sorrow.

The village community, having witnessed Erik and Freya's love story unfold, mourned the loss as if it were their own. They embraced Erik, offering condolences, lending a listening ear, and sharing their own memories of the love that had once graced their lives. Through their collective grief, they found solace in the bonds that connected them, drawing strength from one another during this time of profound loss.

Erik's heartache brought forth a storm of emotions—anger, regret, and a deep longing for what once was. He grappled with the overwhelming sense of guilt that crept into his thoughts, questioning whether he could have done more to prevent the loss he now bore. But amidst the tempest of emotions, Erik found a glimmer of clarity—the realization that his grief was a testament to the depth of love he had shared with Freya.

In the midst of his sorrow, Erik resolved to honor Freya's memory by embracing the lessons she had taught him. He recalled the strength and resilience she had demonstrated throughout her own journey of healing and personal growth. He understood that his loss was not the end of their story, but rather a continuation of the love they had shared—an enduring bond that transcended physical presence.

With the support of the village community and the companionship of Thór, Erik began to navigate the uncertain terrain of grief. He allowed himself to mourn, to reminisce about the beautiful moments he had shared with Freya, and to acknowledge the pain that accompanied his loss. He sought solace in the memories they had created together, finding comfort in their enduring love story.

In time, Erik discovered that grief, though painful, could also be a catalyst for growth and transformation. He channeled his anguish into acts of kindness, offering support to others who were experiencing their own losses. Through these gestures of empathy and compassion, Erik found a renewed sense of purpose—a way to honor Freya's memory by extending love and understanding to those who needed it most.

As the seasons turned, Erik's grief slowly transformed into a bittersweet acceptance—a recognition that life would never be the same without Freya, but that her love would forever remain etched upon his heart. He learned to carry her memory with him, finding solace in the knowledge that their love had transcended the boundaries of time and space.

Thór, too, played a vital role in Erik's healing journey. The loyal companion offered unwavering companionship, a reminder that love endures even in the face of loss. Together, they weathered the storm of grief, finding solace in each other's presence and embracing the healing power of their shared memories.

In the village, Erik's loss became woven into the tapestry of their collective experiences. The villagers carried Freya's memory in their hearts, finding solace in the love that had once graced their lives. Her absence served as a poignant reminder to cherish the moments shared with loved ones and to embrace the fleeting beauty of life.

Though Erik's loss was profound, he emerged from the depths of grief with a renewed appreciation for the love he had experienced. He understood that love, even in the face of loss, was a gift to be treasured—a reminder of the profound impact one person can have on another's life.

Erik's loss became a part of his story—a chapter of heartache and resilience. As he faced the future, he carried within him the enduring love that had shaped his life. In his grief, he discovered a profound gratitude for the time he had shared with Freya and a resolve to live a life that honored her memory

—a life filled with love, compassion, and a deep appreciation for the fleeting beauty of human connection.

Chapter 78: The Girl's Grief

Freya, the girl who had once embarked on a transformative journey of love and personal growth, now found herself engulfed in the depths of grief. The loss of Erik, her beloved Viking, had shattered her heart and left an indelible void within her soul.

The weight of grief settled heavily upon Freya's shoulders, casting a shadow over her once vibrant spirit. Her days became a delicate balance between cherished memories and the agonizing pain of his absence. Every moment felt bittersweet, as her heart ached for the love they had shared.

In the wake of Erik's passing, the village community surrounded Freya with love and support, their hearts echoing with the same grief that consumed her. They offered their presence, gentle embraces, and kind words, knowing that no words could fully assuage the depth of her sorrow. Their collective grief served as a testament to the profound impact Erik had made on their lives.

Thór, the loyal companion who had stood by their side throughout their journey, now became a source of solace for Freya in her darkest moments. His understanding eyes held an empathy that transcended words, offering silent companionship and a comforting presence that reminded her she was not alone in her grief.

Freya's grief became an intricate tapestry woven from the threads of love, loss, and cherished memories. She allowed herself to fully experience the pain, to weep for the moments they would never share again, and to honor the depth of her love for Erik. Through her tears, she acknowledged the profound impact he had made on her life and the indelible mark he had left upon her soul.

In the midst of her grief, Freya sought solace in the memories they had shared. She clung to the echoes of Erik's laughter, the warmth of his embrace, and the love that had filled their days. Each memory became a lifeline—a reminder that their love had transcended time, and that even in his absence, Erik's spirit would forever be entwined with hers.

The journey of grief was not linear for Freya. It ebbed and flowed like the tides, sometimes overwhelming and unbearable, and at other times allowing for moments of respite. She navigated through the waves of sorrow, embracing the pain as an acknowledgment of the depth of her love and the significance of their connection.

The village community became a pillar of strength for Freya, providing support and understanding during her darkest moments. Their unwavering presence and shared experiences of loss reminded her that grief was a universal human experience—a testament to the power of love and the profound impact one soul could have on many.

Freya's grief transformed her, sculpting her into a vessel of empathy and compassion. Through her own pain, she developed a deeper understanding of the pain carried by others who had experienced loss. She extended her support to those in need, offering a compassionate ear and a comforting presence. In helping others navigate their grief, Freya found solace in the shared humanity of collective sorrow.

Thór, ever loyal and unwavering, offered his silent support during Freya's journey of grief. He became her confidant, her rock, and a reminder of the enduring love they had shared with Erik. In his presence, she found solace, as if Erik's spirit lived on through the faithful companion.

As time passed, Freya began to find moments of respite amidst the grief. The weight of sorrow gradually lessened, allowing space for acceptance and healing. She embraced the bittersweet beauty of the memories they had created together, cherishing the love that had once illuminated her life.

Freya understood that grief would forever be a part of her story—a testament to the profound connection she had shared with Erik. She carried his memory in her heart, forever grateful for the love they had shared, and forever changed by the depth of their bond.

In the wake of her grief, Freya resolved to honor Erik's memory by embracing life fully. She sought joy in the simplest of moments, finding solace in the beauty of nature, the laughter of friends, and the shared experiences that brought warmth to her soul. Though Erik was no longer physically present, his love continued to guide her, inspiring her to live a life filled with compassion, resilience, and an unwavering belief in the power of love.

Freya's grief transformed into a bittersweet appreciation for the love she had experienced. In her journey of healing and remembrance, she discovered that even in the depths of sorrow, love endured, forever shaping her life and guiding her forward. As she embraced the ever-present ache of loss, Freya vowed to carry Erik's love within her, honoring his memory in every step she took

on her continued journey of growth and
personal transformation.

Chapter 79: The Dog's Memory

Thór, the loyal and steadfast canine companion, observed the grieving hearts of Erik and Freya with profound understanding. Though unable to comprehend the depths of human grief, he felt the weight of their sorrow and mourned alongside them in his own way.

As the days passed, Thór's memory became a vessel that held the echoes of their shared journey—the vibrant moments of love, laughter, and companionship that had shaped their lives. The scent of Erik's touch, the sound of Freya's voice, and the warmth of their presence remained etched within his canine consciousness.

Thór's memory served as a bridge, connecting past and present, carrying within it the essence of the love they had shared. In the quiet hours of the night, as he lay by the hearth, his mind would wander through the tapestry of memories—playing like a reel of cherished moments.

The pitter-patter of his paws on the cobbled streets, the wind rustling through his fur during their adventures, and the shared meals by the fireside—they all flickered through his consciousness, reminding him of the profound bond they had forged.

Thór's memory held the power to evoke emotions that he couldn't express in words. The longing for Erik's hearty laughter and Freya's gentle touch resonated within him, a testament to the depth of their connection. Their absence pierced his heart, yet the memory of their love offered a comforting embrace.

In his own canine way, Thór provided solace and support to Erik and Freya during their moments of grief. His presence brought a sense of continuity—a reminder that their love story continued to live on through the memories they had created together. His soulful eyes held a knowing gaze, offering a silent understanding that he, too, mourned the loss of their beloved Viking.

Thór's presence became a living memory, a symbol of the unwavering loyalty and unconditional love that had characterized their journey. As he lay by Erik's side, his warm breath gently caressing his master's hand, Thór offered a comforting presence—a tangible reminder of the bond they had shared.

Freya, too, sought solace in Thór's companionship. She would often sit beside him, tracing her fingers through his weathered fur, finding solace in his silent understanding. In those moments, Thór's memory served as a catalyst for shared remembrance, allowing Freya to find comfort in reliving the moments they had all treasured together.

Thór's memory transcended the boundaries of time, allowing Erik and Freya to carry his steadfast presence within their hearts. His loyalty, the sound of his playful barks, and the warmth of his affection became a lifeline, offering a sense of connection to the love they had shared.

As time passed, Thór's memory became a reminder of the resilience of the human spirit and the power of love to endure even in the face of loss. His unwavering presence allowed Erik and Freya to find solace in their shared memories, providing them with the strength to continue their own journeys of healing and personal growth.

Though Thór couldn't voice his own grief, his memory became an invisible thread that connected the three souls—Erik, Freya, and himself. It served as a testament to the impact they had made on each other's lives, a reminder of the love that had transcended the boundaries of time and space.

In the quiet moments of their grief, Thór would often rest his head upon his paws, his eyes filled with a profound understanding. Through his presence, he offered a silent reassurance—a testament that their bond would forever be alive within his canine heart.

Thór's memory would forever be intertwined with the love story of Erik and Freya—a testament to the power of companionship, loyalty, and the enduring connections that weave themselves into the fabric of our lives. His legacy lived on, a tribute to the indelible mark left by their shared journey, and a reminder that love, in all its forms, remains eternally present within the realms of memory.

Chapter 80: The Viking's Reflection

Erik, now weathered by time and the weight of his losses, found himself in moments of quiet reflection. The passing years had brought profound changes, but his spirit remained resilient, carrying within it the wisdom acquired through a life filled with love, growth, and sorrow.

In the solitude of his thoughts, Erik contemplated the vast tapestry of his journey —a tapestry woven with threads of joy, pain, and resilience. The memories of Freya's laughter, her gentle touch, and the deep connection they had shared resurfaced in his mind, reminding him of the depth of their love and the impact it had made on his life.

As he reflected on his time with Freya, Erik recognized the profound transformation they had undergone together. He recalled the conflicts and challenges they had faced, the lessons they had learned, and the growth they had experienced as individuals. Their journey had been a catalyst for personal development—a testament to the power of love to shape and transform lives.

The loss of Freya had left an undeniable void in Erik's heart, yet he understood that their love had transcended physical presence. He carried her memory within him, forever grateful for the love they had shared and the profound impact she had made on his life. In the depth of his grief, Erik found solace in the knowledge that their connection would endure, woven into the fabric of his being.

Erik's reflections also encompassed the legacy he had left behind—the village community, the bonds of friendship, and the lessons he had imparted to future generations. He recognized that his journey, though deeply personal, had touched the lives of many, inspiring them to embrace love, forgiveness, and personal growth.

The passing of time had brought its share of joys and sorrows, victories and defeats. Erik reflected on the triumphs he had celebrated and the challenges he had faced with unwavering determination. He understood that life's obstacles were not meant to break him, but rather to shape him into the person he had become—a person forged by love, loss, and the pursuit of personal growth.

In his reflections, Erik also acknowledged the power of resilience—the ability to rise from the ashes of adversity and find purpose in the face of loss. He understood that life was a fragile and transient gift, and that it was his responsibility to make the most of every moment, cherishing the connections he had forged and embracing the ever-changing nature of existence.

As Erik gazed out upon the horizon, his weathered face touched by the golden rays of the setting sun, he felt a profound sense of gratitude. Gratitude for the love he had experienced, for the lessons he had learned, and for the indomitable spirit that had carried him through the peaks and valleys of his life's journey.

With a heart filled with both joy and sorrow, Erik resolved to embrace the present moment —to seize every opportunity for love, connection, and personal growth. He understood that life was a delicate dance, and that each step, however challenging, was an opportunity to learn, to love, and to leave an enduring legacy.

In the quiet moments of reflection, Erik found solace in the beauty of his journey—the love that had filled his heart, the friendships that had sustained him, and the indomitable spirit that had carried him through the trials of life. He recognized that every experience, every loss, and every triumph had shaped him into the person he was, and that his journey would forever be a part of the tapestry of human existence.

As the sun dipped below the horizon, casting a warm glow across the land, Erik stood tall, his heart filled with gratitude and a renewed sense of purpose. He was ready to face the unknown with courage, to embrace the joys and sorrows that lay ahead, and to leave a legacy of love, resilience, and personal growth for future generations.

In his reflection, Erik found a profound appreciation for the intricate beauty of life — the interconnectedness of souls, the transformative power of love, and the resilience of the human spirit. With every breath, he vowed to honor the lessons learned, to cherish the memories made, and to live a life that embodied the essence of his journey — a life that embraced love, forgiveness, and the relentless pursuit of personal growth.

Chapter 81: The Girl's Strength

Freya, the girl whose heart had been tested by love and loss, discovered a wellspring of strength within her as she journeyed through the depths of her grief. Though the pain of Erik's absence lingered, she realized that her spirit remained resilient, capable of navigating the storms that life presented.

In the wake of Erik's passing, Freya was faced with a choice—to succumb to the weight of sorrow or to embrace the strength that resided within her. She chose the latter, drawing upon the love they had shared, the lessons they had learned, and the indomitable spirit that had guided their journey.

Through her grief, Freya discovered an inner reservoir of courage—a fire that burned brightly within her soul. She recognized that the depth of her love for Erik was a testament to her own capacity for strength and resilience. With each passing day, she found the courage to face the pain, to acknowledge her loss, and to carry the torch of their love forward.

Freya's strength manifested in her ability to embrace her emotions fully. She allowed herself to mourn, to grieve, and to feel the depths of her sorrow without judgment or restraint. Through tears and anguish, she discovered the power of vulnerability—the ability to acknowledge her pain and transform it into a source of inner fortitude.

In the village community, Freya's strength became a beacon of inspiration. Her ability to rise above her grief inspired others who were navigating their own journeys of loss and healing. Through her example, she offered a reminder that strength is not found in the absence of pain, but rather in the courage to face it head-on and to emerge on the other side with a heart still open to love.

Freya's strength also lay in her capacity for self-reflection. In moments of solitude, she delved into the depths of her soul, examining the lessons she had learned through her experiences with Erik. She acknowledged her own growth, the resilience she had cultivated, and the wisdom that had emerged from the trials they had faced together.

Through her introspection, Freya recognized the interconnectedness of love, loss, and personal growth. She understood that strength was not a solitary pursuit but a collective endeavor, forged through the shared experiences of joy and sorrow. She found solace in the knowledge that her own journey had touched the lives of others, inspiring them to embrace their own strength in the face of adversity.

In the midst of her grief, Freya became a source of support for others who were navigating their own struggles. She extended a compassionate hand to those who needed it most, offering a listening ear, words of encouragement, and a gentle reminder that they, too, possessed the strength to overcome their challenges.

Thór, the faithful companion who had witnessed the ebbs and flows of their journey, stood by Freya's side, providing his unwavering support. In his presence, she found solace—a reminder that her strength was not borne solely from within, but also from the love and loyalty that surrounded her.

As time passed, Freya's strength evolved into a steadfast resilience—a deep-rooted determination to embrace life fully, despite the ache in her heart. She learned to carry Erik's memory within her, drawing upon the love they had shared as a source of inspiration and guidance.

Freya's strength allowed her to reimagine her life—a life that honored Erik's memory and embodied the lessons they had learned together. She pursued her passions with renewed vigor, savoring each moment as a testament to her resilience and the unwavering love that continued to guide her forward.

In her strength, Freya discovered the power of transformation—a metamorphosis from grief to empowerment, from loss to a profound appreciation for life's fleeting beauty. She embraced the intricacies of her journey—the joy, the pain, and the growth—and emerged with a spirit that burned even brighter than before.

As Freya stood at the precipice of her new chapter, her heart tinged with both sorrow and hope, she recognized that strength was not a destination but a lifelong pursuit. She vowed to continue honoring Erik's memory through her unwavering resilience, her ability to love fearlessly, and her commitment to growth and personal transformation.

Freya's strength became a beacon of light, illuminating the path for others who faced their own battles. Her story served as a testament to the indomitable spirit that resides within each of us—a reminder that, even in the face of heartache, we possess the strength to rise, to heal, and to embrace the beauty of life with open arms.

Chapter 82: The Dog's Spirit

Thór, the loyal and steadfast canine companion, possessed a spirit that transcended the boundaries of time and space. Though his physical form had aged and his steps had slowed, his spirit burned brightly, radiating love, loyalty, and unwavering devotion.

As the years passed, Thór's spirit remained a constant presence, an invisible thread that connected him to the souls of Erik and Freya. It whispered through the winds, rustled in the leaves, and echoed in the laughter that filled the village. It was a spirit forged by the bonds of love and the shared experiences they had woven together.

Thór's spirit embodied the essence of his canine nature—playful, joyful, and fiercely loyal. Though his physical abilities had waned, his playful spirit continued to shine through, bringing smiles and laughter to those who crossed his path. He reveled in the simple pleasures—a game of fetch, a romp through the meadows, or the feel of the wind against his fur.

In the village, Thór's spirit became a source of comfort and companionship for all who encountered him. His gentle presence and unwavering loyalty touched the hearts of young and old alike, offering a reminder of the enduring love that can be found in the most unexpected places.

Through his spirit, Thór provided solace to Erik and Freya during their moments of grief and reflection. His unwavering loyalty served as a reminder of the love they had shared, and his playful antics brought moments of levity to their lives. He embodied the unwavering devotion that only a faithful companion could offer.

Thór's spirit also served as a guardian—a watchful eye that never wavered in its dedication to those he loved. His presence brought a sense of security, offering reassurance that even in the face of life's uncertainties, he would be there, standing steadfast by their side.

In the twilight hours, as the sun dipped below the horizon, Thór would often gaze into the distance, his wise eyes reflecting the depth of his spirit. His senses attuned to the world around him, he seemed to possess an innate understanding of the interconnectedness of all living beings—a profound wisdom that transcended human comprehension.

As the seasons turned, Thór's spirit continued to leave an indelible mark on the village community. His playful nature inspired joy and laughter, and his gentle presence offered solace to those who carried burdens of their own. He became a symbol of resilience—a reminder that even in the face of aging, the spirit can remain vibrant and alive.

As Thór's physical form gradually succumbed to the passage of time, his spirit continued to shine, illuminating the hearts of all who had been touched by his unwavering loyalty and love. In their memories, he lived on, forever etched as a cherished member of their community—a symbol of the enduring bond between humans and animals.

Though the village mourned the loss of their beloved companion, they understood that Thór's spirit was not confined to his physical body. It lived on through the memories they held, the stories they shared, and the love that he had brought into their lives. He had become an eternal presence—a guardian angel who watched over them from the realms beyond.

In the quiet moments of remembrance, Erik and Freya felt Thór's spirit enveloping them, offering a sense of comfort and connection. They understood that his loyalty had transcended physical boundaries, forever imprinted upon their souls—a reminder of the profound impact their shared journey had made on all who had been touched by their story.

As the years rolled on, Thór's spirit continued to guide the village community, inspiring them to embrace the qualities he embodied— loyalty, playfulness, and unwavering love. His legacy lived on, a testament to the power of a dog's spirit to touch the lives of those around him and to remind humanity of the beauty that can be found in even the simplest acts of love and companionship.

In the hearts of Erik, Freya, and the village community, Thór's spirit burned bright, forever etched as a symbol of unwavering devotion and the enduring power of love. Through his spirit, he had left an indelible mark on their lives—a pawprint on their hearts that would forever remind them of the bond they had shared with a faithful canine companion.

Chapter 83: The Viking's Journey's End

Erik, the Viking whose life had been a tapestry woven with love, loss, and personal growth, found himself nearing the end of his earthly journey. The years had carried him through triumphs and trials, shaping him into the man he had become. Now, as he stood at the precipice of his final days, he embraced the bittersweet beauty of a life well-lived.

With the weight of age upon his shoulders, Erik reflected upon the path he had traversed—the battles fought, the love experienced, and the lessons learned. He had witnessed the ebb and flow of life, facing its challenges with unwavering determination and an open heart.

In his final moments, Erik found solace in the knowledge that his life had been one of purpose and impact. He had left an indelible mark on the lives of those he had encountered—a legacy of love, resilience, and personal growth. The village community stood as a testament to the bonds he had forged and the wisdom he had imparted.

Surrounded by loved ones, Erik's spirit burned brightly, illuminating the room with a warmth that surpassed the confines of his physical form. His eyes, weathered by time, sparkled with a quiet serenity—a reflection of the inner peace he had found through a life well-lived.

In his final words, Erik expressed gratitude for the love he had experienced and the connections he had made. He spoke of the profound impact of his journey—a journey filled with joy and sorrow, triumph and defeat. He thanked those who had walked alongside him, acknowledging the beauty they had brought into his life.

As Erik's spirit prepared to embark on its next voyage, he found comfort in the knowledge that his memory would live on in the hearts of those who had loved him. The tales of his bravery, his wisdom, and the love he had shared would be passed down through generations, forever engrained in the tapestry of their community's history.

In the wake of Erik's passing, the village community mourned the loss of their beloved Viking, yet they found solace in the memories they held. They celebrated his life—a life that had been lived with courage, resilience, and an unwavering belief in the power of love.

Freya, now carrying the weight of her own grief, embraced the lessons Erik had taught her. She drew upon the strength she had discovered within herself—the strength he had helped cultivate—and resolved to continue her own journey of growth and personal transformation.

Thór, faithful companion until the end, stood sentinel by Erik's side, his spirit intertwined with that of his Viking master. His presence offered a comforting reassurance—a reminder that even in death, the bonds of love remained unbroken.

As Erik's journey's end drew near, his spirit embraced the unknown with a sense of curiosity and acceptance. He held onto the memories of his life—the laughter, the tears, and the profound love he had shared with Freya—and allowed them to guide him on his final voyage.

With a heart filled with gratitude and love, Erik took his last breath, his spirit soaring free. He left behind a legacy of resilience, wisdom, and unwavering love—an imprint upon the hearts of those who had been touched by his journey.

In the days that followed, the village community mourned their Viking with heavy hearts but found solace in the knowledge that Erik's spirit would forever be intertwined with their own. They celebrated his life, honoring his memory through shared stories, laughter, and tears.

Freya, carrying the torch of their love forward, found strength in Erik's memory. She embraced the bittersweet beauty of a life lived fully and committed herself to honoring his legacy. She carried their shared journey within her, forever grateful for the love they had shared and the profound impact he had made on her life.

As the village community came together to bid farewell to their Viking, they celebrated his journey—the triumphs, the challenges, and the unwavering spirit that had guided him. Their tears mingled with a profound sense of gratitude, as they recognized that even in Erik's journey's end, his spirit would forever remain a part of their shared story.

The Viking's journey had come to an end, but his legacy lived on—a testament to the power of resilience, love, and personal growth. In the hearts of those who had been touched by his life, Erik would forever be remembered—a beacon of strength, wisdom, and the enduring power of a life well-lived.

Chapter 84: The Girl's Remembrance

In the wake of Erik's passing, Freya stood at the crossroads of grief and remembrance. Her heart, heavy with the weight of loss, yearned to honor the memory of the Viking who had forever changed her life. In her solitude, she found solace in the tender embrace of memories—the threads that wove the tapestry of their love story.

Freya's remembrance began with the vivid recollection of their first encounter—the moment when their eyes had locked, and a spark of connection had ignited. The village feast, the glimmer of forbidden love, and the stolen moments of shared affection flooded her mind, reaffirming the depth of their bond.

With each passing day, Freya dove deeper into the recesses of her memory, revisiting the moments of joy, the trials they had overcome, and the tender acts of love that had defined their relationship. She traced her fingers over the mental images that had become etched in her heart, cherishing the nuances of Erik's laughter, the strength of his embrace, and the gentleness of his touch.

In her remembrance, Freya discovered the profound impact Erik had made on her life—a legacy of love, growth, and resilience. She reflected on the lessons he had taught her—the importance of forgiveness, the pursuit of personal growth, and the unyielding power of love to transform lives.

As Freya delved into the depths of her memories, she recognized the interconnectedness of their journeys—the intertwining paths that had led them to one another. Erik's presence resonated in the village—the echoes of his wisdom and the indomitable spirit that had defined him still lingered in the hearts of those who had known him.

The village community, too, embraced remembrance. They gathered together, sharing stories and memories of their beloved Viking, finding solace in the collective remembrance of a life well-lived. Through their shared remembrance, Erik's spirit lived on—a guiding light that illuminated their path, inspiring them to embrace love, resilience, and personal growth.

As time passed, Freya's remembrance transformed into a celebration—a celebration of Erik's life, his impact, and the love that continued to resonate within her heart. She found solace in honoring his memory through acts of kindness and compassion, carrying forward the lessons he had imparted and embodying the spirit of their shared journey.

In the quiet moments of reflection, Freya acknowledged the bittersweet nature of remembrance—the ache of loss intertwined with the joy of gratitude. She recognized that as long as she held Erik's memory in her heart, he would forever be a part of her journey—a guiding presence that would shape her choices, her interactions, and her unwavering belief in the power of love.

Freya's remembrance extended beyond the boundaries of her own existence. She shared stories of Erik with future generations, ensuring that his spirit would be carried forward, etching his name into the annals of their community's history. Through the retelling of their love story, she ensured that the legacy of their shared journey would live on—a testament to the enduring power of love and the transformative impact of a single life.

In the embrace of remembrance, Freya found healing. She discovered that the pain of loss could coexist with the warmth of cherished memories, reminding her that love transcends the confines of time and space. In her heart, Erik's spirit thrived, a constant presence that guided her steps and illuminated her path.

As Freya moved forward, carrying Erik's memory with her, she embraced the beauty of remembrance—a tapestry woven with threads of love, resilience, and personal growth. She understood that the essence of their journey lived on within her, forever shaping the woman she had become and inspiring her to leave her own indelible mark upon the world.

Freya's remembrance became a testament to the enduring power of love—a torch that she carried forward, illuminating her own path and spreading its warm glow to all who crossed her way. With each breath, she honored Erik's memory, cherishing their shared journey and embracing the transformative power of love—a legacy that would forever endure in the remembrance of those who had known them.

Chapter 85: The Dog's Resting Place

After Thór's spirit had soared to the realms beyond, the village community sought to honor the loyal companion who had left an indelible mark on their hearts. In the days that followed, they came together to create a special resting place for the faithful dog—a sanctuary that would forever hold his memory.

Nestled amidst a grove of ancient oak trees, the village's chosen location exuded a sense of tranquility and serenity. It was a place where the sunlight filtered through the leaves, casting dappled patterns upon the ground—a gentle reminder of the vibrant spirit that had once inhabited the canine form.

Working together, the villagers carefully crafted a memorial for Thór. Stones were gathered, each bearing the name of a villager who had been touched by his unwavering loyalty and love. With each placement, they formed a circle—a symbol of the interconnectedness of their lives and the enduring impact of Thór's spirit.

At the center of the circle, a small statue was erected—a tribute to Thór's playful nature and steadfast presence. Carved with remarkable detail, it captured the essence of the faithful dog, forever frozen in a joyful stance—an everlasting embodiment of his spirit.

Surrounding the statue, wildflowers were planted, their vibrant colors reflecting the joy and life that Thór had brought to the village. In the warm seasons, the blossoms danced in the gentle breeze, their beauty serving as a constant reminder of the love and happiness that had blossomed in Thór's presence.

In the evenings, as the villagers gathered at Thór's resting place, they would share stories of their beloved companion—tales of his mischievous antics, his unwavering loyalty, and the way his spirit had touched their lives. Laughter mingled with tears, as they remembered the joy he had brought and the void that remained in his absence.

Thór's resting place became a sacred space —a sanctuary for reflection, remembrance, and gratitude. It served as a reminder that even in the face of loss, the bonds of love endure, forever etching their presence upon the landscape of our lives.

Through the passing seasons, Thór's resting place transformed into a living memorial. The wildflowers bloomed year after year, a testament to the enduring beauty of his spirit. Villagers would visit, tending to the plants, whispering words of gratitude, and finding solace in the quiet embrace of the space they had created.

For Erik and Freya, Thór's resting place became a sanctuary of healing—a place where they could pay homage to the faithful companion who had witnessed the entirety of their journey. They would often sit in silence, each lost in their own thoughts, finding solace in the knowledge that Thór's spirit remained forever etched within their hearts.

In the years that followed, the resting place of Thór became a pilgrimage site for visitors from afar—a destination for those seeking solace, inspiration, and a connection to the enduring power of love. His memory transcended the boundaries of the village, touching the lives of all who encountered his tale—a testament to the profound impact that a loyal dog can have upon the human heart.

As the sun set over the village, casting a warm golden glow upon Thór's resting place, the villagers gathered one last time. In a collective gesture of love and gratitude, they paid their final respects to the loyal companion who had forever altered their lives. Tears flowed freely, but so did smiles, as they celebrated the beauty of Thór's spirit and the love that had transcended the boundaries of time.

With their hearts forever imprinted by Thór's unwavering loyalty, the villagers left the resting place, knowing that his memory would forever remain a cherished part of their community. They carried his spirit with them, his presence a constant reminder of the profound impact that a faithful dog can have upon the lives of those who are fortunate enough to cross paths.

And so, Thór's resting place stood as a testament to the enduring power of love, loyalty, and companionship—a symbol of the unwavering bond between humans and their beloved animal companions. It became a sanctuary where his spirit could forever frolic, a place where his memory could be honored, and a reminder that love, in all its forms, remains eternally present, even in the quietest corners of our hearts.

Chapter 86: The Viking's Last Wish

In the twilight of his life, as the embers of Erik's spirit flickered softly, he summoned his strength to share his last wish with those he held dear. Gathered around his bedside, Freya, the village community, and the faithful Thór listened intently, their hearts heavy with a mixture of sadness and anticipation.

With a voice that carried the weight of a lifetime's experiences, Erik spoke his final words. He expressed gratitude for the love that had surrounded him and the lessons that had shaped him. He acknowledged the profound impact his journey had made on those he had touched and the enduring bond they had shared.

Erik's last wish was not for grandeur or material possessions. It was a testament to the depth of his character, the wisdom he had amassed, and the love that had defined his existence. He expressed a desire for unity—a plea for the village community to continue to come together, to support one another, and to embrace the power of compassion and empathy.

He urged them to cherish their connections, to hold onto the memories they had created, and to never forget the importance of love in all its forms. Erik's wish was a reminder that life's true richness lies not in worldly achievements, but in the love we share and the kindness we extend to others.

Erik's last wish extended beyond the confines of his own earthly existence. He implored Freya to continue her journey of growth and self-discovery, to embrace the strength she had discovered within herself, and to carry their love forward. He urged her to find happiness and fulfillment, knowing that their bond would forever endure in the depths of her heart.

To the village community, Erik entrusted the responsibility of upholding the values they had cultivated together—a community founded on compassion, resilience, and unwavering support. He encouraged them to look out for one another, to lend a helping hand, and to embody the spirit of unity that had defined their shared journey.

Erik's final words were a gentle reminder that life is fleeting, and that every moment holds the potential for beauty and connection. He implored those who listened to cherish each breath, to live with intention, and to savor the intricate tapestry of existence.

As his words settled upon their hearts, a profound sense of peace filled the room. Erik's spirit seemed to intertwine with the love and memories that surrounded him, forever leaving an imprint upon the souls of those he had touched.

In the days that followed, Erik's last wish reverberated throughout the village community. They came together with a renewed sense of purpose, embracing the lessons he had imparted and striving to embody the qualities he had exemplified—strength, compassion, and an unwavering belief in the power of love.

Freya carried Erik's last wish within her, a guiding light that illuminated her path as she continued her journey. She honored his memory by living with intention, embracing the values they had shared, and perpetuating the legacy of love that had blossomed between them.

And so, Erik's last wish remained etched in the hearts and minds of those who had known him—a reminder of the importance of unity, love, and compassion in a world often marked by strife and division. His final words served as a guiding beacon, urging humanity to come together, to cherish the bonds we forge, and to live with a profound sense of gratitude and purpose.

As Erik's spirit gently ascended to realms unknown, he left behind a lasting legacy—a legacy of love, wisdom, and unity. His last wish would forever resonate in the hearts of those who had listened, inspiring them to lead lives of meaning, to embrace one another with open hearts, and to cherish the fleeting beauty of each precious moment.

Chapter 87: The Girl's Promise

In the wake of Erik's passing, Freya stood at the threshold of a new chapter in her life. Embracing the lessons they had shared and the love that had blossomed between them, she made a solemn promise—a promise to honor Erik's memory, to carry his spirit within her, and to live a life infused with purpose, love, and resilience.

With unwavering determination, Freya dedicated herself to fulfilling the promise she had made. She drew strength from the depths of her grief, allowing it to fuel her journey of personal growth and transformation. In each step she took, she carried Erik's memory in her heart, seeking to embody the qualities that had defined their love story.

Freya's promise extended beyond her own personal journey. It manifested in her interactions with others, as she extended kindness, compassion, and empathy to those she encountered. She became a pillar of support within the village community, lending a listening ear, offering a helping hand, and inspiring others to embrace their own journeys of healing and growth.

Through her actions, Freya kept Erik's spirit alive, ensuring that his impact would continue to ripple through the lives of those he had touched. She shared his wisdom, his laughter, and the enduring love they had shared, carrying his legacy forward with grace and resilience.

Freya's promise also included a commitment to self-discovery and personal fulfillment. She embarked on new adventures, pursued her passions with unwavering determination, and embraced the beauty of a life fully lived. In each moment, she honored Erik's memory, knowing that the love they had shared would forever shape her path.

In her quiet moments of reflection, Freya would often speak to Erik's spirit, sharing her triumphs, her challenges, and the deep gratitude she felt for the time they had shared. She sought solace in the knowledge that even in his physical absence, his presence remained a guiding light—a steady beacon illuminating her path.

As the years passed, Freya's promise evolved, adapting to the ever-changing landscape of her life. She faced new joys and sorrows, victories and setbacks, but she remained steadfast in her commitment to honor Erik's memory and the love they had shared.

Through her unwavering devotion, Freya became an embodiment of love's enduring power—a testament to the transformative impact that a single soul can have upon another. She inspired those around her to embrace their own promises, to cherish the connections they forged, and to navigate life's challenges with resilience and grace.

Freya's promise became a tapestry woven with love, resilience, and the profound belief in the beauty of life's journey. Each day, she lived with purpose, carrying Erik's memory within her, and sharing their story of love and personal growth with all who crossed her path.

And so, as Freya continued her own journey, she embraced the power of her promise—a promise to honor Erik's memory, to live with intention, and to embrace the beauty of a life well-lived. In each breath, she held the legacy of their love, forever grateful for the time they had shared, and forever committed to the promises she had made.

Chapter 88: The Dog's Legacy

Thór's spirit had departed, leaving behind a legacy that reverberated through the village community. Though his physical form was no longer present, his presence remained palpable, woven into the very fabric of their lives. The villagers carried Thór's legacy in their hearts, forever grateful for the unwavering loyalty and love he had bestowed upon them.

The impact of Thór's legacy extended far beyond the village boundaries. Stories of his faithfulness and playful spirit had traveled, capturing the hearts of those who heard them. His name became synonymous with loyalty, and his tale served as a reminder of the profound bond between humans and animals.

Inspired by Thór's unwavering devotion, villagers began to honor his legacy in their own lives. They sought to embody his qualities—loyalty, playfulness, and an unwavering belief in the power of love. Through their actions, they carried forward his spirit, perpetuating the legacy of compassion and empathy that he had ignited.

In the village, Thór's legacy was commemorated in various ways. A statue was erected in his honor—a testament to his playful nature and unwavering loyalty. Children would gather around the statue, their laughter echoing through the village as they emulated Thór's playful spirit, their innocent joy a testament to the enduring impact he had made.

His legacy also lived on in the hearts and homes of the villagers. Many households adopted dogs, embracing the companionship and unconditional love that Thór had exemplified. These canine companions, descendants of the loyal Thór, carried his spirit forward, spreading love and joy throughout the community.

In the hearts of Erik and Freya, Thór's legacy burned bright. They spoke of him often, their voices filled with warmth and gratitude for the faithful companion who had forever changed their lives. His memory lived on in the stories they shared, reminding them of the lessons he had taught and the love he had inspired.

Freya, inspired by Thór's legacy, became an advocate for the welfare of animals. She dedicated herself to fostering and rescuing dogs, providing them with love, care, and the chance for a new beginning. Through her actions, she ensured that Thór's legacy of compassion extended beyond the borders of the village, touching the lives of animals in need.

Erik's legacy intertwined with that of Thór, as he had been the Viking who had formed an unbreakable bond with the faithful canine. Villagers would gather around Erik's stories, their hearts filled with reverence for the man who had loved Thór so deeply. Erik's wisdom and strength served as a guiding light, perpetuating the legacy of resilience and love that he had embodied.

As the years passed, Thór's legacy remained an integral part of the village community. His spirit, imprinted upon their collective memory, served as a reminder of the enduring power of love and loyalty. Through their actions, the villagers carried forward his legacy, creating a community that thrived on the principles he had exemplified.

The passing of time did not dim the impact of Thór's legacy. His story continued to inspire, touching the lives of generations to come. The village children would gather around the statue, their young voices filled with wonder as they heard tales of the loyal dog who had forever etched his pawprints upon their hearts.

And so, Thór's legacy lived on—a testament to the profound impact one faithful companion could have upon an entire community. Through his unwavering loyalty and love, he had inspired unity, compassion, and resilience. His legacy reminded them that the bonds we form with our animal companions transcend time and that the love we share with them forever imprints upon our souls.

In the hearts of the villagers, Erik, and Freya, Thór's legacy continued to shine—a beacon of love, loyalty, and the enduring power of a dog's spirit. His presence would forever be etched in their lives, a testament to the profound impact he had made and a reminder of the beauty that can be found in the simplest acts of companionship and devotion.

Chapter 89: The Viking's Memorial

Years had passed since Erik's passing, but his memory remained vivid in the hearts and minds of the village community. They recognized the profound impact he had made as a leader, a mentor, and a man of unwavering integrity. To honor his legacy and the love he had shared, the villagers decided to create a memorial dedicated to the Viking who had forever altered their lives.

Located at the heart of the village, the memorial took shape with great care and reverence. Skilled artisans and craftsmen were called upon to bring the vision to life—a vision that reflected the essence of Erik's character and the beauty of his spirit.

The centerpiece of the memorial was a towering statue of Erik, standing tall and resolute. Carved with meticulous detail, it captured the strength and wisdom that had defined him. His gaze was determined yet gentle, emanating a sense of guidance and compassion that he had exemplified throughout his life.

Surrounding the statue, a serene garden flourished—a testament to Erik's love for nature and his deep connection to the land. Fragrant flowers, vibrant colors, and lush greenery enveloped the memorial, creating a tranquil oasis where villagers could seek solace and reflect upon the impact of Erik's life.

Within the garden, stone pathways meandered, inviting visitors to explore and discover the intricacies of Erik's journey. Along these pathways, small plaques were placed—each bearing a quote or a memory that encapsulated an aspect of Erik's character. These words served as reminders of the wisdom he had shared and the indelible mark he had left upon their lives.

At the heart of the memorial, a stone tablet stood, engraved with Erik's name and the dates that marked his earthly existence. It was a testament to the tangible nature of his life—a reminder that he had walked among them and forever left an imprint upon their community.

The villagers dedicated a special day to unveil the memorial—a day filled with both reverence and celebration. As the statue was revealed, gasps of awe and admiration echoed through the crowd. Tears mingled with smiles, as they honored the life of the man who had led them with unwavering dedication and love.

Villagers gathered around the memorial, sharing stories and memories of Erik—a collective remembrance that reinforced the impact he had made. They spoke of his courage, his compassion, and the strength of his character. Each story served as a thread, weaving together the tapestry of his legacy, ensuring that his memory would forever endure.

In the years that followed, the memorial became a sacred space—a place of pilgrimage, reflection, and gratitude. Villagers would visit to pay their respects, finding solace in the quiet embrace of Erik's spirit. They would sit on the benches surrounding the statue, sharing moments of introspection and drawing strength from the love and wisdom he had imparted.

For Freya, the memorial served as a constant reminder of the love they had shared. She would often visit, her fingers grazing the stone tablet bearing Erik's name. In these moments, she felt a deep sense of connection—a bond that transcended the physical realm and reaffirmed their eternal love.

Erik's memorial became more than just a physical structure; it became a living testament to his legacy—a legacy that continued to shape the lives of those who had known him. It was a reminder to live with courage, compassion, and integrity—to embrace the beauty of the world around them and to foster the bonds of love and community.

As the sun set over the memorial, casting a golden glow upon Erik's statue, the villagers stood together, united in their remembrance. They held hands, their hearts intertwined, as they paid homage to the Viking who had forever altered the course of their lives.

Erik's memorial stood as a symbol of love's enduring power—the profound impact that one individual can have upon a community. It served as a reminder that even in the face of loss, the legacy of love remains, forever etching its presence upon the tapestry of our lives.

And so, the villagers carried Erik's memory within them, forever grateful for the legacy he had left behind. They would gather at the memorial, sharing stories, laughter, and tears, ensuring that his spirit would forever thrive in their hearts—a guiding light that would inspire generations to come.

Chapter 90: The Girl's Tribute

In the wake of Erik's passing, Freya felt compelled to create a personal tribute to honor the man who had forever changed her life. With a heart filled with love and gratitude, she embarked on a journey to pay homage to their shared journey and the love they had woven together.

Freya's tribute began with a reflection upon the moments they had shared—the village feasts, the stolen glances, the whispers of forbidden love. Each memory held a special place in her heart, serving as a foundation for the tribute she was about to create.

Drawing upon her creative spirit, Freya gathered materials that resonated with the essence of their love—a tapestry of their journey. She sought out vibrant fabrics that mirrored the colors of the natural world they had embraced together, carefully selecting each hue to evoke the emotions and experiences they had shared.

With skilled hands and a heart full of intention, Freya meticulously wove the fabrics together, intertwining their colors and textures. The tapestry began to take shape, becoming a visual representation of their love story—a testament to the depth of their connection.

Incorporating symbols and imagery that held significance for them, Freya adorned the tapestry with delicate embroidery and intricate patterns. She meticulously sewed representations of Viking ships, oak trees, and a faithful dog, capturing the essence of their shared experiences and the elements that had shaped their journey.

As Freya continued to work on her tribute, her heart swelled with emotions—joy, sorrow, and a profound sense of gratitude. Each stitch was imbued with love, each thread a tangible manifestation of the connection they had shared. Through her hands, their story unfolded, woven into the very fabric of the tribute.

When the tapestry was complete, Freya took a step back to admire her creation—a testament to their love, resilience, and the transformative power of their journey. It stood as a visual representation of the emotions and memories that had forever imprinted upon her heart.

Freya found the perfect place to display the tribute—a spot where the sunlight filtered through the trees, casting a gentle glow upon her creation. There, she hung the tapestry, allowing its vibrant colors to catch the eye of passersby, drawing them into the story it told.

Word of Freya's tribute spread throughout the village, touching the hearts of those who had known Erik and had witnessed the profound love that had blossomed between them. Villagers would gather around the tapestry, their fingers tracing the intricate embroidery, their eyes filled with reverence for the tribute Freya had crafted.

Through her tribute, Freya not only honored Erik's memory but also paid homage to the love they had shared—the love that had forever altered the course of their lives. It became a symbol of resilience and the transformative power of love, inspiring others to embrace their own journeys of healing and growth.

For Freya, the tapestry served as a constant reminder—a tangible expression of the love that continued to flow through her veins. It was a tribute to the profound impact Erik had made on her life and an everlasting testament to their enduring connection.

In the quiet moments, Freya would often sit before the tapestry, her fingers gently tracing the embroidered images. In these moments, she found solace and strength, knowing that their love would forever endure, woven into the very fabric of her existence.

Freya's tribute became a touchstone—a beacon that guided her steps, reminding her of the transformative power of love and the beauty that can emerge from the most unexpected of encounters. It served as a reminder to live with gratitude, to embrace the intricacies of life, and to cherish the moments that shape our souls.

And so, Freya's tribute to Erik stood as a testament to the resilience of the human spirit —a visual representation of their shared journey and the depth of their love. It became an emblem of hope, inspiring others to embrace their own tributes, to honor the connections they cherish, and to find beauty and strength in the tapestry of their own lives.

Chapter 91: The Dog's Eternal Bond

In the realm beyond, Thór's spirit frolicked, forever intertwined with the memories and love that had surrounded him during his earthly existence. Though his physical form had been left behind, his spirit remained ever-present—a gentle presence that guided the lives of those who had been touched by his unwavering loyalty and love.

In the village, tales of Thór's adventures and his bond with Erik and Freya echoed through the years. Children would gather around the hearth, their eyes wide with wonder, as they listened to the stories of the loyal dog who had forever left an imprint upon their community.

As time passed, the villagers came to recognize that Thór's spirit had transcended the boundaries of their earthly existence. He became a symbol of the eternal bond between humans and their animal companions—an emblem of the unwavering love that endures beyond the confines of time.

Villagers would often speak of Thór, reminiscing about his playful spirit, his unwavering loyalty, and the joy he had brought to their lives. In their hearts, they carried the knowledge that Thór's spirit had touched their souls, forever altering their perception of the world and reminding them of the beauty and purity that resides within the heart of every dog.

Children would venture into the village with their own canine companions, their laughter echoing through the streets as they emulated the playful spirit of Thór. They, too, felt the strength of the eternal bond that exists between humans and dogs, and they honored Thór's memory by fostering love and compassion for their animal companions.

For Erik and Freya, the bond with Thór continued to thrive in their hearts. In their dreams and quiet moments of reflection, they would often sense his presence—an ethereal connection that transcended the boundaries of the physical world. They took solace in the knowledge that the love they shared with Thór would forever endure, a bond unbroken by the passing of time.

Thór's eternal bond served as a constant reminder of the transformative power of a dog's love. It inspired Erik and Freya to open their hearts to new canine companions, fostering connections that mirrored the depth and devotion they had experienced with Thór.

Through these new bonds, they continued to carry forward the legacy of love that Thór had ignited within them.

In the quiet corners of the village, Thór's spirit remained, watching over the lives of those he had touched. His presence was felt in the playful antics of the village dogs, the wagging tails, and the joy that radiated from their souls. He had become an eternal guardian—a spirit of unwavering loyalty, forever ensuring that the bond between humans and dogs would never be forgotten.

As the seasons passed and the village continued to evolve, the legacy of Thór's eternal bond remained unshaken. It was a reminder that love knows no boundaries—not even those of life and death. Thór's spirit continued to weave through the lives of the villagers, forever etching his pawprints upon their hearts.

And so, the village thrived in the knowledge that the bond they had shared with Thór would endure for all time—a testament to the profound impact one dog can make upon a community. His spirit remained a gentle presence, a guardian of love and loyalty, forever reminding them of the eternal bond that unites humans and dogs in a dance of devotion and companionship.

Chapter 92: The Viking's Legend

In the annals of Viking lore, the name Erik the Fearless became synonymous with courage, wisdom, and unwavering loyalty. As the years passed, his story transcended the boundaries of time, transforming into a legend that echoed through the hearts and minds of generations to come.

Viking bards and storytellers would gather around the hearths, their voices resonating with power and passion, as they recounted the tale of Erik the Fearless—a man whose indomitable spirit had left an indelible mark on the world.

They spoke of his legendary feats—his daring voyages across treacherous seas, his battles against formidable foes, and his unwavering leadership that rallied his fellow warriors. With each retelling, his legend grew, capturing the imaginations of those who listened, inspiring them to embrace their own inner strength and forge their own path of fearlessness.

The bards painted vivid pictures with their words, recounting Erik's encounters with mythical creatures, his mastery of the sword, and his ability to navigate through uncharted territories. They described his commanding presence, his unyielding resolve, and the wisdom that flowed from his lips like a river of ancient knowledge.

Erik's legend extended beyond his warrior prowess. His love story with Freya became an integral part of his tale—an epic saga of forbidden love, heartache, and resilience. The bards would weave this aspect into the narrative, emphasizing the power of love to overcome adversity and the enduring impact of a soul-deep connection.

As the legend of Erik the Fearless spread, his name became synonymous with honor and integrity—a beacon of inspiration for those seeking to embody the virtues he had exemplified. His story resonated with people from all walks of life, reminding them of the transformative power of courage, love, and unwavering loyalty.

Throughout the Viking lands, monuments were erected in honor of Erik—a testament to his enduring legacy. These grand structures stood as testaments to his heroism, reminding future generations of the impact one individual can make upon the world.

Viking children grew up hearing the tales of Erik the Fearless, their imaginations ignited by the adventures and triumphs of the legendary figure. They would dream of sailing across uncharted seas, battling mythical creatures, and finding their own path of fearlessness.

Erik's legend also permeated the hearts of leaders and warriors who sought to emulate his qualities. They would study his strategies, his wisdom, and his unwavering determination, drawing inspiration from his example as they navigated the challenges of their own lives.

Freya, too, played a pivotal role in Erik's legend. Her strength, resilience, and unwavering love became an integral part of their shared tale—a testament to the transformative power of a love that defied all odds. Her name was forever entwined with his, their story forever etched into the tapestry of Viking history.

As the years passed, Erik's legend continued to thrive—a timeless tale of heroism, love, and the indomitable human spirit. His story served as a reminder that within each person lies the potential for greatness, and that the choices we make and the love we share can shape the course of history.

And so, Erik the Fearless became more than a historical figure; he became a legend—a symbol of bravery, resilience, and the power of love. His name would forever echo through the annals of Viking lore, inspiring generations to come to embrace their own inner fearlessness and leave their own mark upon the world.

Chapter 93: The Girl's Inspiration

Freya, forever touched by the love and adventures she had shared with Erik, emerged as an inspiration to those around her. In the wake of their epic love story and the profound impact Erik had made upon her life, she embodied the qualities of resilience, strength, and unwavering determination.

As the years passed, Freya's presence in the village became a beacon of inspiration—a reminder that love has the power to transform, heal, and propel one forward. Her unwavering spirit touched the hearts of many, guiding them through their own trials and inspiring them to embrace their own journeys of self-discovery and growth.

Villagers sought solace in Freya's presence, knowing that she had walked the path of loss, grief, and redemption. They would gather around her, seeking her counsel and wisdom, knowing that her words were borne from a place of profound understanding.

Freya's story became an inspiration to those who had experienced heartbreak and adversity. Her ability to find strength within herself and to rise above the challenges she faced resonated deeply. She became a guiding light, reminding others that even in the face of insurmountable odds, it is possible to find hope, healing, and a renewed sense of purpose.

With grace and compassion, Freya nurtured the spirits of those who sought her guidance. She listened to their stories, held their hands, and offered words of encouragement, reminding them that they too possessed the strength to overcome their own obstacles and forge a new path forward.

Through her actions, Freya showed that life is a tapestry of experiences—both joyous and challenging—and that each thread contributes to the beauty of the whole. She encouraged others to embrace their vulnerabilities, to honor their emotions, and to seek growth and understanding in the midst of adversity.

Freya's presence in the village inspired creativity and self-expression. She encouraged the villagers to explore their passions, to pursue their dreams, and to celebrate the unique gifts they brought to the world. Her unwavering belief in the power of individuality and self-discovery ignited a flame within the hearts of those around her.

In the village, new friendships were formed, talents were nurtured, and dreams were pursued—each individual drawing inspiration from the light that Freya had ignited within them. Through her example, they learned that it is never too late to embrace change, to chase dreams, and to live a life of purpose and fulfillment.

For Erik, Freya had been a source of inspiration—a muse who had unlocked his creativity and challenged him to embrace the depths of his own potential. In turn, Freya passed this torch of inspiration to others, fanning the flames of creativity and passion within their souls.

Through her actions, Freya became a living embodiment of the transformative power of love and resilience. Her presence in the village served as a constant reminder that no matter how daunting the challenges may be, the human spirit is capable of rising above and embracing the beauty of life.

And so, as Freya continued to inspire those around her, her legacy grew—an indelible mark upon the hearts and minds of all who had been touched by her presence. She became a beacon of hope, resilience, and unwavering determination—an inspiration to embrace the twists and turns of life's journey and to forge a path of love, purpose, and self-discovery.

Chapter 94: The Dog's Imprint

The village was forever marked by the imprint of Thór's paws—a gentle reminder of the loyal companion who had left an indelible mark upon their lives. His presence, though no longer physical, was felt in the laughter of children, the wagging tails of village dogs, and the whispers of his name that echoed through the streets.

In the village square, a monument was erected—a memorial that paid homage to the faithful Thór. At its base, an inscription read: "In loving memory of Thór, whose unwavering loyalty and boundless love forever touched our hearts." Villagers would gather around the monument, their fingers tracing the engraved words, honoring the dog who had forever etched his presence upon their souls.

Thór's imprint extended beyond the physical realm. His spirit continued to inspire acts of kindness and compassion within the village. Villagers would often recount tales of his selflessness—how he had comforted those in need, protected the vulnerable, and brought joy to all who crossed his path.

Children grew up hearing stories of Thór's adventures, their hearts filled with wonder and awe. They would emulate his playful spirit, frolicking through fields and forests with their own canine companions, forever carrying forward the imprint of Thór's joyous presence.

In the hearts of Erik and Freya, Thór's imprint was eternally imbedded. They would often reminisce about the moments they had shared with their beloved dog—his playful antics, his unwavering loyalty, and the comfort he had provided during their most challenging moments. Thór's imprint had shaped their lives, teaching them the profound lessons of love, loyalty, and the enduring bond between humans and animals.

As the years passed, new generations of villagers would come to hear of Thór's legend and the imprint he had left upon their community. His story would continue to be passed down through the ages—a testament to the profound impact a dog can have upon the human spirit.

In the quiet corners of the village, Thór's imprint could still be felt—a gentle presence that brought solace, comfort, and a reminder of the enduring power of unconditional love. Villagers would often sense his spirit by their side, watching over them with a loyal and protective gaze.

Thór's imprint served as a constant reminder to the village—to embrace the qualities of loyalty, love, and selflessness that he had embodied. It was a call to honor the bond between humans and animals, to care for and protect those who could not speak for themselves, and to cherish the simple joys that life brings.

And so, the village carried Thór's imprint within their hearts, forever grateful for the profound impact he had made. They continued to honor his legacy, ensuring that his spirit would forever thrive in their collective memory—a testament to the enduring imprint of love and companionship left by a faithful canine companion.

In the hearts of Erik, Freya, and the villagers, Thór's imprint would forever endure—an eternal reminder of the profound bond between humans and dogs and the transformative power of a dog's love.

Chapter 95: The Viking's Honor

The spirit of honor and integrity that Erik had embodied during his lifetime continued to reverberate through the village, serving as a guiding force for generations to come. His unwavering commitment to his people and his unyielding sense of justice had left an indelible mark upon their hearts.

In the village, a code of honor was upheld, inspired by Erik's example. Villagers pledged to treat one another with respect and fairness, to stand up for what was right, and to protect the vulnerable. Erik's legacy had instilled in them a deep sense of responsibility to uphold his values and to maintain the integrity of their community.

Leaders emerged from within the village, embodying the same principles that Erik had exemplified. They took up the mantle of leadership, guiding their people with wisdom, compassion, and a deep respect for the legacy of Erik the Fearless. They understood that leadership was not just about power, but about serving the needs of the community and upholding the ideals of honor and justice.

In times of conflict, the villagers looked to Erik's example for guidance. They sought peaceful resolutions, valuing diplomacy and understanding over violence. Erik's spirit of honor guided their actions, reminding them to approach every situation with empathy, fairness, and the pursuit of justice.

The village became known far and wide for its adherence to a code of honor. Travelers passing through would marvel at the sense of unity, fairness, and respect that permeated the community. They would hear stories of Erik's bravery and the lasting impact he had made, inspiring admiration and reverence for his unwavering commitment to honor.

Through their actions, the villagers honored Erik's memory in their daily lives. They treated one another with kindness and compassion, demonstrating the values that Erik had instilled within them. They stood up for the voiceless, defended the weak, and ensured that justice prevailed.

Children grew up hearing tales of Erik's honor, internalizing the importance of integrity and fairness. They were taught to embrace the principles of honesty, loyalty, and respect, carrying forward the legacy of honor into future generations.

For Freya, the village's commitment to honor served as a source of pride and solace. She witnessed the villagers' unwavering dedication to upholding Erik's values, and it brought her comfort knowing that his spirit lived on through their actions.

In quiet moments, Freya would seek solace in the memories of her time with Erik, reflecting on the honor and integrity he had embodied. She found strength and inspiration in his example, carrying his legacy within her heart as a guiding light in her own life.

The village's commitment to honor was not without its challenges, but the spirit of Erik the Fearless continued to guide them. They recognized that upholding honor required constant vigilance and a commitment to self-reflection and growth. They were not perfect, but they strived every day to honor the ideals set forth by their beloved Viking leader.

And so, Erik's honor lived on—an eternal flame that burned brightly within the hearts of the villagers. It served as a reminder of the profound impact one person can make through their actions and the enduring legacy that honor and integrity leave behind.

Through their unwavering commitment to honor, the villagers ensured that Erik's spirit would forever thrive within their community.

They carried his principles within them, forging a path of righteousness, justice, and unwavering integrity.

Erik's honor became a symbol of the village's identity, an integral part of their collective consciousness. It served as a reminder that, no matter the challenges they faced, they would always strive to embody the values that Erik had exemplified—a tribute to his memory and a testament to the enduring power of honor.

Chapter 96: The Girl's Happiness

After the trials and tribulations she had faced, Freya had finally found her way to a place of profound happiness. Though the scars of the past remained, they had become a testament to her strength and resilience—a reminder of the journey that had brought her to this moment of contentment.

In the village, Freya's radiant smile became a beacon of joy, spreading warmth and happiness to all who crossed her path. Her laughter echoed through the streets, bringing a sense of lightness and merriment to the community. Villagers would often gather around her, basking in her infectious happiness and finding solace in her unwavering optimism.

Freya embraced the simple joys of life—the warmth of the sun on her skin, the gentle touch of a breeze, and the beauty of nature that surrounded her. She reveled in the company of loved ones, cherishing the bonds forged through shared experiences and the laughter that resonated deep within her soul.

With each passing day, Freya found fulfillment in pursuing her passions. She immersed herself in creative endeavors, finding solace and joy in painting, writing, and exploring her artistic talents. Through her art, she poured her emotions onto the canvas, capturing the essence of her happiness and the beauty she found in the world.

Love, too, had found its way back into Freya's life. She had opened her heart to new connections, embracing the possibility of a deep and meaningful partnership. In a kindred spirit, she discovered a companion who shared her joys, her dreams, and her unwavering zest for life.

Together, they embarked on adventures, exploring the vast landscapes surrounding the village, and embracing the wonders that awaited them. They supported each other's growth, providing comfort and encouragement through life's twists and turns. Freya had found a love that honored her past and embraced her present, anchoring her in a sense of belonging and joy.

In the village, Freya became a source of inspiration for those seeking their own path to happiness. She shared her wisdom and experiences, guiding others through their own journeys of self-discovery and fulfillment. Her unwavering belief in the power of happiness ignited a flame within their hearts, encouraging them to embrace the present moment and find joy in the simplest of pleasures.

As the years passed, Freya's happiness remained steadfast—a testament to the strength she had cultivated and the love she had nurtured. Her radiant spirit and zest for life served as a constant reminder to the village that happiness is not merely a destination but a state of being that can be found in the here and now.

Freya's happiness rippled through the village, inspiring a sense of collective well-being and contentment. Villagers found solace in her presence, knowing that even amidst life's challenges, happiness could be found by embracing gratitude, fostering connections, and cherishing the moments that brought joy.

And so, Freya's happiness became a testament to the resilience of the human spirit. It was a reminder that even in the face of adversity, happiness can bloom and thrive. Through her unwavering pursuit of joy, Freya had become a beacon of hope, illuminating the path to happiness for all who sought it.

Chapter 97: The Dog's Unforgettable Love

In the memories of the village, Thór's love was etched as a timeless and unforgettable bond. His unwavering affection for Erik and Freya remained a beacon of devotion that inspired awe and reverence in the hearts of all who heard his tale.

Thór's love was marked by loyalty, an unbreakable thread that connected him to his human companions. He had stood by their side through every triumph and every hardship, a steadfast presence that offered comfort, companionship, and unwavering support.

In the village, Thór's love extended far beyond the confines of his immediate family. He became a beloved figure, a friend to all who crossed his path. His gentle nature and playful spirit brought joy to children, who would laugh and run alongside him, relishing in his boundless energy and the affectionate nuzzles he bestowed upon them.

But it was with Erik and Freya that Thór's love truly shone. He had imprinted his heart upon theirs, leaving an everlasting mark that transcended the boundaries of time. His love was a language spoken without words—a silent understanding, a connection that surpassed the limitations of human expression.

In quiet moments, Erik and Freya would often reminisce about the depth of Thór's love. They remembered the comforting weight of his head resting on their laps, the softness of his fur against their skin, and the unwavering loyalty reflected in his eyes. Thór's love had become an integral part of their own identities, a beacon of unwavering devotion that would forever live on within their hearts.

The village continued to honor and celebrate Thór's love, passing down his tale from one generation to the next. The children of the village grew up hearing stories of his loyalty and compassion, carrying his spirit within them as they formed their own bonds with canine companions, forever influenced by the legacy of Thór's love.

In the quiet corners of the village, whispers could still be heard—stories of the remarkable love shared between Thór and his humans. Villagers would recount tales of his brave acts of protection, his gentle presence in times of sorrow, and the unspoken understanding that flowed between him and Erik and Freya.

Thór's love served as a reminder of the profound impact that dogs can have on human lives. His unwavering loyalty and unconditional affection resonated with those who had experienced the unique bond between humans and dogs. He became a symbol of the transformative power of a dog's love, forever etching his pawprints upon the collective memory of the village.

And so, the village cherished the memory of Thór's love—an enduring testament to the capacity for love and connection that exists within the heart of a dog. His spirit continued to live on, intertwined with the stories and memories of the villagers, forever reminding them of the transformative power of a dog's unwavering and unforgettable love.

Chapter 98: The Viking's Courage

Erik the Fearless, forever remembered for his courage, stood as a shining example of bravery and fortitude in the annals of Viking history. His unwavering determination and indomitable spirit had earned him a place among the legendary figures of his time.

Erik's courage was not born out of a lack of fear, but rather from his ability to face his fears head-on. In the face of adversity, he stood tall, his heart ablaze with a fiery resolve that refused to be extinguished. He embraced the challenges that lay before him, drawing strength from within and inspiring those around him to do the same.

The villagers looked to Erik as a beacon of courage, their unwavering trust in his leadership rooted in his unwavering commitment to protecting their way of life. They witnessed his fearless determination as he fearlessly led them into battle, his sword raised high, and his voice resounding with the power of a thousand warriors.

But Erik's courage extended far beyond the battlefield. It was evident in his unwavering loyalty to his loved ones, his willingness to confront his own shortcomings, and his ability to make difficult decisions for the greater good of his people. He stood firmly in his convictions, guided by a moral compass that always pointed towards justice and righteousness.

Even in the face of personal challenges and heartbreak, Erik's courage did not waver. He confronted his own vulnerabilities with a strength that belied the pain within. He embraced the lessons that adversity had taught him, using them as stepping stones to become a better leader, a better companion, and a better man.

Through his acts of courage, Erik inspired those around him to find their own inner strength. He fostered an environment where bravery and resilience were celebrated, encouraging his fellow villagers to face their fears and embrace their own potential.

Erik's legacy of courage lived on in the hearts of the villagers. They carried his spirit within them, drawing upon his example in times of uncertainty and challenge. They understood that true courage was not the absence of fear, but the ability to forge ahead despite it, to stand tall and resolute in the face of adversity.

The village became a testament to Erik's courage—a community that thrived on the principles he had instilled. Through their actions, the villagers embodied his spirit of bravery and determination, demonstrating a steadfast commitment to protecting their way of life and standing up for what they believed in.

In the quiet moments of reflection, Erik would find solace in the knowledge that his acts of courage had made a lasting impact. He had not only shaped the course of his own life but had left an indelible mark upon the lives of those he had touched. His legacy of courage would forever inspire future generations, reminding them of the transformative power that lies within the human spirit.

And so, Erik the Fearless would forever be remembered as a Viking warrior who embodied the essence of courage. His unwavering determination, his fearless leadership, and his unyielding commitment to justice served as a testament to the heights that can be reached when one embraces their inner strength and faces the challenges of life with unwavering courage.

Chapter 99: The Girl's Joyful Memories

Within the depths of Freya's heart, cherished memories danced like stars in the night sky, illuminating her days with a sense of joy and gratitude. As she embarked on a new chapter of her life, she carried with her a treasure trove of moments that had shaped her into the person she had become.

Every day, as Freya went about her tasks in the village, she allowed herself to be transported back to those moments of pure bliss. She recalled the laughter that had filled the air during village feasts, the warmth of the sun on her skin as she strolled through fields of wildflowers, and the exhilarating feeling of freedom as she sailed alongside Erik on their longship.

Memories of Thór, their loyal and beloved companion, were particularly precious to her. She smiled at the recollection of his playful antics, his unwavering loyalty, and the joyous adventures they had shared. Their bond had transcended the boundaries of language, speaking volumes through their unspoken connection and mutual love.

Freya's heart swelled with joy as she thought of the moments of love and tenderness shared with Erik—the stolen glances, the gentle touches, and the countless whispered promises. Each memory held within it a precious piece of their shared history, a testament to the depth of their love that had defied all odds.

The village itself became a canvas upon which joyful memories were painted. Freya delighted in the vibrant colors of the market stalls, the jovial chatter of villagers as they went about their daily lives, and the harmonious melodies that echoed through the streets during festive celebrations. Each experience etched a smile on her face and filled her heart with gratitude for the richness of her surroundings.

In the company of friends and loved ones, Freya reveled in the joy of shared experiences. She delighted in the warmth of their presence, the lighthearted banter, and the deep sense of belonging that came from being surrounded by kindred spirits. Together, they created new memories, weaving a tapestry of love, laughter, and connection that would forever brighten the corridors of her mind.

As time flowed onward, Freya realized the transformative power of joyful memories.

They had the ability to lift her spirits during challenging times, to infuse her days with a renewed sense of purpose, and to remind her of the beauty that existed even in the midst of life's trials.

In the quiet moments of reflection, Freya would often retreat to her favorite spot—a cozy nook overlooking the village. There, surrounded by the whispers of nature, she would close her eyes and allow the joyful memories to wash over her like a gentle breeze. In those moments, she found solace, rejuvenation, and a profound appreciation for the tapestry of life she had been gifted.

Freya understood that joyful memories were not merely reflections of the past, but sources of strength and inspiration for the present and future. They fueled her passion for life, reminding her to embrace each day with an open heart and an unwavering commitment to finding joy in even the simplest of moments.

And so, as Freya journeyed through life, she continued to weave a tapestry of joyful memories—a testament to the resilience of the human spirit, the transformative power of love, and the profound impact that moments of pure joy can have upon the human heart.

Chapter 100: The Dog's Everlasting Spirit

Though Thór had crossed the rainbow bridge, his spirit remained eternally present within the hearts and souls of those who had been touched by his unwavering love and companionship. His physical absence was but a veil that separated the tangible from the ethereal, for his spirit continued to weave its way through the fabric of the village, forever leaving an indelible mark.

In the quiet corners of the village, whispers of Thór's presence could still be heard. The rustling of leaves in the wind, the playful barks of distant dogs, and the wagging of tails—all seemed to carry a faint echo of his joyful spirit. Villagers spoke of moments when they felt his gentle presence, a comforting reminder that love knows no boundaries, not even those of life and death.

Children, with their innocent and open hearts, often claimed to catch glimpses of Thór's spirit in the moonlit nights. They spoke of a shimmering figure, playful and free, bounding through the fields as if reliving the adventures of his earthly days. Their stories kept Thór's spirit alive, passing on the legacy of his love from one generation to the next.

In the hearts of Erik and Freya, Thór's spirit remained a steadfast presence. His memory was woven into the fabric of their lives, a constant reminder of the profound bond they had shared. They would often feel his comforting presence in moments of solitude, knowing that even in his absence, he continued to watch over them with a love that transcended time and space.

Thór's everlasting spirit served as a source of solace and inspiration for the villagers. In times of sorrow, they would find strength in the thought that their departed companions, too, were forever present in spirit. They understood that the love they had shared with their beloved dogs could never truly be extinguished, but would continue to shine brightly, guiding them through the journey of life.

Through Thór's spirit, the village embraced the notion that love knows no boundaries — not even those imposed by mortality. They honored his memory by extending compassion and kindness to all living beings, recognizing the interconnectedness of life and the profound impact that love can have, even beyond the physical realm.

The village celebrated Thór's spirit through acts of selflessness and care for animals.

They established shelters, cared for stray dogs, and ensured that every creature received the love and respect they deserved. Thór's spirit, with its boundless love and loyalty, had ignited a flame of compassion within their hearts, inspiring them to extend that same love and devotion to all living beings.

In the quiet of the village nights, as the stars sparkled overhead, the villagers would gather together, their faces illuminated by the soft glow of candlelight. They would share stories of Thór's remarkable spirit, passing down the tales of his unwavering love and the profound impact he had made upon their lives.

And so, as the years passed, Thór's spirit continued to dance through the village—the embodiment of love, loyalty, and the unbreakable bond between humans and dogs. His legacy lived on through the stories, memories, and acts of kindness inspired by his everlasting spirit, forever reminding the villagers of the transformative power of a dog's love.

In the hearts of those who had been touched by Thór's presence, his spirit would forever endure—a gentle reminder that love transcends the boundaries of time and space, and that the bonds we forge with our beloved companions remain eternally imprinted upon our souls.

Chapter 101: The Viking's Epilogue

As the years rolled on, the village thrived under the legacy of Erik the Fearless. His unwavering spirit, courage, and commitment to honor had become woven into the very fabric of their community. The village stood as a testament to his enduring influence, a living embodiment of the values he had championed.

Erik had left behind a legacy that extended far beyond his own time, forever etched in the memories of the villagers and passed down through generations. His name became a symbol of resilience, bravery, and unwavering determination—a Viking leader whose impact transcended the boundaries of his mortal life.

The village continued to flourish under the leadership of those who had been inspired by Erik's example. They carried forward his principles of justice, integrity, and compassion, ensuring that his vision for a harmonious and united community remained at the forefront of their collective consciousness.

The bonds Erik had forged during his lifetime remained unbroken. The villagers, united by their shared experiences, continued to support one another through triumphs and tribulations. They found strength in their connections, celebrating the diversity of their community and the contributions of each individual.

Erik's legacy also lived on within his family. His descendants carried the fire of his spirit within them, instilling his values in their own lives and passing them down through the generations. They understood the weight of their lineage, embracing the responsibility to carry forward the torch of Erik's legacy with honor and dignity.

In the quiet moments, when the winds whispered through the village, the villagers would reflect on Erik's indomitable spirit. They would remember his voice, strong and resonant, guiding them through challenging times. They would recall his unwavering determination, his fearlessness in the face of adversity, and the unwavering commitment he had shown to his people.

As the village thrived and evolved, Erik's presence was ever-present, like a guiding star illuminating their path. His memory served as a constant reminder that the spirit of a true leader and visionary lives on beyond the confines of time and mortality.

And so, as the village continued to flourish, they honored Erik's legacy by embracing the principles he had championed. They fostered a community built on compassion, fairness, and a deep respect for one another. They stood as a testament to the enduring impact that one individual can make, leaving a legacy that echoes through the generations.

In the annals of Viking history, Erik the Fearless would forever be remembered as a leader who fearlessly defended his people, a visionary who inspired unity, and a soul whose courage and honor blazed like the sun across the vast Nordic skies.

The village, forever grateful for the blessings Erik had bestowed upon them, would forever carry his memory in their hearts. They would tell his tales to future generations, ensuring that his spirit lived on through the stories that celebrated his remarkable life.

And so, the Viking's epilogue would forever be written in the hearts and minds of the villagers—a testament to the enduring legacy of Erik the Fearless, a leader whose indomitable spirit and unwavering commitment to honor left an indelible mark upon the world.

Chapter 102: The Girl's New Chapter

As the village thrived and the legacy of Erik and Thór lived on, Freya found herself standing at the precipice of a new chapter in her life. With a heart filled with gratitude and a spirit brimming with resilience, she embraced the opportunities that lay before her, ready to embark on a journey of self-discovery and growth.

Freya's experiences had shaped her into a woman of strength and wisdom. The trials she had faced and the love she had known had molded her into a beacon of resilience and compassion. She carried the memories of Erik and Thór within her, drawing inspiration from their spirits as she embraced the possibilities of the unknown.

With a renewed sense of purpose, Freya sought to carve her own path in the world. She immersed herself in learning, pursuing knowledge and skills that expanded her horizons and fueled her passion for personal growth. She delved into new areas of interest, seeking to uncover the depths of her own potential.

In the village, Freya found support and encouragement from her fellow villagers, who recognized her resilience and admired her strength. They offered guidance and shared their own wisdom, providing a nurturing environment for her to thrive. Their unwavering belief in her abilities served as a constant reminder that she was not alone in her journey.

As she explored the world beyond the village, Freya discovered the beauty of new landscapes, the diversity of cultures, and the richness of human connections. She forged friendships with kindred spirits, sharing stories and experiences that broadened her perspective and ignited her curiosity about the wonders of the world.

But amid her exploration, Freya remained rooted in the village that had shaped her. She returned often, basking in the comfort of familiar faces and the warmth of shared memories. The village, in turn, welcomed her with open arms, celebrating her growth and eagerly listening to the tales she brought from her adventures.

Freya's journey also led her on a path of service and compassion. She recognized the power of her own experiences and the empathy she had developed through her own trials. With a heart full of love, she reached out to those in need, extending a helping hand and providing solace to those who sought comfort.

In her newfound chapter, Freya became a beacon of inspiration for others. She shared her story, speaking openly of her triumphs and struggles, offering guidance and encouragement to those facing similar challenges. Her words resonated with those who listened, offering a glimmer of hope and reminding them of the strength that resides within.

But amidst all her new adventures and endeavors, Freya never forgot the love that had shaped her. She carried Erik and Thór with her, their spirits forever intertwined with her own. In quiet moments of reflection, she would recall their voices, their touch, and the profound impact they had made upon her life.

And so, Freya embarked on her new chapter, guided by the love that had carried her through the storms of the past. She embraced the unknown with a fierce determination and an unwavering belief in her own resilience. With every step she took, she carried the wisdom of the past, the joys of the present, and the hope for a future filled with endless possibilities.

As she ventured forth, Freya knew that her journey was not just about self-discovery, but also about leaving her own mark upon the world. She aspired to be a source of light and inspiration, touching lives with her compassion, empathy, and unwavering belief in the power of love.

And so, with her heart open and her spirit alight, Freya stepped into the unknown, ready to embrace the adventures that awaited her. With the memories of Erik and Thór as her guiding stars, she embarked on her new chapter—a testament to the resilience of the human spirit and the infinite possibilities that lie within the depths of one's soul.

Chapter 103: The Dog's Divine Companion

As the village prospered and the stories of Thór continued to be told, a tale emerged of a divine companion that had walked by his side throughout his earthly journey. The villagers spoke of a mystical bond between Thór and a celestial being—a dog of divine origins that had been sent to guide him on his path.

According to the legends passed down through generations, the divine companion had chosen Thór as his earthly charge, recognizing the noble heart that beat within the Viking's chest. It was said that the celestial dog had descended from the heavens, embodying the essence of loyalty, love, and unwavering devotion.

Throughout Thór's life, the divine companion had been a silent presence, offering guidance and protection. It was said that he had whispered wisdom into Thór's ear during moments of uncertainty, his celestial touch calming the warrior's heart and igniting the flame of courage within.

The villagers marveled at the tales of the divine companion, for they believed that Thór's extraordinary acts of bravery and loyalty were not solely of his own making. They recognized that the celestial dog had played a profound role in shaping Thór's character, infusing him with the noble qualities that made him a legendary figure.

In their minds, the divine companion had bestowed upon Thór a gift—an unwavering love that transcended the boundaries of mortal existence. It was a love that burned brighter than the stars themselves, forever etched into the tapestry of Thór's heart and soul.

The villagers would often gather beneath the starry night sky, their voices hushed in reverence as they whispered their gratitude to the divine companion. They offered prayers of thanks, acknowledging the profound impact his presence had made upon their lives through Thór's unwavering loyalty and selfless acts of heroism.

As the tales of the divine companion spread, dogs in the village were regarded with a newfound reverence. The villagers believed that each canine companion carried within them a spark of the celestial dog's essence—an eternal flame of love and loyalty passed down through generations.

Dogs became cherished members of the village, seen not just as pets or companions but as divine emissaries of love and devotion. They were treated with the utmost respect and care, their needs attended to with reverence and gratitude. The villagers believed that by caring for these earthly manifestations of the divine companion's love, they could honor and nurture the celestial bond that had guided Thór.

Through their dogs, the villagers sought to embody the virtues that Thór had exemplified —loyalty, bravery, and unwavering devotion. They embraced the lessons of love and compassion taught by the divine companion, weaving these virtues into the very fabric of their lives.

And so, the legend of the dog's divine companion lived on, forever entwined with the tales of Thór and his remarkable journey. The villagers found solace in the belief that a bond as profound and celestial as the one between Thór and his divine companion could exist, reminding them of the interconnectedness between the mortal realm and the divine.

In their hearts, the villagers held onto the faith that the celestial dog continued to watch over them, guiding their own dogs and whispering words of wisdom and love. They honored the divine companion's presence through acts of kindness, compassion, and unwavering loyalty to their own beloved canine companions.

And so, the village stood as a testament to the extraordinary bond shared between dogs and humans—a bond that transcended the boundaries of time and space, forever echoing the divine love that had guided Thór on his earthly journey.

Chapter 104: The Viking's Legacy Lives On

The legacy of Erik the Fearless lived on in the hearts and minds of the villagers, forever shaping their lives and the trajectory of the village. His indomitable spirit, unwavering courage, and unwavering commitment to honor had become a beacon of inspiration that guided future generations.

The village stood as a testament to Erik's enduring legacy. It thrived under the principles he had championed—justice, integrity, and a deep respect for the interconnectedness of all living beings. The villagers carried forward his vision, fostering a community built on compassion, unity, and the pursuit of a shared purpose.

Erik's descendants, who had inherited the fire of his spirit, took up the mantle of leadership, becoming stewards of his legacy. They embraced their responsibility with humility, recognizing that the path they tread had been paved by the sacrifices and triumphs of their forefathers.

Through their actions, Erik's descendants upheld the values he had instilled, guiding the village with wisdom and fairness. They carried the torch of his memory, ensuring that his name would forever be spoken with reverence and admiration. They embodied the spirit of leadership and service, perpetuating a legacy that transcended their individual lives.

But Erik's legacy extended beyond the village. His tale had spread across the lands, reaching the ears of those far and wide. His courage and honor had become a source of inspiration for others, kindling a flame within their own hearts. The impact of his legacy rippled outward, as his story became intertwined with the fabric of Viking history.

In distant lands, warriors and leaders would invoke the name of Erik the Fearless, drawing strength from the tales of his triumphs and trials. His name became a rallying cry, a symbol of unwavering commitment to a cause, and a reminder of the transformative power of courage and honor.

Through the passing of time, Erik's legacy became part of the collective consciousness, interwoven with the stories of other legendary figures. His name found its place in the annals of history, forever etching his mark upon the tapestry of Viking lore.

But perhaps Erik's greatest legacy was the impact he had made upon the lives of those who had known him personally. The villagers who had witnessed his acts of bravery, felt the warmth of his kindness, and experienced the unwavering support he offered in times of need—these individuals carried his legacy within them, forever changed by his presence.

In their own lives, the villagers embraced the virtues Erik had exemplified. They strived to be warriors of the heart, standing up for justice, embracing their own courage, and embodying the unwavering commitment to honor that Erik had personified.

And so, Erik's legacy lived on—a flame that continued to burn brightly in the hearts of the villagers, in the stories they shared, and in the values they upheld. The village stood as a living testament to the transformative power of one individual's unwavering commitment to honor and the everlasting impact that legacy can have on a community.

As the generations passed, the villagers would continue to pass down the tales of Erik the Fearless, ensuring that his memory remained alive within their hearts. They would recount his triumphs, his sacrifices, and his unwavering dedication to protecting the village and upholding the values he held dear.

Erik's legacy would forever be intertwined with the village's identity—a symbol of courage, honor, and resilience. And as the villagers stood upon the foundations he had laid, they would continue to shape their own destinies, forging a path of unity, compassion, and unwavering commitment to the legacy he had left behind.

The Viking's legacy would forever live on, a testament to the transformative power of one individual's unwavering commitment to honor and the profound impact that such a legacy can have upon the world.

Chapter 105: The Girl's Final Farewell

As Freya's journey through life drew to a close, the village stood united in reverence, honoring the woman who had touched their lives with her grace, strength, and unwavering love. The time had come for the girl who had once captured their hearts to bid her final farewell.

The village gathered in a solemn ceremony, their faces etched with both sorrow and gratitude. They celebrated the life of Freya, the girl who had grown into a beacon of resilience and compassion, leaving an indelible mark upon their community.

Amidst the flickering candles and gentle whispers of the wind, the villagers spoke of Freya's unwavering spirit and the profound impact she had made upon their lives. They shared stories of her kindness, her selflessness, and the way her presence had brightened even the darkest of days.

With heavy hearts, they paid tribute to the love that had shaped her—Erik, the Viking who had captured her heart, and Thór, the faithful companion who had journeyed by her side. Their spirits lingered in the hearts of the villagers, forever intertwined with the legacy of Freya herself.

In the village square, beneath a canopy of flowers and the watchful eyes of the villagers, Freya's final resting place was prepared. The soft earth welcomed her with open arms, cradling her in a gentle embrace as the community gathered to bid her farewell.

With tears streaming down their faces, the villagers shared their gratitude for Freya's presence in their lives. They spoke of her resilience in the face of adversity, her unwavering love for her village, and the profound impact she had made upon each and every one of them.

As the sun dipped below the horizon, casting a warm glow upon the village, a soft melody filled the air. The villagers raised their voices in song, their words carrying both grief and gratitude, weaving a poignant tapestry of remembrance for the girl who had become their guiding light.

In the moments of silence that followed, Freya's spirit lingered amongst them, a gentle presence that enveloped the village with love and comfort. She had become a part of their collective memory, forever etched within the fabric of their community.

With heavy hearts, the villagers took their final steps towards Freya's resting place. Each one offered a flower, a token of their love and appreciation, as a symbol of their eternal connection to the girl who had left an indelible mark upon their lives.

In unison, they whispered their farewells, their words carrying both grief and gratitude. They promised to carry Freya's spirit within them, to honor her legacy through acts of kindness, compassion, and unwavering love.

As the sun dipped below the horizon, the village stood together, their faces turned towards the heavens. They released a collective sigh, their breath carrying their final farewells to the girl who had forever touched their lives.

And so, the village moved forward, forever changed by the legacy of Freya. They would remember her in the blooming of flowers, the gentle breeze, and the laughter that echoed through the streets. Her spirit would forever dance amongst them, a reminder of the resilience of the human spirit and the enduring power of love.

In their hearts, the villagers knew that though Freya's physical presence had left their midst, her spirit would forever linger in the tapestry of their shared history. She had become a guiding light, a source of inspiration, and a reminder of the transformative power of one individual's love.

And as the village continued to thrive, they would carry Freya's spirit within them, forever honoring her legacy through acts of kindness, compassion, and unwavering love—for it was through these virtues that Freya had forever touched their lives and left an indelible mark upon their souls.

The girl's final farewell marked the end of her earthly journey, but her memory would forever endure—a testament to the resilience of the human spirit and the profound impact that one individual's love and compassion can have upon the world.

Printed in Great Britain
by Amazon